Deep Harbour

Deep Harbour

TOVE ALSTERDAL

translated by Alice Menzies

faber

First published in the UK in 2024
by Faber & Faber Ltd
The Bindery, 51 Hatton Garden
London ECIN 8HN
Originally published as *Djuphamn* in Sweden in 2023 by Lind & Co

Typeset by Typo•glyphix, Burton-on-Trent DE14 3HE
Printed and bound by CPI Group (UK) Ltd, Croydon CRO 4YY

A CIP record for this book
is available from the British Library

ISBN 978–0–571–37213–3

Printed and bound in the UK on FSC® certified paper in line with our continuing
commitment to ethical business practices, sustainability and the environment.
For further information see faber.co.uk/environmental-policy

2 4 6 8 10 9 7 5 3 1

The last of the ice had melted or drifted out to sea, and there was a light, south-easterly breeze. They exchanged a few final words before going under.

'Stick together down there, OK? And let me know the minute you run into any trouble.'

'Absolutely, OK.'

The other diver seemed as comfortable in fins as regular shoes. Ylva had met him for the first time the evening before, after her bus arrived in Lunde and she checked in at the guest house. She was grateful, so grateful to get to go out with them, that this spring would be nothing like the last.

Yes, she was aware of the dangers. And yes, she was qualified to dive to eighteen metres and had put in the requisite number of hours.

No, she hadn't realised just how cold the river would be at five in the morning in late April, but she didn't mention that.

Ylva fastened her buoyancy compensator, various hoses looping back to her tank. Mask on, regulator in, check that the air is flowing and the gauges are working properly – they went through the silent routine she liked so much. Signalling that everything is OK, I'm ready. I'm going down now, you follow me. We've got each other's backs, and I'm here for you no matter what.

Visibility was poor just beneath the surface, and she dumped air from her buoyancy compensator in order to descend. Slowly, not too fast. Breathing calmly, deeply. The water was the colour of unfermented beer, sediment swirling in the fast-flowing current, and she could feel the chill, despite her thick drysuit.

It was a far cry from the exotic adventures people liked to boast about on social media; no sign of the bright shoals of fish that looked like they belonged in some Disney film.

During her final outdoor dive on the training course two years ago, it was as though the world had opened up to her. There was so much left to explore, dimensions of the future she hadn't been expecting.

The whole thing had started with a man, of course. They dated for a few months, shared their hopes and dreams for the rest of their lives. Ylva wanted to cut back her hours and possibly even buy a summerhouse, something simple somewhere, but the man whose name she would rather forget had wanted to go diving along the coral reef in Tahiti, to sail around the islands by the Great Barrier Reef; he said he knew of places mass tourism hadn't reached yet. In her quiet moments, she had started googling diving courses, afraid she wouldn't be able to handle it. That she would panic, be unable to breathe. She couldn't afford for that to happen on a boat in Australia, she had decided, and so she secretly enrolled in diving lessons at the local pool that winter.

Eight metres, nine, but they still hadn't quite reached the bottom. Ylva could no longer tell that her gloves were red; all colours disappeared at these depths.

She allowed herself to sink a little deeper.

The final outdoor dive had been all that stood between her and her qualification when the man stopped responding. Everything had moved a little too fast, he wrote, when he finally replied to her long thread of messages. She was a nice girl, but he needed time. Wasn't quite done with his ex yet.

And so there she was, unable to hold on to someone, yet again. A lifetime of loneliness stretching out in front of her. She had also blown thousands of kronor she would never get back, learned to breathe underwater and wrecked her hair with all the chlorine.

No, she had told herself. She would get her certificate. That way she could post about it on Facebook, tell everyone: look what I've gone and done!

And then she did her final dive and discovered the new world that opened up to her, and from that point on it no longer had anything to do with him. After that, she had taken every opportunity she could to go diving in the Stockholm archipelago, and that was when she heard all about the many unexplored wrecks up north, in the Ångerman River.

Ylva caught sight of something at the edge of her beam of light. Posts of some kind. Huge lumps of wood that seemed to be straining towards her. She checked her depth – fourteen metres – and realised what it was.

The sunken bridge.

The broken spans had been forced up in the middle, forming an angular arch a bit like the entrance to a cathedral.

In the diving community, it was known as the Church.

Ylva turned around to make contact with her dive partner, who was busy with his camera off to one side. I'm going this way, she gestured. Is that OK? He raised his hand, which she took as a yes.

A sense of reverence settled over her as she swam through the opening. The silence. The expanse of darkness all around her, shrinking the world to a solitary beam of light. To think that it had been there all this time, the old Sandö Bridge, which collapsed during construction so long ago. Lost to the depths of memory as the twentieth century progressed and the new millennium dawned. Ylva felt an urge to reach out and touch the broken wooden structure as she swam a short way along the other side. The past wasn't gone; it was real.

As she turned to head back, she realised she was no longer sure which way was which. The darkness was so compact, her torch reaching only a few metres. She had gone too far, and the bridge was suddenly nowhere to be seen. Ylva was both icy cold and red hot, she couldn't tell which; everything felt different down here.

A diver was supposed to spend two minutes looking for their partner before heading back up to the surface, that was the rule, but Ylva wasn't sure how much time had already passed. She had just started her ascent when she noticed something big in the darkness up ahead, and she paused. Her first reaction was fear, but she quickly told herself that was stupid. There was nothing to be afraid of here. Angling her beam of light forward, she could make out the side of a boat. She swam slowly towards it, switching to a frog kick to avoid disturbing the sand and sediment.

It was impossible to say how long the wreck had been

down there. In the brackish water of the Baltic sea, ship-worms didn't thrive the way they did in saltier environments, which meant that many wooden vessels remained largely intact. Ylva tried to remember what she knew about the wrecks in the river. Those on this side of the Sandö Bridge had been mapped by another team just last summer, which was a dizzying thought. What if she was looking at something no one else had seen close up before, not for 100 years or more? She squinted in through a hole in the hull and saw an overturned chair, something broken – was that china? – and a wall-mounted bed. She moved slowly along the edges of the vessel. There was something on the riverbed, and she swam around the object and experienced a sudden lack of oxygen, as though someone had blocked the hose.

She gripped her regulator, breathing, breathing.

A skull. A human skull, half submerged in the sludge. She felt giddy as she thought about the objects that had once been inside the boat: the book someone was reading, the bowl that had shattered as the boat sank. All of it became real somehow. Life, death, they merged into one. Ylva heard or imagined a roar in her ears, and she exhaled and swallowed in an attempt to even out the pressure, but she couldn't quite shake it. Why did it feel like she couldn't breathe when she must have several hours' worth of air left? She searched for the button to inflate her buoyancy compensator and start the ascent – not too quickly, that could be fatal – but she couldn't tell the red one from the grey, what was up and what was down. She kicked as hard as she could, causing the sediment to swirl around her, a haze without direction or end.

Allan Westin missed the smell of tar as he approached the dock area. He could still hear the whistle that had once sounded at that time every morning, just before seven, as the workers raced down Lunde's hills towards the shipyard on their bikes.

Turpentine and diesel, the clanking and the thumping and the lapping of waves as the tugs arrived to have their hulls painted after the winter. He could just see them. There was the *Stufvaren* and there were the old whaling boats, *Björn* and *Backe*, reconfigured to haul logs. There was the *Dynäs II*, a little grander than all the others with her velvet couches like the *Orient Express*. King Gustaf VI Adolf himself had travelled in her. There was a thrill in the spring air, something that still brought a sense of life to the area, even though all that was now long gone and the river flowed by empty and quiet.

Ghosts and shadows, wherever he went. The engineer's villa at the bottom of the hill was gone too, as were the little girls who once sat on the porch and made paper dollies. Not to mention the beer house where the old men played cards and a young Allan might earn himself five öre by running over to tell the missus that her husband had to work late.

The hills were hard on his old knees and hips, especially

the last steep slope down to the river, where Rabble started tugging on his lead. The dog had never been given much in the way of training – that was one thing they had in common.

A need for freedom, to be able to go wherever they liked.

No following orders from managing directors, as the sawmill bosses called themselves when they decided one name or another wasn't good enough. Men who bought themselves titles like Vice Consul of Venezuela, just to make themselves sound a little more important than they were.

He unclipped the lead and sat down on his usual bench, breathing in the slightly salty air from the river, which was flowing freely once again. It spent the winter frozen and mute, but come spring it flooded back to life. Allan had heard the faint sound of the ice beginning to crack and sing a week or two back, loosening and breaking up without much fuss. It had none of the violent force he remembered as a lad, when the ice seemed to crash and rumble its way downstream, towering up on the banks.

Rabble was splashing about in the cold mountain water, barking and lunging at all the sticks that floated by.

Was that a boat out there?

Yup, a small motorboat, approaching from the south cape of Sandö. Heading straight for Lunde, it looked like.

Allan squinted, not that it helped much with his old eyes. It wasn't until the rickety little thing reached the former dock area that he managed to make out the people on board.

He clipped the reluctant dog back onto the lead and got up.

* * *

A young man, lithe in his movements, jumped down from the gunwale and secured the lines. He could have been anywhere between twenty and fifty given the way people carried on these days, thought Allan. There was another man there too, slightly older but just as supple, plus a woman sitting perfectly still in the stern. She was no spring chicken, but that's not to say she was old. Still in her drysuit, though she'd peeled it down to the waist and wrapped a coat around her shoulders. Allan could see all sorts of tubes and kit lying on the deck.

'Nice weather for diving!' he called over.

The two men said polite hellos and shook his hand. Probably told him their names, too, but that kind of thing went in one ear and straight out the other. There'd been far too many names over the years, he couldn't be expected to remember every damn one. Allan thought they said they were marine biologists, but they corrected him. Marine *archaeologists*. They were in the area to dive the wrecks, had already mapped over three hundred between Sandslån and the High Coast Bridge.

'Hell's bells,' said Allan. 'Three hundred?'

He knew there was all sorts of junk on the bottom of the river, of course, he just hadn't realised it was something that might interest educated folks like these. Fishing for logs had always been more popular among the poor, who built their ramshackle houses from sunken timber and other bits of wood they found bobbing around.

'Right,' he stuttered. 'You found anything good, then?'

The young man glanced over to his friends, seemingly unable to speak for himself. Allan got the sense they were hiding something, as though he had caught them red-handed

8

smuggling booze. The woman was still in the boat, hunched over with her head in her hands. She looked like she was seasick.

'I'm not sure it's the best idea to start shouting about it,' said the older of the two men. 'We don't want anyone to go down there, you know? Before the police have time to come out, I mean. We know what we're doing, and we never touch anything, but with some of these hobby divers there's always a risk.'

'Eh? A risk of what?' Allan looked around. Did they really think the area was crawling with people desperate to get into the river in late April? Just for the fun of it? He'd seen a few loopy winter swimmers over the past few months – something they'd started doing during the pandemic – but they were in and out in a few seconds, woolly hats firmly on their heads.

'What've you found, then?'

More damned mumbling. He didn't want to ask them to repeat it, like some sort of idiot. They'd found a body, he'd caught that much.

'Ah, hell. A person?'

They nodded.

A skull, half buried in the sediment on the bottom of the river, partly hidden beneath the bow of what they thought must be a boat from the early twentieth century.

'So he could be from back then?' said Allan. 'Whoever you found?'

'Impossible to say on first glance,' one of them said. 'We're scientists; we don't like to speculate before there's been a proper investigation.'

They were planning to report it, had dug out a phone and were discussing whether to call the coastguard or 112. It was hardly an emergency, after all. If they were further south, they could have called the Marine Police, but there was nothing of the sort north of Stockholm.

'If you call 112, you'll get someone a hundred odd miles away, up in Umeå,' Allan spoke up. 'Bloody centralisation.'

His stomach turned as he gazed out across the river. So many souls had been lost to its depths over the years.

'But we've got police here,' he said.

E ira Sjödin tugged down her sweatpants, put on a fresh pair of underwear and desperately rummaged through her wardrobe for something slightly more appropriate for an investigator with Violent Crimes. Her top was stained and probably smelled slightly of sweat, but these were the sorts of things she rarely thought about while she was sitting alone in front of her computer at home, relegated to so-called desk duty.

She brewed a pot of coffee and took some sliced bread out of the freezer.

A body in the river, her neighbour had said on the phone. He was with the divers who'd found it right now.

'Have you called it in?' Eira had already found her shoes and was on her way out before Allan Westin had time to explain that the person was very much dead.

'OK,' she said. 'Bring them over.'

A cool breeze blew through the kitchen as she opened the window to let some fresh air in. Strictly speaking, a body in the river wasn't a case for Violent Crimes. Not unless they suspected there was foul play involved. It fell under the jurisdiction of the local police, and she no longer worked for them. Just the thought of her old job made Eira long to get back out on the road, driving mile upon mile, never knowing what might be waiting around the next bend.

She moved her laptop to one side and cleared the case files from the kitchen table. Bank statements, names, telephone numbers. A large drug ring that grew bigger and bigger the more she pulled the thread. It was important work, vital for building a case against their prime suspect down in Sundsvall, but Eira hadn't become a police officer in order to sit in front of a computer all day. It left her feeling restless and drowsy, whether she was in her cramped booth at the station or at the kitchen table – the latter of which had become perfectly acceptable since the pandemic.

Sure, a pregnant woman could go out and speak to a harmless witness on the fringes of a case every now and then, but it was often hard to know what posed a risk, and her bosses took her safety incredibly seriously. That meant desk duty from day one in her new job, because Eira was already pregnant when they offered her the role. It had been so overwhelming and new then, on the boundary between late autumn and winter, and she hadn't been showing, but she knew she still had to let them know.

There were moments when she worried that she had duped them, taking advantage of the section of law that prevented discrimination, even though they insisted that it was her they wanted, that she wouldn't be pregnant forever. Her union rep had three children of her own, and she could vouch for that.

'Hello?' a voice called from the hall.

As ever, Allan Westin let himself in without knocking; they were neighbours, after all. Rabble came bounding in after him, leaving a trail of mud and wet pawprints on the floor.

They were followed by three people who shook Eira's hand, two men and a woman. Jesper, Lars and Ylva. She could make a note of their surnames later.

Eira told them all to take a seat, but Allan remained standing by the hob. The aroma of coffee and toast drifted through the kitchen as the woman explained that she had given in to the temptation to swim under the collapsed Sandö Bridge and then lost her bearings. She was in her fifties, grey hair with blonde highlights.

'It was like I was in a daze.' She hadn't touched her toast, and she let the coffee go cold in her mug. 'Or a dream. I was just staring at the skull and I forgot everything else. Time is so different down there. I couldn't tell you how long I was there for.'

'Nine minutes,' said Jesper, the youngest of the three. Judging by his accent, he came from down south, Värmland. 'I lost sight of her while I was filming the remains of the bridge. That's not so uncommon – it's dark, and visibility is only a few metres. If we lose each other, the protocol is to spend two minutes looking before heading back up to the surface. There was no sign of her up there, so we went down again.'

'It was all my fault,' said Ylva. 'I was so moved by what I'd seen that I completely forgot what I was doing. I thought maybe I'd found . . .' Her eyes began to wander, and she trailed off.

'Tell me what you saw,' said Eira.

It took a while; the woman kept mixing facts with feelings. She had seen death down there.

'It's rare for us to find remains in sunken vessels,' the man named Lars explained. 'Much less common than you might think. People usually manage to get out. Either that or their bodies are carried away on the tide or the current. When we do find someone, it's usually deeper inside the vessel, often because they were asleep at the time of the sinking.'

Scenes from *Titanic* flashed through Eira's head, the third-class passengers trapped in the lower decks, Leonardo DiCaprio handcuffed to a pole. She also remembered the old Evert Taube song about the *Blue Bird* of Hull, the young cabin boy bound to the helm and forgotten. Sinking with no chance of survival.

Once they had found Ylva and established that she was OK, one of the men had dived back down to document what she had seen. Eira leaned in over the camera. Something blurry and pale in the sand, or whatever the sediment on the bottom consisted of. Blue clay, perhaps. She had dealt with that in previous investigations, and she knew that both it and the weakly saline water had a preservative effect.

'Do you know anything about the boat?' she asked.

'No, it's not one we've dived before,' said Jesper. 'But it's big, bigger than most of the others down there.'

Possibly a steamboat, a ferry, a large tug. Most of the finds in the Ångerman River remained unexplored, he explained. It was only in the last few years that they had started to map the wrecks using sonar. From the surface, the soundwaves were able to produce images of objects down to a depth of thirty metres. He took out a laptop to show Eira. The images on the screen looked more like works of art than reality. Shades of brown, almost sepia-coloured, the shadows and silhouettes of scattered vessels.

It was something of a record to have found three hundred wrecks in such a short space of time. Eira thought it looked like someone had thrown a pack of cards into the water, the riverbed littered with the square barges that once used to transport timber to the ferries. They had become obsolete once the steamboat docks were built, and the easiest and most cost-effective solution was simply to sink them.

Some of the finds were marked 'wreck-like object' and required further investigation, and judging by the size and shape of others, they might date back to the seventeenth century. There had been shipyards along the river during the Thirty Years' War, after all.

Eira pointed to a yellowish band stretching across the river, from Lunde to Sandö. It looked like a matchstick that had been snapped in the middle.

'Is that the bridge?'

'That's the bridge.'

She had never really thought about the fact that it was still down there. The tragic collapse of the bridge was one of many wounds that had never fully healed in the area. Using her finger, she traced a line to the spot where they had found the body.

'The current can be pretty strong here . . .' Eira had grown up with the warnings: stay close to shore when you're swimming, and never go in alone.

'Yes, the body could easily have been carried quite some way, if that's what you're thinking.'

She exchanged a glance with Allan, who was leaning back against the woodburning stove with his coffee, and realised he was probably thinking the same thing. The missing.

Those whose names had never been carved onto head-stones, who had lost their lives or fallen into the river – been thrown into it, in some cases. Names she was already sorting through in the back of her mind, that would form a list.

Eira pushed Rabble away. The dog was desperate for attention, his coat stinking of everything that came seeping out in the spring thaw. She made a note of the exact coordinates of the find, at a depth of sixteen metres. That wasn't so bad, considering there were areas where the riverbed was a hundred metres below the surface.

'I'm sorry to ask, but when do you think we can head out again?' Jesper spoke up. 'I know that probably sounds insensitive, but we really want to try to avoid losing too much time.'

Marine archaeology was an underfunded specialism; that was why they set out so early in the morning: to maximise their time in the water.

The lengthening hours of light that arrived with summer, nights that would soon become almost indistinguishable from day.

'It's fine, providing you stay away from this area.' Eira used her finger to draw a circle on the chart they had spread out on the table, a good distance from the wreck. It covered almost the entire stretch of river between Sandö and Lunde. 'Consider this the crime scene.'

She met the woman's wide eyes.

'Routine procedure,' Eira added. 'Just to be on the safe side, until we know more.'

As the others got up to leave, Ylva asked if she could use the toilet.

'When do you think you'll know more?' she asked.

The workload at the National Forensic Centre had gone through the roof lately, which meant the police often had to wait weeks for DNA results – even in cases involving firearms.

'I don't know,' Eira replied. 'It really depends on what we can recover. If we don't find any clothes, for example, or other objects, it could be a while before we even know what century we're looking at.'

'I'm not going to be able to stop thinking about him,' said Ylva, her eyes sweeping out across the river. 'What if he still has family somewhere, someone who misses him?'

Or her, thought Eira.

The police divers arrived three days later, and the flurry of activity on the banks of the river immediately drew a crowd. It was rare for something so big to happen in Lunde.

An idyll, it might seem, at least to those who didn't know about everything people concealed and kept to themselves.

Their voices surrounded Eira as she squinted out at the river, blending together.

What've they found, then?

Some poor sod, apparently. Down on the bottom.

Could it be . . . ?

Too early to say. They haven't even got 'em up yet.

Still.

Yup, oof. Imagine.

There were pauses, silence and mumbling, things that were implied but no one dared actually utter. Eira thought she heard someone saying a prayer, one of the women still involved in the free church.

Bestow thy peace on the lost, still our fears . . .

With each new arrival, they went through the whole charade again. Explaining why there were so many unfamiliar cars parked down by the docks, who the people in overalls were, why they were setting up a table and a white tent over by the edge of the wharf.

No one had argued when Eira offered to arrange the recovery of the body. This was Norrland, a place where limited resources had to cover an enormous area. People helped one another; they weren't too precious about over-stepping boundaries. The overworked Kramfors police were grateful for any help they could get, and her boss in Sundsvall was perfectly happy to lend her out for half a day given she was already on the scene.

Possibly a little too happy.

It would be hard to find a less risky case, thought Eira, but at least it was a chance to get out and about. She heard the sound of a motor and saw the boat coming back in to shore. She'd borrowed it from the coastguard in exchange for promising them a training session at the police shooting range.

Again, this was Norrland.

'Could you all move back, please,' she shouted to the crowd of onlookers. 'And no photographs. Show some respect.'

Eira heard an embarrassed murmur as at least a couple of mobile phones were returned to their owners' pockets. Most of those who had gathered were pensioners, people who had nowhere better to be on a Monday morning, but she was sure they were active on Facebook, on the local forums, in group chats with their grandkids.

The river was calm, not a breath of wind disturbing the surface as the divers carefully carried their cargo ashore. Water poured from the drainage holes in the recovery bags, and the crowd fell silent, craning their necks. One older man actually took off his cap and held it to his chest. Eira wouldn't have been surprised if the elderly church ladies had broken out in song, 'Glorious is the Earth' or something along those lines, but everyone kept quiet.

The forensic technician took the bags and carried them the few metres to the tent. Eira had asked specifically for Shirin ben Hassan, who had been present when they dug up a skeleton in Lockne a few years earlier. Shirin had studied archaeology before realising that what she really wanted to be was a crime scene investigator, applying to police college and continuing her training in the U.S. As luck would have it, she was also an osteologist, an expert in bones. And despite all her training, she didn't look a day older than twenty-seven.

Shirin slowly opened the first of the bags and peered into the void inside the skull, the holes where a pair of eyes had once sat.

'So, what happened to you, my friend?'

That was one of the things Eira liked about Shirin, that she was always on the side of the dead. It was her job to give a voice to those who had been silenced, as she had once put it. To tell the world: this is what happened to me.

'Did you manage to retrieve everything?'

'We don't know,' said one of the police divers, Mira, who had driven down from Umeå. 'Parts of it were scattered, so there could well be more down there, either in the sediment or further downstream.'

Valentin, the other diver, was from the local force in Sundsvall. Both were regular police officers who also happened to be qualified divers, and they were called out whenever the need arose.

They had each been handed a cup of coffee and a cheese sandwich.

'We definitely got most of the torso,' said Valentin, nodding to the other bags. 'One arm, too. And the pelvis.'

'Any clothes?'

'Nope, sorry.'

Eira remembered the Doc Martens boot in the water by Lockne; the way the laces were tied, where it had most likely been bought. That kind of information could speed up the identification process by several weeks. Still, the deceased's teeth looked relatively intact, so with a bit of luck they would be able to find a match from the dentistry register.

Shirin stroked the skull's forehead with something verging on tenderness.

'And what was your impression of where you found him?' she asked. 'Could he have gone down with the boat?'

'He?'

Shirin nodded and pointed to the brow ridge above the eye sockets, then gently turned the skull over and showed them the slope of the crown.

A man, no doubt about it.

'If he was thrown overboard when it sank,' said Mira, 'then I guess the body could have ended up where we found it. Or he could have drifted there, from somewhere upstream, and come to rest against the hull.'

Shirin carefully transferred the bones into a specialist bag for bodies recovered from water, studying each of them in turn. The sun was warm, bright and springlike, and the air inside the little tent quickly grew stuffy. Everything seemed to be taking so long.

'Now, this is just a guess,' she said, her eyes on the remains of the man's upper body, his shoulder blades; she had already examined his arm. 'But I'd say he was a relatively young adult.'

She pointed at several of the bones as she explained. At the sword-like breastbone, 'a sneaky bone it's easy to forget', and his elbow, which was almost completely ossified, something that happened around twenty. At his clavicle, which wasn't quite fully developed, meaning he was under thirty.

Eira glanced over to the huge arch beneath the Sandö Bridge, over forty metres high. As a girl she had thought it reached right up into the sky, at one time the largest concrete arch bridge in Europe. A modern masterpiece which, when it was built, had replaced the need for the ferries and linked the two halves of Sweden. It was still too early to ask, but she knew she had no choice.

'If someone was thrown from a bridge,' she said, 'possibly by force, could they have ended up where he was found?'

'I assume you're thinking about something specific?'

'The day the bridge collapsed.'

'What?' asked Valentin, who was too young to know any better. No, he wasn't much younger than Eira, but he wasn't from the area. He hadn't grown up with the stories. It was an event that probably wasn't mentioned in the history books. No monument had ever been raised to the dead.

'It happened on 31 August 1939, in the afternoon. They'd completed the wooden framework and were ready to pour the concrete. No one knows why it happened.'

The old folks remembered the roar, the screaming, people cycling and running and shouting, *it's collapsed, the bridge*

22

has collapsed. The chaos as sections of bridge and bodies were flung through the air, the simmering water as it all came crashing down, the twenty-metre wave that washed in over Sandö. They remembered that everyone with a boat had gone out, risking their own lives amid the currents and the wreckage in an attempt to save those who were fighting and sank.

The next day, on 1 September, Germany invaded Poland and the worst industrial disaster in Swedish history fell from the front pages.

Eighteen people had died that day, and two of them were never found.

'One of them was pretty young,' Eira continued. 'Around twenty, I think.' She waited for the penny to drop with the others. 'His dad worked there too, but he'd finished his shift that afternoon. When they started work on rebuilding everything, he was there. He wanted to finish the job that killed his son.'

'Jesus,' said Valentin, who had sat down in one of the camping chairs with a Coke Zero. 'I can't even imagine how that must have felt.'

'Maybe he found a sense of meaning in it, despite every-thing.' Eira could hear her father's voice, talking about the value of work, of not giving in, of finishing what you started.

'It's too early to say,' said Shirin, confirming what they already knew: that they couldn't tell whether the bones were twenty years old or eighty – or even older than that. She sealed the last of the evidence bags just as the black van arrived to collect them. 'Send over whatever pictures you've got from down there as soon as you can.'

S omeone must have had their phone out after all, taking a
photograph that they shared on social media or flogged
straight to the local papers, where it was splashed across the
front pages two days later.

Eira snatched up the copy of *Sundsvalls Tidning* in the
waiting room at the clinic. She nibbled on a biscuit and took
a sip of water as she studied the image.

It wasn't especially intrusive or revealing, no visible body
parts. Her own face was in sharp focus, however. The photograph had been taken just as she turned around, possibly at
the exact moment she was telling the crowd that had gathered
to put their phones away.

'Police Assistant Eira Sjödin oversaw the recovery of the
body,' she read underneath. It always made her slightly
uncomfortable to be in the public eye like this, but it was the
headline inside the paper that made her choke on her biscuit.

BODY FOUND IN LUNDE – IS IT MISSING LINA?

The other women's glances shifted from irritation to anger
as Eira kept coughing and spluttering, and she felt like she
had no choice but to explain that it wasn't Covid, it wasn't
even a cold; she just had something stuck in her throat.

From the page in front of her, Lina Stavred smiled her
sweet sixteen-year-old smile. The last known picture of her
before she disappeared one night in early July 1996.

Murdered, according to the officers who spent hours interrogating the fourteen-year-old boy who was eventually charged with her death. Of course the media had run with this angle.

Eira skimmed through the text, which regurgitated the same things as ever. The theory that the boy, Olof, had dumped Lina's body in the river – as he had eventually confessed. The fact that he had been driven out of the area only to reappear three years ago, tearing open old wounds.

That her body had never been found.

Eira wasn't sure whether it was a contraction that made her lean forward with a sharp intake of breath, or whether it was just the usual anxieties surrounding the Lina Stavred case. All the tangled, twisted parts that had never been investigated.

She wished she had spoken a little louder down by the dock in Lunde, in any case. Or that instead of asking people to back up to a respectful distance, she had let them hear what Shirin had to say. In the article, the police spokesperson had announced – quite correctly – that they had to wait for the pathology report before they could make any statements. These procedures were vital in upholding the rule of law and the integrity of their investigation, but it also meant that the news that the dead body was a man was not common knowledge.

All it took was one reporter to have a hunch or receive an unfounded tip, and the whole circus got under way again. A quick search in the archive for terms like Lina, missing, rape, murder, Marieberg and 1996, and the article would practically write itself. Every single person in the area would click on the headline, which meant they would be celebrating their readership figures in the newsroom today.

'Eira Sjödin?'

She shoved the newspaper into her bag and got up.

It was like a tumble drier in there. High-octane noise, disharmony. A motorway tunnel was the other image that came to mind as the midwife moved the wand over the taut skin on her belly and paused.

There it was.

A tapping sound. Quick and persistent, like an angry woodpecker.

Life, beyond all reasonable doubt.

Until now it had all been so abstract. The nausea and the changes to her body, even the ultrasound images showing the contours of a foetus. But listening to a heart beating at its own rhythm, that was something else entirely. All the other things that came with it, none of that mattered any more. The pulsing was more important, her child's frantic gallop towards freedom.

It was alive.

'Everything sounds just perfect.'

The thudding of the baby's heart faded away as the midwife turned her attention to measuring Eira's bump instead.

Eira wanted to ask her to press the wand to her skin again, needed time to catch up with her feelings, but the woman simply handed her a wad of paper to wipe the gel from her skin.

Week twenty-three, almost six months gone.

'I don't see anything about Dad here,' said the midwife,

26

reading through the notes as Eira got down from the bed and reached for her knickers. Another new face on the ward; it wasn't the first time she had been asked. The staff shortages in maternity and neonatal care were so severe that they would be heading for disaster by summer. Things were bad all over the country, but Västernorrland always seemed to be the worst.

'Sorry, maybe he isn't involved?' The woman gave Eira a forced smile. As though every pregnancy involved a father, as though there weren't countless other ways to do things now.

'No, he is,' said Eira. 'I'm just not entirely sure which one of them he is.'

The station was only ten minutes away, that was the main reason she had chosen that clinic.

Eira closed the door to her office.

She gripped her phone, knew she should ring August. She should tell him she had just heard the baby's heartbeat for the first time, how energetic and healthy it was, but he was probably out on a call somewhere. It was better to wait. Eira suspected he would be annoyed that she hadn't asked him along, but if she did that she would have to invite the other possible father, too, in the name of fairness.

And Ricken still had no idea about the baby.

She put her phone down and opened the file on the man from the river instead. No match for his dental records, as yet nameless, and no report from forensics. Eira was debating whether or not to bring up the careless speculation about Lina Stavred with her boss when she heard a knock, a quiet drumroll on the door.

27

'Do you have a minute?'

GG was standing in the doorway, his navy shirt unbuttoned at the neck. Now that he had stepped down as head of the unit, he almost never wore a jacket.

'Sure,' said Eira, scooting to one side to make room for him.

The ventilation in the building had stopped working sometime last century, and the same air had been circulating for decades. Her swollen belly felt uncomfortable around him.

'Everything OK?' he asked.

'Yup.'

She wasn't sure whether he meant her pregnancy or the investigation into the drugs ring, but she took out the list she had compiled.

'We've got small transactions, mobile payments. I've checked all the names against the database, and these are the ones who don't have a record.'

GG scanned the list of names Eira had found from the bank statements, people suspected of buying drugs through the dealer's network. There were plenty of family men with healthy finances helping to keep the business afloat, it seemed. It reminded Eira of a raid on a small-scale brothel she had been involved in when she worked in Stockholm, the messages they had found on one of the Eastern European women's phones. *Hey! Horny, STD-free, all-Swedish economist here – would love for you to give me a great blowjob at 17.30 today xxx*

A few of the names on the list were homeowners, in management positions. One was a successful businessman, another a student of engineering science. They were people who had plenty to lose, in other words, which meant they might be willing to talk.

'Perfect,' said GG. 'You coming?'

'Do you want me to?'

'Unless you've got something else to do?'

'I'm pretty much on desk duty.'

'Right, of course.' He glanced at her bump with a smile that made her feel all warm inside.

Eira bent down and rummaged for something in her bag, she wasn't sure what. Lip balm, perhaps. Winter had left her lips dry and chapped. GG studied the list again.

'I don't think there's much risk of physical violence at the bank.'

Eira didn't care that it was blowing a gale from the sea. She just grabbed her scarf and wound it once more around her neck. Rubbish and sand swirled through the air as they cut across the square. As ever, it was usually a mistake to believe that spring had finally arrived.

'So, how are you doing?' asked GG.

'Really well.'

'Good.'

'And you?'

'Good.'

It felt strange to be walking alongside him. Eira picked up on so many subtexts in everything he said and didn't say. Perhaps that was why she dropped back, ending up half a step behind him. Or maybe it was just that he had a longer stride.

29

That night last autumn, when she had found him locked in a root cellar, hovering on the boundary between life and death. They had been so close then. Eira had used her body to warm him up, trying to share some of her own life with him until the emergency services arrived, whispering words she had never said to anyone before.

People in her family didn't say words like that. She couldn't remember ever hearing her parents utter the words 'I love you', whether to each other or their children. It took someone being unconscious, practically dead, for her to manage it. GG had thanked her when he came round, but he didn't remember anything. That night was always there between them, and yet in some ways it didn't even exist.

'Have you seen what's in the paper today?' she asked, taking out the article about Lina Stavred as they walked. GG stopped and gripped her hand for a few seconds in order to hold the page steady.

'Well,' he said. 'Looks like someone was feeling imaginative.'

'It's true that the forensic examination isn't complete yet,' said Eira. 'But we know that the body is male. Don't you think we should release that information?'

GG read the empty statement from the police spokesperson, who almost certainly didn't have the full story. There were some things that weren't shared across the organisation: investigations that never led to charges and therefore weren't made public; truths that were deliberately kept within a close circle. Like the fact that Lina Stavred was still alive, for example. She hadn't died that night twenty-six years ago; she had left the area and been living under the radar in Stockholm ever since, adopting different identities and being supported by various men.

GG was one of only a handful of people who knew. That was something else he and Eira shared.

'Are her parents still alive?' he asked.

'I don't know. They went to live with family in Finland; I guess they couldn't face staying here. They also had her officially declared dead a year after she disappeared. I mean, according to the police report there was no other explanation.'

GG folded the newspaper and handed it back to her.

'Let them write their stories,' he said. 'If we release the news that it's a man then they'll just find some other poor sod in the archives and dredge up his story again.'

They had reached one of the large banks, a grand stone building with columns and lion heads.

'When did drug dens get so classy?' GG muttered.

Kramfors had once been known as Powder City on account of the high number of drug users there, but that was nothing compared to the reach the drugs now had. Across every generation and social class, far beyond the less salubrious areas of town. The postal service had emerged as the country's biggest drug mule in recent years, enabling people to order whatever they liked online or over the phone and have it delivered straight to their homes in padded envelopes.

Eira and GG were shown through to a small room where loan applications were usually approved or refused. The man in the shiny suit was called Rasmus.

'That must've been the skis I bought for the kids,' he said

when they confronted him with the transaction. 'I found an ad online. I don't know who the seller was.'

'Expensive skis,' said GG.

'I guess it might've been all the hockey gear, actually.'

'For a four-year-old?'

'They've got to get started early. Honestly, you wouldn't believe the pressure the sprogs are under these days.' The banker loosened his tie a little. 'I don't like it, but you want your children to stand a chance, you know?'

'Where did you find the ad?'

'Can't remember. It could've been on Blocket or Facebook Marketplace, I really don't know. The kids grow so fast, I'm always buying and selling stuff.'

'Do you use cocaine at work, too?'

Eira felt the mood change as GG leaned forward, something aggressive lurking just beneath the surface. He was both taller and stronger than the younger man.

'Or is that just for Friday nights?' he continued, his tone much cooler now. 'When you want to unwind and take it easy? How do you feel about the fact that you're funding the criminal gangs? How do you think your employer might feel about it?'

The man's reaction was hard to read, his face as stiff as a film star with too much Botox, eyes drifting off to one side.

'I don't know whether you've seen it on TV, but kids are shooting other kids,' GG went on. 'Don't you think the people who recruit them, who give them the guns, should go down for that?'

'Yeah, I . . . Of course I do.'

'So are you prepared to testify? To tell us what you

bought and who you bought it from? And I'm not talking about skis here.'

The banker glanced down at his watch. An expensive thing, the kind the police had begun to seize from gang members' wrists.

'Am I suspected of anything here? I think I'd like to speak to my lawyer.'

An hour or so later, they had managed to crack the student. He started crying, said they had no idea just how much pressure he was under, how was he supposed to pass his exams if he couldn't stay awake at night. The CEO of an IT start-up also folded, slumping back on a huge sofa.

'I mean, fuck . . . it's not like I'm a *junkie*,' he told them. 'And it's actually much less dangerous than alcohol. Society is so hypocritical about all this stuff.'

'Would you be willing to testify at trial?'

'About what? The hypocrisy?'

'About the fact that the money you earn through this company is funding organised crime.'

GG lit a cigarette in the doorway as they came out, right beneath a no smoking sign.

'What's wrong with these people?' he asked, blowing the smoke away from Eira. It swung back on the breeze, wrapping her in his breath. 'When did we stop seeing ourselves as part of the bigger picture? Kids are getting shot, for fuck's sake.'

S hirin called while Eira was on her way home. She had just pulled over in Älandsbro, overcome by a sudden craving for a hot dog with mash and pickles from the grill there.

'I've got some news about our friend from the river.'

'What is it?'

'I'm in Umeå; the pathologist wanted to discuss a few things.'

'Did you drive all that way for an accidental drowning?'

'Had some other business, too,' said Shirin. 'Are you at your computer?'

'I can be in about twenty minutes.'

Eira stepped on the gas the last twenty or so miles back to Lunde. She called Shirin the minute she was sitting at the kitchen table, grabbing a pack of biscuits from the cupboard as she downloaded the images.

Ribs, a section of spine.

'It probably wasn't a drowning accident,' said Shirin. 'Or a jumper, for that matter.'

'What am I looking at here?'

Eira clicked between the images as Shirin talked about a damaged cervical vertebra that had caught the pathologist's eye. There was, she explained, a minute notch in the bone. One they had double checked under the microscope.

Crumbs from Eira's biscuit dropped to the keyboard as she zoomed in and enlarged the image. An indentation, a small nick.

'We both agree that it could have been caused by a bullet,' said Shirin. 'It also seems to have grazed the breastbone on the way out. The angle fits.'

Eira felt the baby's racing heart. Or maybe it was her own, pounding at the same speed.

'A shot to the back of the head?'

They were sitting outside the People's House, by the road past the monument to the Ådalen shootings, its stumbling bronze horse forever frozen in the moment before the military opened fire on a group of protesters. Allan knew several of them, which meant he had to stop and chat.

Bettan Ljung was there, the old crone who'd won big on the scratch cards and refused to say what she'd done with the money. She clearly hadn't blown it all on expensive clothes, at any rate, always wearing the same shabby coat to flap around Lunde. Kalle Molin was there, too – Allan had often come to blows with him in his younger days, about the politics of betrayal and the powers that be – plus a couple of summer visitors who'd come up early this year.

Remote workers, so Allan had heard. Apparently it made no difference whether they were here or in Stockholm. One of them was leaning back against the wall of Café 31, staring down at their phone.

'Makes you wonder whether it's that lass they've found, young Lina,' said Bettan. 'It's all I can think about.'

'She's not said anything, has she? Your neighbour, Veine Sjödin's girl,' asked Kalle Molin, turning to Allan. 'They'd have to tell us if they knew anything, wouldn't they?'

Allan cleared his throat as he debated whether or not it

would be stupid to say anything at all. Eira had become something of a bonus daughter to him over the years. He often thought that if he died in his sleep, she would be the one to find him. After he failed to drop the dog off, to take the paper in. There was talk that they were planning to cut back to three editions a week, which meant he could well be lying there for some time before she noticed.

'What they've been writing in the papers is a load of rubbish, I'll tell you that much,' he said, keen that it didn't seem like he knew nothing. 'It's not Lina Stavred, they're sure of that.'

Eira had mentioned that after Allan asked a few questions when he went over to get the dog. She had been annoyed that the press were writing things they knew nothing about.

'If only it was,' said Kalle. 'So her poor parents could finally be at peace – if they're still alive, that is.'

'Who could it be, then?' asked one of the newcomers.

'We'll find out soon enough.'

'Unless the poor sod's been down there a long time, of course. It'll probably be impossible then.'

'No, remember the Stone Age woman they've got on show over in Härnösand? They managed to work out what she looked like.'

'Rubbish, no one knows what she actually looked like.'

'I saw a thread online,' the newcomer spoke up. 'Someone said the body was a man. That he was murdered.'

'How did they know that?'

'There's always someone who knows.'

Rabble was sniffing around Kalle's dachshund, and he

was reluctant to leave when Allan discreetly tugged on the lead. The gossip made him uncomfortable. Allan was born and raised in the area, he knew what it could be like. One day people were shouting and screaming, and the next they turned away and refused to speak.

He had been trying to keep himself busy and had done a bit of tidying in the garage, a few other odd jobs. Anything to avoid having to face up to death, as he had on Monday when he watched them lift the remains of a person out of the river. Pieces of bone. Broken but still understandable, voids where a pair of eyes had once been.

'Everything OK with Maarit?'

Kalle again, poking his nose into things that had nothing to do with him.

'Sure, she's just fine.'

'She coming up here at all this summer?'

Allan mumbled something that was neither a yes nor a no and managed to drag Rabble away, saying, *bye, see you when I see you*, and continuing down towards the river.

A few more acquaintances had gathered by the old customs house, but he spotted them from a distance and turned the other way, up the steep slope past Wästerlund's Café, still shuttered after the winter.

Rabble tugged on his lead, wanting to walk the same route as usual.

'Heel!' Allan snapped, though the unruly pooch had never been taught any real commands. Once they were far enough away from the main road, he unclipped the lead and let the pest of an animal loose.

Up at the top of the slope, God's house was also boarded

up. Sold, or so he'd heard, no doubt to someone who would turn it into a home. It did have a great position on the hill, after all. The Bethania Chapel had been built by volunteers, back when Lunde was a melting pot for sinners and drunks in need of the Baptists' salvation. According to the stories, even the worst of the booze hounds had helped carry wood up to the site, hoping their efforts would balance out some of the misery they had caused in the event that Judgement Day really did come.

There was a bench outside the chapel, a place for people to rest their weary legs and look out at the river that wound through the landscape. *March evenings' blue hour in Ådalen*, as Birger Norman, the poet of Svanö, once wrote. *What do I care about Paris?*

It had been five years since Maarit left Lunde, five years since Allan began telling anyone who asked that yes, he would be joining her. There was just so much to do first, with the house and everything else.

Loneliness had taken root inside him – somewhere just behind his ribs, if he were to try to put a finger on it – like a dull ache.

She had made up her mind one day, and that was that. Packed her bags and moved to Stockholm like some sort of overgrown teenager, though of course it wasn't work or study that had lured her down there. Not at the age of seventy-five, no. It was because of the grandkids. They had four of them, which was a miracle in its own way. Two great-grandkids, too. All living in different areas of the capital. Allan had been to visit, but he'd never quite managed to get his bearings there, to wrap his head around where Hökarängen was in relation to Helenelund, and so on.

He had said he would join her.

He still wore the ring on his finger, too – had done for fifty-four years – but deep down he knew she had broken free.

There was nothing he could do about it.

Rabble disappeared into the bushes down by the old substation where Allan and his brother, his late brother, had once played football and met girls.

The truth was that Maarit had only ever been visiting. If it had been down to her they never would have lived in Lunde in the first place, nor Ångermanland. They wouldn't have moved into the house on his grandparents' farm, and the kids wouldn't have played in the same overgrown meadows he had as a boy. Maarit's family were up in Luleå, and there was nothing she wanted more than to be close to them. He had been willing to move there with her, but he also had his job to think about. He needed to work, to bring in money, but Umeå had given him a firm no.

And so she'd had to uproot herself instead.

'These mountains,' she sometimes said, when she was feeling down. It often happened around this time of year, in early spring, when she got her annual bout of the blues. 'I can't see past them. They're like towering walls all around me. I can't breathe here.'

Allan had never come out and said it, but he assumed she knew. He could hear it in her voice, in the lengthening silences in their conversations.

The distance between them.

He sat on the bench, watching as the dark blue of the sky merged with the mountains, erasing them from view. The truth was that he would never be able to leave this place.

He was bound to it in ways he couldn't explain.

E ira picked out a Monica Zetterlund album, soft jazz at a low volume. She had found peace in these visits to the care home, a sense of timelessness where memory didn't have to get in the way. Coping was simply a case of adapting.

Accepting things as they were and ignoring how they might have been, particularly now that she really could have done with having her mother around. Someone to share the happy news with, to help out, be a grandmother.

She poured a sherry for Kerstin, a coffee for herself.

'Bottoms up!' said Kerstin, raising her glass in a toast and then knocking it back in one go.

Eira hadn't dared keep alcohol in the house while her mother was still living at home; not because she had a drink problem, but because she often forgot what time it was. She would drink in the morning, have a few glasses too many. But now that she was here she would be safe even if she did drink a bit too quickly, the lack of moderation that had come hand in hand with her dementia.

'Aren't you going to join me? You don't need to drive home, you know. You can stay here tonight.' Kerstin's eyes scanned the room as though she was looking for a guest bed, as though her life hadn't been reduced to eighteen square metres.

'I'm pregnant, Mum, you know that. I've told you.' Eira moved her chair closer and took her mother's hand, pressed it to her belly. Telling her, *feel this, surely you can understand this, it isn't the kind of thing a person forgets.* 'Six months in May.'

Kerstin pulled her hand back and shook her head.

'Oh, I never thought you'd get yourself into this sort of mess, having a little one at your age. But I suppose it's too late now.'

'I'm almost thirty-five, Mum. I'm hardly too young. I know what I'm doing.'

'Can I have another?'

Eira got up to grab the bottle of sherry, pausing for a moment with her back to Kerstin. She had known right away that she wanted this baby. Mostly for her own sake, but still. It was an opportunity to make her mother happy. To get closer to her. One last chance.

She filled the glass and reached for a couple of photo albums from the shelf. Pictures from the sixties and seventies. The past was much easier to handle. They flicked through snaps from her parents' honeymoon to Florence, young Kerstin posing like Botticelli's Venus on the Ponte Vecchio, one hand over her crotch and the other half-heartedly covering her breasts. The wind tugging at her hair.

'Look how beautiful you were, Mum.'

There were photographs of her posing in front of a sculpture of a naked man, in the seating area outside a bar, by an enormous church door. No captions, just the images, colour prints that had faded over time. If this was a police investigation, Eira could have googled the places and put names to locations, followed in her parents' footsteps, but it wasn't.

On the next page, they had reached the sea, Kerstin emerging from the waves. Her father was always the one behind the camera.

Their travels quickly gave way to the first pictures of Magnus as a baby, the young mother with the child in her arms.

'What a chubby little thing he was,' said Eira.

'Nine stone, four pounds.'

'Nine pounds, four ounces, surely?'

'Yes, good grief. Yes.' Kerstin laughed, but Eira wasn't sure she had really understood the mistake. 'Seven hours I laboured, split right open down there.'

These detailed memories still came out from time to time, with crystal-clear precision. Or maybe they were just things she had talked about so many times that she knew the story by heart.

More photographs flicked by: Magnus learning to crawl, to walk, holding his first kitten.

'Oh, look, that's Tusse. Or is it Nicke? The one who got run over. Do you remember?'

Eira didn't mention that the cat had died before she was born, picking up another of the albums to avoid having to talk about Magnus. Kerstin rarely remembered that he was currently in prison in Umeå, serving a sentence for manslaughter, and Eira had largely stopped reminding her. It was easier to dodge the issue with lies, telling her mother that he was busy, that he'd gone on holiday, that he would no doubt be coming to visit next week.

By then Kerstin would have forgotten anyway.

Time took another lurch backwards, to Kerstin's childhood in the fifties. It looked like an old film; teenagers, a camping holiday. Kerstin with friends; this must have been later, during her time in high school, sitting on a lawn with flared jeans and messy hair. Eira liked seeing her mother like that, young and wild. The version of her that was still in there somewhere.

'Look at this one, you're smoking! I didn't know you were a smoker.'

'What about him.' Kerstin jabbed a sticky finger at a boy with long dark hair. He was gazing straight at the camera. 'He's a real looker, huh?'

'Check out your outfit, Mum! Those sunglasses. You look like Yoko Ono.'

Her laughter felt like a shimmering moment of mercy.

Eira kept turning the pages, uncovering pictures from a trip to Stockholm, taken in front of the palace and with her friends by the water; snaps from her high-school graduation. Her grandparents, proudly dressed up for the occasion. Kerstin was the first member of the family to have completed upper secondary school. She was the future, their bright hope.

Her chin slumped down against her chest as she dozed off in her armchair.

When the staff came in to say that dinner was ready, Eira stayed behind to wash the cups and go through her mother's clothes. Were they clean? Did she need anything else? Something had usually gone missing, but she had stopped asking about that.

She took out her computer to read through the pathologist's report, which had finally arrived after four days. They had managed to narrow down the man's age. He was somewhere between twenty and twenty-five, and he had broken his wrist no more than a couple of years before his death. The break had healed nicely, which meant he had lived during a time with access to sophisticated medical care, and the fact that his teeth were also in good shape suggested he hadn't lived a disorderly life. These were all things that could help to identify him going forward. Dental records were kept for seventy years in Sweden, often much longer than that if you really delved into a dentist's own archives, but that assumed you knew who you were looking for.

They had successfully extracted a small amount of DNA from inside his teeth and his thigh bone, but it would be a while before they knew whether that had yielded any results.

So far, their searches of the missing persons' register hadn't brought them any closer to the young man's identity, but they had shared everything they had internationally.

Because of the trace left by the bullet, the investigation was now officially a murder inquiry. Eira scrolled down to see who had been assigned the case and was surprised to find her own name there. The new group leader hadn't said anything about that.

'Gosh, are you here already?'

Kerstin was back in the doorway, though no more than ten minutes had passed since she left. Her trousers looked loose, thought Eira. Had she eaten anything at all?

Anxiety in her eyes as she peered around the room.

'Where's Magnus? Is he late again?'

Winter seemed to have reared its head again that morning in mid-May, when Eira finally managed to get the police divers back into the river.

She went out with them this time. Stood on deck and felt the cold air bite her cheeks, fingers growing stiff as they struggled into their gear. Gloves, rubber shoes, no more than a narrow chink of bare skin once they were done. The water temperature, they had told her, was only seven degrees.

Between the frigid trunks of the birches on Sandö, Eira could make out a couple of strange-looking buildings. They belonged to the rescue training school based on the little island, and were used to teach the students how to save people from burning buildings and put out raging fires.

The divers gestured to each other and tipped back over the edge of the boat. Just a few seconds later, all trace of them had vanished from the surface of the water.

The river was cold and grey.

Eira took shelter in the cabin, moving over to the screen and waiting until the divers had reached the right depth. Visibility would be poor for the first few metres, they had told her, but below that the water was clear. They had access to much more advanced equipment this time.

The officer from the coastguard handed her a mug of coffee, and the screen came on. They had contact. No sound, but a swaying image. The diver holding the camera moved slowly alongside the wreck, following the edge of the vessel where it was resting on the riverbed. They hadn't gone down there to do any digging, simply to take a better look around now that they knew there was a crime involved.

The camera paused by the side of the boat, and the diver gently ran a hand over a plaque on its hull, wiping away the sand and clay. Eira could make out something birdlike, possibly a coat of arms. Was that an eagle?

A shudder passed through the cabin. The officer was leaning over her, following everything, and he was the first to speak.

'That's a double-headed eagle,' he said. 'I'll be damned if the boat's not Russian.'

The second diver came into shot and made a gesture, and they moved on. An unsteady journey over the uneven river-bed. There was a log, another, a mass of timber that had sunk over the years, then back to the boat again. They had now reached the bow, and the camera swung around and moved closer, right up against the vessel where it tilted sharply towards the depths.

They worked carefully to uncover their find, and before long Eira could make out the bones of a foot. It was followed by something else, some sort of rod or hook.

'What is that?' she asked.

'Not sure,' said the officer. 'But if you look at this angle here . . .' He pointed to the bottom corner of the screen. Smooth lines curving upwards, metal rather than wood.

'An anchor?'

* * *

Bringing it up to the surface was a slow process. Eira held the lift bag while the divers took off their masks. A brief drink break before they headed back down.

They were confident they could recover the anchor without having to bring in extra help, estimating that it weighed somewhere around ninety kilos.

'That sounds pretty light,' said the officer. 'Given the size of the boat, I'd expect it to be upwards of a hundred and fifty.'

They had taken a number of photographs down there, and Valentin plugged the camera in to the computer to show them on a larger screen. The resolution was better than the video, the camera much closer.

He shuffled to one side to make room for Eira.

There was the foot, half buried in the sediment. And there was the anchor, which seemed to be surrounding it.

'We had to lift it off to get the leg loose,' he explained.

'No chain?' asked the officer.

'Nope.'

'Rope? Line?'

The two divers shook their heads.

Their silence was loaded, with something Eira couldn't quite understand. She had grown up by the river, close to the coast, but that didn't mean she was all that comfortable in the world of boats. Young people got themselves reconfigured pickups and longed for a proper car so that they could get to Kramfors or Härnösand, but where would she have gone by boat? To Lugnvik or Klockestrand on the other side of the river? Sleepy communities that were no different to her own?

'What does that tell you?' she asked.

'If it was used to anchor a boat then it should be attached to a fifty-, maybe even a hundred-metre-long chain,' said Mira, glancing over to Eira. 'It's what helps the anchor settle so it can dig down into the riverbed.'

She scrolled back several images.

'And if you look here, you can see that the object is partly underneath the bone. That could be a coincidence, but . . .'

'You mean it could have been used to sink the body?' Eira leaned in, trying to imagine a rope being wound, clothes that might have disintegrated over time. A shot to the back of the head and a body that had to be hidden, whatever the cost.

She called Shirin as the divers went back down. The crime scene investigator said she could leave Sundsvall in the next hour or two.

By then, the divers had managed to haul the anchor up onto the deck. The skipper started the engine and they headed back to the shore.

Eira could see that a crowd of onlookers had gathered by the docks, and she grabbed a pair of binoculars. There were several cars there, parked just outside the fence by what some in the area still called the Clink, after the old drunk cells. The buildings were long gone, but the name lived on, the words much more powerful than the thing they had once described.

She spotted the logo of the local paper on the side of one of the cars, TV4 on another. They must have been reporting on something else in the area to have come to Lunde for this, she thought.

'Let's keep going upstream,' she said. 'I'd really like to avoid the cameras until we know more.'

The speculation around Lina Stavred had stopped since the police opened a murder inquiry and released the information about the body being male, but several regional papers had already picked up the story, which meant that they were keen to cover any updates in the case.

Headlines shouting brutal murder, who is the mystery man in the river, and so on.

'Where are we heading?' the officer shouted as they passed beneath the Sandö Bridge.

Eira glanced up at the sky, the clouds grey and heavy above the concrete arch. Her hands were cold and stiff as she scrolled down to his number. She wasn't used to making the big decisions, to facing the press, leading others and assigning jobs, and perhaps that was why her thoughts had turned to her old colleague.

A cabin by the water, with its own private jetty and a veranda where they could work in peace, away from the prying eyes of the public and the media. Someone who understood what was what.

'Just give me a minute.'

One small part of her still wasn't sure as she listened to the phone ring, but she couldn't come up with a better idea.

'Could you go under the bridge between Sandö and Svanö?' she asked once she hung up.

'No problem.'

'There's a private jetty we can use in Klockestrand.'

E ilert Granlund had taken Eira under his wing when she
was a new recruit at the station in Kramfors, never
missing an opportunity to share the things he had learned
over the course of his long career as a police officer, always
encouraging and believing in her.

For a brief moment before he picked up, she had managed
to convince herself he was dead and felt terrible for missing
the funeral, but Eilert was alive and well and was now
standing on the jetty outside his summerhouse, waving his
arms to show them where to go.

'You think you've escaped once you retire, but no,' he
said, laughing loudly as the officer moored the boat to a
rickety post. 'If it's not the crooks who come knocking, it's
you lot.'

There was a fire burning in the hearth as they came
inside, and Eira noticed a photograph of Eilert's wife on the
sideboard, surrounded by candles.

'I didn't know . . .'

'She passed just before Christmas. But she was in so
much pain it almost came as a relief.'

'I'm sorry.'

Shirin pulled up on the driveway and immediately laid
claim to the veranda. The officer got back into his boat and
set off for the coastguard station in Härnösand.

Eilert started making coffee.

'Almost choked when I saw what they were writing in the paper, that it could be Lina's body they'd found,' he said. 'I was hoping the press had finally got it right this time.'

'We already knew it wasn't her,' said Eira.

Through the window, she saw that the previously so well-tended garden was starting to become overgrown, dotted with weeds she recognised from her own flowerbeds.

She had always been able to talk freely with Eilert in the past, but now it felt like she was tiptoeing around him, walking on eggshells. He was the one who had led the investigation into Lina's disappearance in the nineties, who had interrogated the teenage boy suspected of having killed her. Eira had sat through hours and hours' worth of footage, and had watched them pile pressure on the boy until he finally cracked and confessed.

You remember, Olof. We know you remember.

'Do you have any milk?' she asked.

As she helped him fill the thermos with coffee, taking out the flatbread, butter and cheese, she told Eilert what little they knew about the man whose bones they were busy unloading onto his veranda.

'So have you got any theories on how he died?'

'Looks like a shot to the top of his neck,' said Eira.

'Christ. And the timeframe? Even the foggiest idea when it might've happened?'

'Not yet, and considering how overworked they are at the lab it'll probably be a while before we know any more.'

On the other side of the patio doors, Shirin had spread a plastic sheet over the recently oiled deck. They watched her movements as she picked up and studied the parts of a foot, a leg.

'We think the body might have been deliberately sunk,' Eira said after a moment. 'But that's not something we've released yet.'

'Oof,' said Eilert. 'Not your average drunken brawl, in other words – especially not with the shot from behind. Are we talking about an execution here?'

He glanced over to her when she failed to reply.

'You don't think you need to worry about me keeping quiet, do you?'

'No, of course not.'

Eira heard his heavy breathing behind her as she opened the patio doors, caught a slight whiff of whisky that followed her out.

Shirin was in the process of uncovering the anchor. Cast iron and rust, probably the most common model of admiralty anchor. She carefully picked away the remaining sediment from the ring where the chain should have been attached.

'If the body was tied to the anchor somehow, then the rope or line could easily have come loose over time,' she said, straightening up to take the coffee.

He was dead when he entered the water, thought Eira. Shot from behind. He wouldn't have felt himself being dragged down.

'With the caveat that I'm not exactly an expert on nautical antiques,' Shirin continued, 'I'd guess this anchor is last century, possibly even older. That doesn't necessarily mean much, of course; it could have ended up in the water at any point.'

Eira let Eilert take over, asking questions about the man's teeth, the spot where he had been found, the sediment at that depth. It didn't matter how much experience she now had, how much progress she had made, she was and always would be a novice in his presence. She also liked seeing him step back into his former role.

'So, either no one missed the bloke or he never bothered going to the dentist?'

That bullish laugh, all the jokes she had heard before.

Eilert started talking to Shirin about the latest advances in DNA technology, which he now followed from a distance, but still with great interest. About how remarkable it was that genealogists had managed to solve a random double murder by tracking down the killer through relatives as far back as the eighteenth century – not to mention that it was now possible to produce a picture of a person's face using only their DNA, a process developed in the U.S.

'I read that the police down south somewhere tried to identify a murder victim that way, but how sure can they really be?'

'I'm guessing it'll be a while before it's admissible as evidence,' Shirin agreed. 'And we'll still need the Americans' help. People think that just because the technology exists, we should be all over it, but the cost isn't the only issue. It has to hold up to scrutiny, too.'

She grabbed the last of the bags containing the bones just as the rain began pattering on the tin roof overhead.

'Christ, I miss this sometimes,' said Eilert.

S pring didn't seem to have reached Strinne yet, and there were patches of snow still dotted about the property. As Eira got out of the car, she realised that it wasn't snow at all. It was foam.

Was he seriously washing his old bangers?

The red Cadillac was definitely gleaming in the fading evening light, a well-tended Eldorado. Unlike the other rust buckets, it actually looked roadworthy.

She found Ricken out back, sitting with a blanket wrapped around his shoulders and a small fire in the barbecue to stave off the chill.

'I can throw some food on if you're hungry?'

'No, don't worry.'

'Sit down.'

Eira was still wearing her bulky anorak, less because of the weather than because it hid her growing belly. For a moment or two, the setting sun made the river look like it was ablaze; the thick clouds from earlier had blown away.

Spring. A constant back and forth.

'Who've you locked up today, then?' Ricken asked, flashing her his irresistible smile.

'No one,' said Eira. 'But there's still time.'

'Anyone you want me to squeal on?' He held out a beer, but she shook her head; wouldn't be sleeping over, not this time. She sat down on a rickety camping chair, and he draped the blanket over her legs. It couldn't be much more than six or seven degrees, but he had to be outside, free.

'I was just passing by,' she said. 'I'm not on duty.'

'You're a cop,' he said. 'Are you ever off duty? Aren't you all cops through and through, loyal to the powers that be?'

'Come off it, I don't have the energy.' Eira looked down at the book lying beside him, in last year's muddy, trampled grass. *The Prince* by Machiavelli, a dog-eared paperback. She had never read any of the books Ricken read, not even when she was young and dizzy and in love.

'Don't think you get away with it just because you're good,' he continued. 'Even the good have to become a tool of the powers they serve, otherwise you're a traitor, which you don't want to be because your privilege and prosperity depend on your loyalty to the power.'

'There's something I need to talk to you about,' said Eira.

'Hey, don't get upset, I mean in general terms. Power takes over our lives unless we actively shut it out. They've been keeping an eye on us up here ever since the king decided to have a sheriff of Ångermanland, and after that it was the Security Service and their secret spies in the IB. The names might change, but they're basically the same. And these days that's all they need,' said Ricken, pointing to the phone she was spinning round in her hand. He must have noticed that she was nervous. 'They don't need to send anyone out to watch over us now, we do it all ourselves.'

Eira let him babble away as she searched for the right words. She had already tested them all out in her head, tried different ways of saying it.

There weren't many things that scared her, but this . . . Getting the words out.

How he might respond.

Just like the last time, when she was seventeen, when Ricken broke up with her and her period failed to arrive in the weeks that followed.

What was it he used to say back then, when they were younger?

That it was wrong to bring a child into this world. He wanted a different kind of life; he wanted freedom, not the shackles of a relationship. He didn't want to have power over anyone else.

Eira had dealt with it in secret back then; only her best friend knew. And Kerstin, of course, though she had probably forgotten about it by now. Her mother hadn't questioned or judged her – on the contrary. She had trusted that Eira's decision was the right one, that life had different plans for her.

We didn't have that option, you know. When I was your age.

Eira couldn't bring herself to look at Ricken as she said it.

'I'm pregnant.'

She sensed rather than heard him shudder, a bit like a deer when it smells danger. Ears pricked and skin quivering, followed by a rapid dash into the bushes. Gone, taking cover. That reaction.

'You don't have to be involved,' she continued before he had time to catch his breath. 'I'm not even sure it's yours.'

'A baby?' He gripped her hand, forcing her to look at him. That smile, the twinkle in his eye. She was so damn defenceless when it came to his laugh. 'Am I going to be a dad?' Ricken leapt up from the stray car seat where he had been sitting, taking a ridiculous leap onto the grass. 'Are you serious? Are you sure? Can I see?'

Eira tried to stop him from pulling her up from the chair, had no choice but to let him open her anorak and put a hand on her stomach.

'Shit, you're really showing. I can feel it. Is she kicking?'

'What makes you think it's a she?'

'Because she's going to be just like you.'

What else could she do but laugh?

'So, who's the other guy?' Ricken continued once he was sitting down again. 'Do I know him?'

He didn't sound angry, but then again why would he? They had never talked about being exclusive; this thing between them was nothing like that, nothing that could be called a relationship. It was sporadic, whenever Eira felt like coming over. Ricken never called her.

'A colleague,' she said. 'You don't need to know. Like I said, I can do this on my own.'

He was holding her with both hands now, his face serious, trying to force her to look him in the eye.

'I don't give a shit about genes and all that crap,' he said. 'We'll do this together either way, you hear me? You know how it is, you know me. I'm not the best at living with people. I never thought I'd have a kid.'

Her voice betrayed her, as though she was still seventeen.

'I didn't think you wanted to,' she managed to stutter.

'You never asked.'

Eira got up.

59

'I've got to go.'

He followed her back to the car, gave her a long hug and ruffled her hair. There was nothing that made her feel both so little and so secure, though she knew this wasn't a place of safety.

As Eira drove away, cold from sitting outside, she felt a flicker of that old fear of being trapped. She slowed down as she approached the sharp bends in the road, known locally as the death curves after a nasty accident there in the sixties. It happened the day after Sweden switched over to driving on the right, when the driver in the approaching car forgot. Several young people had died.

The rockface rose sharply at one side of the road. Growing up, her life had been shaped by the desire to get away, a fear of getting stuck, of losing sight of the alternatives. She remembered her mother's voice in the distant past: *don't forget you can do whatever you want to do, but be careful not to get stuck with someone just because he wants you.*

And yet there had been moments when she had longed for that baby. Not to be a mother at the age of seventeen, but a confusing dream that maybe, just maybe, it would be enough to get him to stick around.

Rabble was curled up at the foot of the bed, smelling softly of damp fur and bad breath. Allan had got into the habit of bringing him over in the evenings. He hadn't said anything, but Eira knew it was because she was pregnant, because of a belief that a woman shouldn't be left alone in that condition, at least not at night. A quiet gesture of consideration that didn't require any thanks or fuss, but which also ignored what *she* wanted. Not having a dog in her bed, for example. A dog that leapt up without warning and whose nose tickled the backs of her knees.

She had tried to get to sleep, she really had, but Lina Stavred just kept swirling through her head whenever she closed her eyes.

Eira was now sitting up with her laptop instead. No lights, just the pale moonlight and the bright glare of the screen. She had held off long enough.

It wasn't against the law for her to access investigations in other regions, but all logins were registered and would be visible to anyone who went to the effort of checking. Still, Eira just couldn't resist.

At first glance, the case looked like a drunken brawl.

Grubby, and of no real interest.

November last year.

A fifty-two-year-old man, the middle manager at a

telecoms company, had been found dead at his home in Täby on the outskirts of Stockholm. Stabbed to death. Bottles and mess everywhere, alcohol in his system. There were no witnesses, but several neighbours reported that a woman seemed to have been living there for a while. No one knew her – they didn't even know her name – but the National Forensic Centre had found a hit for her fingerprints.

Matching a young woman who had been declared dead, whose body had never been found.

Lina Stavred.

The preliminary investigation into her disappearance contained various pieces of evidence, which meant that the police in Stockholm had been able to confirm the match using DNA.

Eira spent a long time studying the images of the forty-two-year-old woman her colleagues in the capital had managed to dig up from the dead man's online presence. Her eyes were as pale and blue as ever, like a river in the morning once the ice melts in spring. Eira thought she could see the same coldness in them, a hint of danger, but perhaps that was just because she knew too much. Lina the adult was much plumper than she had been as a teen, her longish hair dyed dark and with no discernible style.

No one would recognise her as Lina Stavred if they bumped into her on the street.

The alert the Stockholm police put out had been internal, which made sense. No one could be sure whether the woman was the perpetrator or simply another victim who had fled the scene. For all they knew she could be lying dead somewhere too. They had chosen to share the latest images of

Lina with the public, but they had withheld her name, pre-sumably because they knew that a media circus wouldn't help their case. Stockholm had also reached out to the police in Finland for help finding her parents. Lina's father was still alive, but unresponsive following a severe stroke.

It had been five months since Eira heard about the case, in December, just after GG woke up from his nightmare out by Högbonden lighthouse, and it had been eating away at her ever since. No, that probably wasn't the right word. Haunting her? Terrorising her at night, sometimes, to the extent that she had to get up and log in to this damn investigation where nothing ever seemed to happen.

Back in December, when GG first told her about the match, Eira had spoken to the Stockholm police, told them she had more information, that Lina Stavred had a tattoo on her left arm.

That she had probably killed before.

A transcription of that conversation was right there on the screen in front of her, and it felt so strange to read her own words.

LG: How long have you known that Lina Stavred is alive?
ES: I found out during an investigation three years ago.
LG: How?
ES: I came across some suspicious posts on Facebook, among other things, and then I followed that line of enquiry to Stockholm. I think I might have met her there, in a café, but I didn't realise it at the time. She was calling herself Simone; she could have had various names over the years.

LG: And you never reported any of this?

ES: We had no proof it was definitely Lina, and even if it was it's not exactly a crime to be alive. There just wasn't enough to justify reopening the case.

LG: And you believe that before she disappeared in the nineties, she killed someone. A man by the name of . . .

ES: Kenneth Isaksson.

Eira could just picture the young police assistant, hear his warm voice. Linus Gustafsson, who had been sent north to take her statement. She remembered him scrolling on his iPad, utterly clueless.

LG: A crime your brother confessed to and was later convicted of?

ES: Magnus did that to protect Lina. He felt guilty, but that doesn't mean he—

LG: According to Magnus Sjödin, Lina Stavred wasn't even there.

ES: She was. I know she was.

LG: We've spoken to your brother. He maintains his version of events.

(Pause)

Seeing it written in black and white, there was no escaping just how weak it was. They had no evidence, only what Magnus had told Eira late one evening while they were alone, and never again. By that point he had already confessed to manslaughter, and there had been nothing she could do about it.

Or had there?

If she had refused to be drawn into his warped logic and studied the whole thing with her police officer's hat on, if she hadn't fallen for his threats of confessing to even worse crimes, could she have prevented the death of a man in Täby three years later?

Whatever the answer, her information didn't seem to have made any difference to the investigation. Eira logged out, assuming that no one would notice if she accessed the files every single day; they were far too busy with all the shootings down there.

When they arrest Lina, she thought, the whole thing will come crashing down. Loyalty won't protect her this time. A prosecutor in Stockholm will take over the case, and facts will be the only things that matter, not half-truths and old lies.

Eira curled up with one hand on the sleeping dog, the warmth of another living creature. He really did smell terrible.

'And how's it going with our murder victim from the river?'

They had already dealt with the most pressing issues when Silje Andersson turned to Eira during the morning briefing.

'Are we any closer to putting a date on it yet? Any idea who he is?'

Silje had taken over as team leader when GG stepped back. Eira had always felt a certain admiration for her slightly older colleague. She was cool and analytical, with a background in psychology and all sorts of other academic disciplines. Last time they were out in the field together, they had got drunk one evening, shared certain confidences, though that felt extremely distant now. Eira wasn't sure whether it was Silje who had sought out that distance or whether she had done it herself; it just seemed to have happened.

'The carbon-14 dating will probably take a while,' she said. 'Ditto narrowing down the age of the anchor, if that's even possible. I sent a few questions to the forensic genealogist in Linköping, but I haven't heard back yet.'

Almost a month had now passed since the first discovery. It had become one of those backburner cases, one Eira took out whenever she had a spare moment.

'So nothing new, in other words?' Silje was an efficient boss and didn't waste any energy trying to be liked.

'This could be something,' said Eira, turning her computer so that the others could see the images from the riverbed. 'The boat where the body was found seems to be a Russian destroyer, the *Berkut*.'

'Wow,' said a voice from the corner of the room. There was a whistle from another, and one of the young police assistants, Ville, leaned forward over the table.

'What happened?' he asked. 'It looks so well preserved.'

Eira had reached out to the marine archaeologists and their contacts, and they had found more information in the archives. She enlarged the image so that the crest was visible to everyone. The two-headed eagle, a symbol of the Russian empire's dual nature, with one head facing west, towards Europe, and the other east, towards Asia. It was something the Tsars had adopted from the Byzantine Empire – that was the sort of information she had learned over the past week.

Around the table, her colleagues listened with interest, throwing out questions. These secrets from the bottom of the river appealed to their boyish thirst for adventure and one-time dreams of becoming pirates; they offered a moment of respite from fighting organised crime.

Boats and ships were almost as well documented as people, with every change in ownership and route recorded somewhere. The *Berkut* had sailed the Baltic on behalf of the Russian empire and had been damaged by the Reds during the Finnish Civil War in January 1918. After that, it had been salvaged by a scrap dealer in Umeå and given extensive repairs. It then sailed over to Åbo in Finland before being sold on to Kramfors AB, a forestry company that was looking for spare parts. Stripped of its engine, the shell had remained at the wharf in Lunde, and the *Berkut* had been used as accommodation for strike breakers in the 1920s.

'It probably wasn't the easiest of jobs to find someone who was willing to rent them a room round here,' said Eira.

'Why did it sink? Was it sabotage or something?'

'Reported as an accident in October 1930,' said Eira. 'But it could just as easily have been the owner that sank it. Once they built housing for the strike breakers on land – which was available from May 1931 – it probably lost all value.'

Peace in the labour market, regulated working conditions. The shooting in Ådalen had consigned the use of scabs to the dark annals of history, giving way to a spirit of consensus and cooperation, and the rise of the Swedish welfare state.

'So if the wreck stopped the body from drifting downriver,' said Silje, 'then we can be pretty sure he wasn't there before October 1930, at the very least.'

'Exactly.'

'Which means there's a chance the statute of limitations hasn't run out. For the time being, let's assume that's the case.'

When Eira got back to her desk after lunch, there was a message from the National Board of Forensic Medicine waiting in her inbox.

Dark hair, blue eyes. Southern European descent.

68

She spent a while on hold, being transferred from department to department, but she eventually managed to get through to the right person from the department of forensic genealogy. Eira had specifically asked for this information; it wasn't part of the usual process. The Board of Forensic Medicine was an independent authority, and genetics was a sensitive area. It was a question of personal privacy, bound by all sorts of rules and regulations. The answers it provided were far from certain, too. DNA technology could be incredibly helpful if the person in question had a criminal record, when there was evidence to be found at the crime scene or relatives who could provide samples. But without those things, a person's genetic make-up was free-floating information, whispers at best, ready to be interpreted or misinterpreted.

'Southern Europe,' Eira said once they had ticked off all the usual pleasantries. 'How confident are you about that?'

'More confident than we are that he had dark hair,' said the woman, Åsa Kovaczs. 'I actually had my own analysis done once, during a course. It said I was blonde, but I was born with red hair.'

'So what does this mean? He was from Italy, Spain?'

'Don't forget Greece.'

That was all they were able to say with any confidence. It was more sophisticated than the kind of DNA tests people bought online, of course. The ones that announced a person was seventy per cent Scandinavian, two per cent Russian, and so on, when all they really showed was how many distant relatives had also paid fifty dollars for the same test.

People rarely found out they had third cousins in the Democratic Republic of Congo, for example, which probably contributed to the ongoing blurring of humankind's African origins.

The more serious genetic science went precisely that far back. Since Europeans were descended from only a handful of individuals who had moved north, the experts could analyse small changes in DNA to determine whether a person was related to those who had stopped in the south of the continent, or those who had kept going.

Eira found herself thinking about Lunde as it had once been. The most sinful place in Middle Norrland, if you believed the stories, somewhere a seaman might spend a night and leave a legacy that stretched generations. Porcelain figurines from the other side of the world that turned up in homes where people could barely afford to eat; news from England and America that reached the area before Stockholm. A poor woman's blouse that might be woven from Chinese silk.

It was a place to which people had been drawn for centuries, looking for odd jobs in the forest or at the sawmills, wandering around as a bum or a tourist, passing through for whatever reason – one of the billions of lost moments in history – perhaps without ever leaving a mark.

Dark hair, blue eyes.

She added that information to the rest. They didn't have much, but still. An outline of an outline of a person.

There was a car she didn't recognise blocking half the driveway, a muddy Saab that had seen better days. No, thought Eira, maybe she recognised it after all. As she pulled in to the kerb, she spotted Eilert Granlund in his fisherman's jacket, chatting to her neighbour over the currant bushes.

'Hi,' said Eira. 'Nice of you to stop by.' The last time she remembered him doing that, he was on duty and had come over to pick her up.

'I guess I should say congratulations,' he said with a grin that stretched from ear to ear, his eyes on her belly. 'You kept that quiet the other day.'

Eira glanced over to Allan. So, he had blabbed. She felt more touched than annoyed; they both looked so happy.

Rabble darted around her legs, a shaggy blur, and she wrenched the stick out of his mouth and threw it, sending him bolting off after it.

'Who's the proud father?'

'Is that why you're here? To investigate?'

'I was just passing through.'

'OK.'

She nodded for Eilert to follow her inside, retrieving a couple of paper bags from the porch on her way in. Baby clothes, a cuddly rabbit. Eira wasn't sure who had left them there. Things had started appearing after she bumped into her childhood friend Stina at the supermarket in Kramfors and told her she was pregnant. They had spoken a few times since, and with that it was like the doors to a parallel world had opened: bags and boxes turning up out of nowhere. Tiny body suits, bouncers and nursing tops, all sorts of things, with no expectation of payment or thanks, just the hope that she would pass everything on once she no longer needed it.

Eilert said no to coffee with a nod towards the clock. It was too late in the day.

'So, why are you really here?'

He sat down on one of the kitchen chairs, the way he always had whenever they interviewed someone at home, comfortably taking over the room.

'Do you mind me asking whether you've found out any more about the anchor?'

'Nope, next to nothing. Incredibly common, a model that's been in use since the late nineteenth century.' Eira paused and drank a glass of water. She knew she shouldn't feel like a failure in front of him; it had been years since he was her mentor and superior. 'And it's hard to know when it ended up there, because obviously it's spent most of its life in the water. That's what an anchor does.'

'I started thinking about where they could have got it from,' he said. Eira recognised the satisfied look on his face, as though what he was about to say was something the whole world had been waiting to hear. 'Would the killer really have used the anchor from his own boat, if he had one? And would one person have been able to drag that thing around – with the body to deal with, too? You can't switch off an old detective's brain, you know?'

Eira sliced cheese onto a crispbread and gestured to see whether he wanted one, but Eilert said no. He clearly hadn't come over for a social visit.

'I did a bit of asking around, chatted to a few blokes. You know the type: old timers who've still got splinters in their palms, who remember the golden era at the sawmills. The stuff they know is the kind of thing that never gets written down, that no one values. But they're always happy to talk, let me tell you.'

'I know,' said Eira. 'You taught me that.'

Eilert didn't seem any less pleased with himself when he smiled.

'Well, we chatted about anchors, which boats might've had one like that. A small tug, they said, and one of the old boys did actually remember a theft.'

'Of an anchor? When? Are you sure it was one like that?'

'I showed them the picture.'

'You took a picture? Of evidence?'

'Like I said, can't change a habit of a lifetime . . .'

Eira swatted at a fly and missed. They seemed to have multiplied over the past few days, and she suspected they might have laid eggs in the vents. What was it Eilert had always said about private detectives? Obsessed with outdoing the police, overstepping boundaries if you let them get too close. But at the same time, she understood him, in a painful way. The arrival of the spring birds and getting to work on the garden was all well and good, but surely it was the same every year? The same flowers, the same chirping.

'So, where can I find this guy with the good memory?'

* * *

73

The man lived in one of the old workers' barracks out on Svanö. They had been renovated at some point, and were now light, bright homes on a slight rise by the shore. People were busy working in their gardens, and the air smelled like earth and bonfire smoke.

'Ninety-six years old, and he can barely walk,' Eilert said as they got out of the car. 'But he refuses to move to a care home. Once the river's got you, it's got you.' Svanö was separated from the mainland by no more than a thin channel of water. 'It's the movement,' he continued. 'The river doesn't give a damn about any of us; it just keeps on flowing. We're not that bloody important.'

Bert-Rune Forslund's apartment was on the ground floor, and he shouted for them to come in. They made their way through to the kitchen, where his walking frame was parked by the kitchen table.

'What'd you say you were called?'

Eira got the usual reaction when she repeated her name, which wasn't really surprising considering where they were. Brune, as he wanted to be called, actually remembered that terrible day over ninety years ago, when her namesake, Eira Söderberg, was carried ashore down by the jetty. Shot and killed by the military. The lass had grown up just next door. He was only five at the time, but that was the kind of thing you remembered: the adults' rage, their fear, the grief that seemed to take root in the walls.

There had been times when Eira wanted to change her name, to escape being associated with a girl who had only lived to the age of twenty. She wanted to avoid the inevitable shift in atmosphere whenever someone older found out

74

what she was called. The pain lurking beneath the surface that she'd been able to sense before she was old enough to really understand why, the friction between neighbours and relatives.

A feeling, deep down, that she was the reason for it, that she needed to do something about it; that she had to be nice to keep everyone happy, to make sure they all got along.

'It must've been the late sixties,' the man said once she had managed to tear him away from his childhood memories to talk about the anchor. 'Back when there were still tugs on the river. It can't have been any later than 1970, anyway, because the Marieberg Mill was still open. That's where the *Åbord* was headed with a load of timber that day, when they had to turn back. She'd been in the shipyard for a while. Engine troubles, if I remember right.'

'There definitely doesn't seem to be anything wrong with your memory.'

Brune's hands were shaking, but he insisted on pouring the coffee himself.

'She was one of the last old tugs,' he said, pointing out towards the river. His eyes kept drifting over there, and he pushed his glasses back onto the bridge of his nose every single time. A pair of swans sailed by outside.

Eira used her sleeve to dry the table as she reached for her cup, subtly wiping up the coffee the old man had spilled in order to spare his blushes.

The *Åbord* had already left the shipyard by the time the theft was discovered. No one understood how an anchor could just disappear like that, and the skipper had been furious.

Ranting and raving once they got back.

'As if any of us would ever think about running off wi' something like that,' Brune muttered, shaking his head. 'I'd guess it'd never happened before, someone stealing an anchor. Little buggers, that's what we thought.'

'How do you think they got into the shipyard?'

'Just walked straight in, most likely. There wouldn't be anyone there at night.'

'Didn't they have a guard? Wasn't it locked?'

'Nope, it was a different time back then.'

Eira held out a picture of the anchor.

'And it could have been this one?'

Brune studied the image, mumbled, could well have been. An anchor was an anchor, he couldn't tell one from another after all this time, but judging by the size – ninety kilos, he'd guess – it could easily have belonged to one of the smaller tugs like the *Åbord*.

'It's like I've always said,' Eilert said once they got into the car to drive back to Lunde. 'Cops these days don't get it; they think they can find all the answers in this.' He waved his mobile phone in the air before droning on. 'But technology can't beat good old-fashioned conversation, the questions we ask, whether it's an interview or just chatting with folk. People always know things we don't think they know; it's just about talking to them, asking the right questions. Not sitting at a computer and calling yourself police.'

Eira pulled over onto the grass verge just before the road continued out across the water to the next island.

'Lina Stavred is alive,' she said.

He stared at her for a moment. 'Are you pulling my leg?'

'I went through the interviews . . .' Eira could barely get the words out, felt sick at what she was about to do to him. 'Olof Hagström just told you what you wanted to hear. You got a fourteen-year-old boy to confess to a crime that hadn't even taken place.'

'What the hell are you talking about?'

'You know exactly what I'm talking about. Repressed memories, all that stuff that was so popular in the nineties, the idea that a child could do something terrible and then forget all about it, you really weren't alone in believing—'

'What a load of guff. We found her clothes. No one else had seen her, the lad *confessed*.'

'Yes, after hundreds of hours in the interview room, just so he could get out of there. I'm sure you believed you were doing the right thing, but she wasn't raped. And Lina Stavred didn't die that evening.'

Eira had turned off the engine, and a couple of gulls screeched overhead. She could feel that Eilert was staring at her, but she looked the other way. The sun hung low between the bare branches, the brush that had taken over. Was it possible that he hadn't known? That he hadn't even suspected it after all these years?

'How long have you known about all this, then?'

His voice was strained, hoarse.

'Almost three years; since I was investigating the murder of Olof Hagström's dad. I had to look through the old case files.'

'And you discussed it with everyone else, I take it? Without coming to me first? No, if I'd known that was how you saw me, I'd never . . .' He made a vague gesture back-wards, to the help he had just given her.

'Don't you want to know what happened to Lina?'

Eira turned the key in the ignition and drove back over to the mainland before she continued.

'She spotted a chance to get away that evening. I don't know if you remember, but her parents were pretty strict, old-school teetotallers. Lina Stavred was already planning on running away before any of this happened. She's been living under the radar ever since, and she probably stabbed a man to death on the outskirts of Stockholm last November.'

'And that's my fault, is it?'

'None of this has come out yet, but I'm sure they'll arrest her sooner or later. I just wanted you to know.'

Eira couldn't bring herself to look at him until they turned off onto her street in Lunde, following a silence that lasted all the way over the bridge. Her old mentor seemed to have aged drastically in the space of just a few minutes. He looked shrunken, grey.

Tired.

'I wonder if it was ever reported,' she said.

'What?'

'The theft of the anchor.'

Eilert struggled out of the car.

'Well,' he said, 'I couldn't say. I'm not an officer any more.'

F amiliar rooms, a sense of homecoming. The local investigator at the station in Kramfors got to her feet with a
cheery hello and gave Eira a hug.

'How are you doing?' asked Anja Larionova.

'Pregnant,' Eira replied, slumping down into the spare
chair.

'Who's the dad? Don't tell me it's the hottie from Violent
Crimes?'

'GG? Are you crazy?' Eira hoped it wasn't obvious that
she was blushing. Nothing had ever happened between
them, it was all just in her mind, things that would never
actually become a reality. 'Of course it's not his. What made
you think that?'

'Just a hunch, I suppose.' Anja studied her as though she
was a thief caught red-handed with the family silver. 'So,
who is he? Come on, I'm a police officer. I can keep a secret.'

'Can we stick to an easier subject?'

'Of course,' the local investigator said with a laugh.
'Such as?'

'A theft fifty years ago.'

'Shoot.'

As she began to explain, Eira saw the older woman's eyes
sharpen. The investigator in her was listening.

Anja Larionova took a certain pride from looking into

79

petty thefts, arguing that what had been lost was about so much more than money. Trust, above all.

'I don't know whether it was ever reported missing,' Eira continued. 'Or whether this is even linked to my case. The time frame is a little hazy, sometime in the late sixties or early seventies.'

'Grab yourself a cup of coffee while I have a look.'

It felt strange to be back in the lunch room in Kramfors, as though years had passed since she left. In truth, it had only been a few months. It reminded her of when she first came back to Ådalen after her time in Stockholm, a shift in perspective. The sense of belonging and yet not, an undertone of betrayal that made people sound slightly awkward around her. She was met by a lot of hellos and 'how's it going, you happy over in Sundsvall?' and she sat down with a few of her old colleagues, quickly finding her feet in their chatter, the gossip about who had come and gone, what they were currently working on.

Anti-social behaviour from the group that hung around outside the supermarket; the arrival of break-in season over in Bjärtrå now that the local addicts had woken from their winter slumber, before the owners of the summerhouses reappeared. And the drugs, of course, the root cause of most of it.

'Hey, what are you doing here?'

There was so much more to August Engelhardt's 'hey' than the others'. Surprise and demands and all sorts of other things Eira hoped weren't too bad.

'Just needed to follow up on a few things.'

He sat down beside her and the others got up. Had they been called out somewhere? Was their lunch break over? Did they know?

'Have you been avoiding me?' August asked once they were out of earshot.

'Of course not.'

'You never called me back.'

'Sorry, I've just had a lot on my plate. On top of everything else I've been put in charge of an investigation on my own.' She wanted to take his hand, for him to hold her. 'You've probably heard about the body we pulled out of the river over by Lunde? The case is colder than cold, and I'm pretty sure they've only given it to me to keep me off the streets. They see me as a walking risk.'

'It's good they're looking out for you,' said August, putting his hand on hers beneath the table.

'Yeah, I know.' Eira gripped his hand, trying to think of something nice to say. That she missed him, something along those lines, but then she saw Anja Larionova approaching and she let go of him again.

Anja was carrying a pale brown folder in her arms. There really was no one better at digging things up from the deepest of archives.

'I've got something for you.'

Eira spent a long time just staring at the date.

September 1968.

It was like music, something that changed everything.

Two measly sheets of paper, the text slightly faded with age.

Written on a typewriter, of course.

The theft had been reported on 7 September, the day after it was discovered, as the *Åbord* left the shipyard where she had spent the past two weeks undergoing repairs.

A timeframe so exact it was dizzying.

Eira didn't recognise the name of the officer who had taken the report – even Eilert Granlund was too young to have been working then. So long ago and yet also so close, she thought. Many of the people who had been around at the time were still alive, they might remember. People like Brune Forslund. There could be witnesses.

The officer had interviewed the owner of the boat and the employees at the shipyard, none of whom had seen anything. All the foreman and his workers could say was where the *Åbord* had been berthed; the rest was a mystery. Eira gave a start when she saw the name Allan Westin. Of course, he'd worked there too.

They had never come up with any suspects.

Between the lines, she got the sense that the police hadn't made all that much effort – though on the other hand they were hardly going to call the crime scene investigators out just for a missing anchor.

Once she had handed the file back, she made a quick detour down the corridor. She found August sitting at a computer in the room closest to the stairs. He didn't hear her come in.

'You're right,' Eira said to the back of his head. His fair hair had grown, and was getting slightly wavy. In a good way. 'I've been avoiding you.'

* * *

On the other side of the shopping street, the windows of the shops that had closed for good during the pandemic were now empty. In contrast, NC Café and Restaurant was packed. It was the kind of place that served latte macchiatos and salmon salad alongside Kurdish tea and falafel, and it seemed to be doing a roaring trade.

'I just feel like we need to deal with this,' August said once they were sitting down. 'I hardly ever see you any more, I don't know what you want.'

'Deal with what?'

'Us. Our relationship, I guess?'

'Wouldn't it be easier to do that once the baby is here and we know whether or not it's yours?'

He stirred his cappuccino, destroying the pretty flower in the froth.

'We're not the only ones this affects,' he said calmly, as though he was talking to a child. 'There's Johanna to think about too. She needs to know what her life's going to be like going forward.'

Eira leaned back in her chair. She had bought a juice, needed to cut back on her caffeine intake. That was the kind of thing she thought about whenever she saw August. She knew he did his research, that he tried to avoid additives in his food, having too much sugar. Too much of anything.

'What do you mean, what her life is going to be like?' she asked. 'Aren't the two of you getting married?'

Johanna was August's fiancée in Stockholm, that had never been a secret. They had an open relationship and were free to sleep with whoever they wanted to sleep with. August had been clear that that wouldn't change just because they were getting married, but Eira couldn't help but feel that some of the no-strings fun disappeared whenever she saw his ring. He'd chosen one person above all else, despite everything he said.

'Should I keep working in Kramfors or try to find a job in Stockholm?' he continued. 'And are you going to stay here, or would you be willing to move down south? We need to talk about these things so we're not totally over-whelmed once the baby is here. It's bad to fight in front of kids. I've been through that before. We don't want that.'

'Obviously we're not going to fight,' said Eira. She liked his outlook on life: not doing what was expected of him, making his own decisions. That was what she had fallen for, over and over again. Not seriously, but a little. She felt a sudden longing for that breezy nature.

'Johanna is coming up to visit the first weekend in June,' he said. 'Don't you think it would be good for the three of us to get together?'

There were downy buds on the willow, flashes of yellow coltsfoot in last year's grass. Dusk was getting later and later, stretching out towards the endless light of summer.

Eira threw a stick out into the water and watched as the dog broke the surface, churning it up and then leaving it to settle again.

She could see the old shipyard further downstream, now nothing but an expanse of tarmac. Eira tried to imagine that night, when someone – or had there been several of them? – stole the anchor. And then what? Did they haul it onto another boat, tie it to the dead man's body?

Damp paws clawed at her legs, and Rabble barked. Eira threw the stick further out this time, making him swim for it, letting him struggle against the current.

1968. She tried to remember everything she had heard or been taught in school, so many things that had taken place elsewhere. Youth protests in cities around the world, the Russians' invasion of Prague. It was long before she was born, and more importantly it was before the assassination of Prime Minister Olof Palme in early 1986. The unsuccessful hunt for his killer led to the statute of limitations being abolished for murder, but unfortunately that didn't apply to crimes committed prior to 1985.

The rush of excitement at finally having a possible

timeframe had lasted no more than fifteen minutes once she got back to Sundsvall.

'So the statute of limitations is up,' Silje had said with a deep sigh. 'Someone shot a twenty-year-old, dumped him in the river and got away with it.'

'But at least it's not hundreds of years old,' Eira had countered. 'There are probably witnesses, close relatives who could still be alive.'

'We could throw hours and hours at this, but we still wouldn't be able to prosecute anyone. We can't do our job here. If we had limitless resources, maybe, just for the sake of it, but I need you elsewhere.'

The drugs case that had begun to swamp everything else, a wife beater in Ånge, a haul of weapons that might be linked to a shooting in Bosvedjan. Eira had looked down at Silje's desk as her boss talked about priorities and a request for reinforcements in Stockholm following the latest wave of violence there, the number of people currently on sick leave. There wasn't a single stray paper, no pictures of her family. She remembered that Silje had chosen not to be in a relationship. What was it she had said that night they got drunk in Härnösand? That she wanted to be in control of her life, not lumped with a *load of shit that just complicates things*.

'Really great work though, Eira. You took it as far as you could.'

The kid didn't look old enough to have finished high school, but maybe he'd just dropped out early. Arms covered in DIY tattoos, which didn't exactly fill her with confidence, but Lina had followed him down to the basement anyway. This was something she should have done a long time ago, and now wasn't the time to put it off.

'Is this your place?'

The kid shrugged and turned the key in the padlock. It was a thin metal door, an ordinary basement storage space. He pulled out an extension lead and plugged it in to a socket further down the hall. Using someone else's power. That was the price for going with someone who wasn't certified, she thought. An amateur who advertised on social media.

'Mobile payments or cash only,' he said.

'I've got cash.'

'Cool, so you got any ideas or do you want one of my designs?'

Lina pushed her sleeve back to show him the embarrassing tattoo that had been there since she was sixteen and didn't know any better. A heart and a couple of birds, flying up towards the crook of her arm. Such a cliché, so meaningless. It had faded over the years, along with the memory of what her younger self had been thinking.

'I don't care,' she said. 'Anything that'll cover this.'

'Gotcha.'

A low buzzing sound, a needle that tickled more than anything, crude patterns covering the old design. It would soon be gone and that was all that mattered. Lina didn't care what she was left with, and she almost dozed off in the chair. It may have been a dingy basement in a drab suburb, but it was far warmer than the tent where she had been sleeping recently.

'There. Hope you like it.'

He taped clingfilm over the new tattoo and mumbled that it would be 1,500 kronor.

'No problem,' said Lina, rummaging through her pockets until he turned around to do something with his equipment, then shoving him so hard that he stumbled forward. She yanked the cable out of the way and slammed the door, snapping the padlock shut.

'What the fuck? Crazy bitch, I'll report you!'

His voice echoed around the basement as he shouted one expletive after another, and she bounded up the stairs two at a time. A kid who ran a black-market tattoo parlour from a basement storage cage was hardly going to report her to the police, and even if he did all he knew was that her name was Anna.

Or was it Maria or Eva? She couldn't actually remember what she had told him. In the past she had always picked names that meant something to her, Simone or Edith or Virginia. Names that transported her to the intellectual circles of Paris or London, transforming her into someone of importance, but she realised now that it was better to opt for something bland and ordinary instead. The kind of name that passed a person by, that was immediately forgotten. She dyed her hair a mousy shade of brown and had even found a pair of drab glasses. The people she lived with didn't ask any questions.

Lina put up her hood and crossed the deserted playground, making her way through the tunnel beneath the motorway and onto the gravel track leading into the woods.

A few caravans and wrecked cars between the trees, heavy drizzle.

'You got anythin' to eat?' asked the guy who owned the tent where she had crashed the past few nights. Not for much longer.

She dug a few cans of soup and some flatbreads out of her rucksack, things she had lifted before she went to the tattooist. Slumped down in the folding chair beneath the awning by the door of the caravan and let him mess about with the camping stove.

Lina peeled back the clingfilm and studied the strange artwork on her forearm. It looked like a cross between the Devil and a Moomin, completely abstract. Still, it covered the heart and the birds and the girl she had once been, all those years ago. She felt an urge to touch the ink, the angry red skin, but it would only get infected.

Lina Stavred, she thought. You little idiot.

You didn't know shit about love.

His face lacked some crucial component, whatever it was that made a person a person.

The faults and imperfections, the irregularities. There were no teenage acne scars or fine lines around his mouth, not a single birthmark to disrupt the perfection.

'Say hello to our friend from the deep,' said Shirin ben Hassan.

'What? This is him?'

The man's hair was certainly dark, almost black, his gaze impossible to meet. His eyes were a deeper shade of blue than most, like the sky on a late summer's evening. They were also completely blank. No hint of any thoughts, feelings or life.

'Maybe not *exactly* how his mum would remember him, but it's probably close enough.'

'And where on earth did you get this?' asked Eira.

'From his DNA.'

'OK, I got that, but this sort of thing is only possible in the States, isn't it?'

Eira felt a sudden jolt of dizziness. Her stomach had been cramping a little that morning. Nothing to worry about, they'd said. She should just take it easy and get back in touch if the contractions came any closer together, if they grew stronger, it if started to hurt.

She was almost seven months gone now.

'The case is more or less shelved,' she said. 'I've been told not to prioritise it.'

Shirin got up and closed the door to her office. She paused then with a strange look on her face, as though she was fighting back a smile.

'Honestly, I don't know what lines I might have crossed here,' she said.

'Was it your idea?'

Shirin nodded.

'It's not something I planned,' she said. 'I would've discussed it with you first if it was.'

She talked about those early days, after they first recovered the body from the river and realised that the anchor had been used to sink it, as one depressing piece of news after another came pouring in. No hits from any of the databases, either in Sweden or abroad. Shirin hadn't been able to shake the feeling that they would never find out who the unnamed man was.

It was the kind of thing that ate away at her when she went home in the evening, that made her mind whirr in all sorts of directions.

But then an email had arrived from the U.S., related to a completely different matter. An invitation to a conference with a research group there. A personal greeting from her old professor, hoping she would be able to make it.

'So I asked them about the project, and since it touched upon a subject I'd been looking into for the past few days – how to identify a person when the usual methods can't help . . .'

Eira took a deep breath, as the midwives had told her to do. Rules and regulations raced through her head. Sharing another person's DNA profile wasn't exactly above board, far from it, but she also couldn't tear her eyes away from the digital face. What was the alternative?

Forgetting about him?

'It's about as far from proper evidence as you can get,' said Shirin. 'But I thought you might still be able to make use of it. I don't know what I was thinking, I—'

'Hang on,' said Eira, 'I'm not sure I understand. I know you studied with this professor, but are you saying you got them to do it for free?'

'As part of their research project.' Shirin's smile finally broke through. 'Complex material like this is incredibly valuable. Finding out exactly how much DNA is needed, that sort of thing. She'd like us to share information with them if it leads anywhere, because his real identity would be a kind of answer key for their work.'

'Have you showed this to anyone else?'

'It's your case. You were the one who recovered him.'

'I don't know how my boss will take this,' said Eira. 'She's pretty strict about following the rules. That's a good thing.'

'Absolutely,' said Shirin. 'As it should be.'

Eira studied the man's face, his smooth features. She tried to imagine him with different hair, wondered what his smile had been like.

'I can always delete it,' said Shirin.

S ome sort of renovation seemed to be under way at the People's House in Lunde. As ever, the work was being carried out by volunteers, and they were currently taking a break on the steps outside. Clothes flecked with paint, the spring sun on their faces. One of the women was handing out paper plates to the others, and Eira could smell soused herring and smoked whitefish. A few of the younger men perched on ladders were relatively new to the area. Eira didn't know them, but she knew exactly who they were, part of the latest exodus from the cities that had been fuelled by the pandemic. She often found herself admiring anyone who made the move like that, people who wanted to be closer to nature, to live different lives. It all seemed so simple. Yes, it might be tricky to find a plumber in July, or to get functioning broadband installed, but they were at peace with themselves.

The small group sitting on the steps were all well over pension age, Lunde residents since time immemorial, which was exactly what Eira had been hoping for.

'Looks like you're doing a great job,' she said. 'And it's so good to see more people getting involved.'

'Yup, they've got plenty of ideas,' someone muttered. 'One of them suggested opening a microbrewery and a bar. That'd be something.'

'The young folks aren't interested in dwelling on the past. They want to keep moving forward, wherever that takes them.'

'To hell,' someone else added, neatly summing up the Ångermanland approach to life: always expecting the worst. If that was how things turned out, then you could dazzle everyone with the fact that you'd been right all along, and if you were wrong then it would be a pleasant surprise. Ultimately, it meant that people could be happy either way.

Eira fended off all the usual questions about how Kerstin was doing and when she was due, the latter of which spurred them to vent their anger at the latest wave of hospital closures, muttering that they hoped she wouldn't have to give birth in the back of an ambulance, and so on.

She tied Rabble to the corner post to stop him getting at the fish and took the paper plate that was held out to her. Sat down on the steps and praised the way they had mixed the smoked whitefish with the soused herring and mayonnaise.

'Were any of you here in the late sixties?' she asked, keeping her tone light-hearted, a question in passing.

One of them had been at sea at the time, and another had moved to the area twenty years ago, but the others all nodded.

'Why do you want to know? Is it something to do with the bloke you found over by Sandö? Do you know who he is?'

'Not who he is,' said Eira. 'But we do know he was here in 1968.'

The date hadn't leaked yet; there had been bigger stories

94

to cover. Russia's war of aggression against Ukraine and Sweden's about-turn in giving up on neutrality and applying to become a member of NATO; the crisis in the healthcare system.

The digital image of the man's face had been gnawing away at her from her phone for the past two days. Eira hadn't mentioned it to anyone, wrestling with the unpleasant prospect of snitching on Shirin, who could well end up in the shit for taking matters into her own hands. Evidence had to be handled properly, that was drummed into them from the day they joined the force, though on the other hand this case would never go to trial. She couldn't *officially* release the picture, but how official was a coffee break on the steps outside the People's House in Lunde?

'Yup, good grief, I must've been twelve then. I'd started at the sawmill in Lugnvik that summer, a general dogsbody, and I was there 'til they shut up shop . . . I've seen plenty of folk come and go . . .'

'I had a wife and kids by that point, so the whole '68 hoo-ha sort of passed me by.' The man scratched his chin, a few strands of grey hair he had missed while shaving. Kalle was his name, wasn't it? From the hill behind the Näslunds' place, one of her father's old friends. Kalle Molin, that was it.

'. . . if you were young and came to town looking for work, you'd probably go straight to the loading docks. There were always new faces there. Seasonal workers, Finns, bums, all sorts.'

'We think he might have been from southern Europe,' said Eira. She added that this wasn't information the police had released, that none of it was set in stone, and that she would appreciate them keeping it to themselves.

'What year did you say it was? '68? That's the year they shot that film! There were a hell of a lot of people round here then.'

Of course, *Ådalen 31*, about the clash between the military and the strikers in Lunde. It had been a real hit the following year – nominated for an Oscar, no less – and practically everyone in the area at the time had been an extra. Her own mother had made clothes for the cast, and her father had been one of thousands of people in the procession of demonstrators.

'And that Bo Widerberg bloke, the director, he ran about the place like a headless chicken. Borrowed a car even though he didn't have a licence, drove straight over the roundabout on the way into Härnösand. All to impress some lass, of course, probably the one playing the rich blonde – as though we had any of those here in Lunde. No, all the fancy folk lived in Härnösand and Sundsvall, that's probably why we don't have the same forelock-tugging mentality over here; we've never had to bow or curtsey to anyone on our own streets . . .'

In the end, Eira brought up the picture. She watched as they passed her phone around, studying their faces.

There were shakes of the head, apologetic frowns. 'No, sorry, how's anyone supposed to remember . . .'

'I wouldn't have forgotten a face like that,' said Vivi Koskela. It was common knowledge that she had been a real beauty back in the day; you could still see it in her eyes. 'In his twenties, you said? If he hung out at the People's House in Frånö or at Parken in Kramfors, I would have spotted him. I kept track of every newcomer, and if an Italian had shown up . . .'

She racked her memory as the conversation drifted over to the political battles of the era, new communist parties that popped up and fizzled out, the Vietnam war. And then they were back to talking about dancing and having fun, like the time Vivi had competed to become Miss Sandö Bridge, a beauty contest like the ones they had in Stockholm, with the girls lined up in bikinis.

'The local drunks' eyes practically popped out of their heads, not to mention the farm boys from over in Nordingrå.'

'Parken in Kramfors was the best. You could sneak in to one of the oldies' dances and bum a drink off them before moving on to one of the more hip ones. Most people went to Babels, though, the mods and that lot. *Shake Time with Chepp Steppers*!'

Eira's mind had started to drift. There were too many memories that had nothing to do with anything, and Rabble was tangled up in his lead, eager to get a bit closer to Kalle's dachshund. She also felt slightly queasy, had eaten too much of everything; Gudrun's cinnamon buns and Susul's fantastic chocolate slices.

'Have you never heard of Chepp Steppers?' Vivi Koskela teased. 'You're too young, I suppose, but I'm sure your mum could tell you a thing or two . . .' She trailed off as time caught up with her, remembering where Kerstin Sjödin was. Vivi patted Eira on the hand, a wordless gesture of sympathy. 'Let me tell you, Chepp Steppers were almost as good as Shanes and the Hep Stars, but they were actually from

Kramfors. They had their own fan club and everything, and they came *this* close to getting onto *Hylands hörna* on TV. You remember that talk show, don't you? I'll never forget the time they played on the roof at Tempo. There must have been thousands of us in the square that day. All these people who moan about the flat roofs in the centre of town being ugly just don't know what to do with them!'

It was the snapshots of her mother that lingered in Eira's mind once she got home, as she lay down on the sofa to rest. For a brief moment, Kerstin had really come to life. Several people had shared recollections of her in order to cheer Eira up, talking about the time she crashed her moped, the dances and drunkenness, how beautiful she had been. *There probably wasn't a bloke in town whose head didn't turn when he saw your mum.* Eira wanted to conjure up that time, the pop bands that made the girls scream and the mods smoking outside the old temperance house. She wanted to see her mother in the middle of it all, and it proved easier than expected. Kerstin's long hair hanging loose, a sense of freedom. The pair of sunglasses that made her look like Yoko Ono, laughing with a couple of unnamed boys, a glimpse of a wooden building – was that Babelsberg?

How old could she have been in that picture? Seventeen or eighteen?

Kerstin was born in 1950.

Eira didn't exactly leap up from the sofa, but she definitely got up much too quickly. Her head spun for a moment, and she had to lean forward and breathe deeply. Low blood pressure was better than high, they had told her.

She grabbed a carton of juice for a quick energy hit as she jumped into the car and drove over to Kramfors.

The old days came back to her as she stepped on the accelerator: stretches of road where she had driven much too fast before she joined the force, moments from her youth, all vanishing from view.

A glimpse of the old temperance house flashed by on the hillside above the railway as she turned off towards the care home, a handsome old wooden building.

Babelsberg.

It was only nine o'clock, but the nightlights were glowing at floor level, and the hallway was quiet.

'I'm sorry, but your mum's already asleep.'

'She goes to bed this early?'

Kerstin had always been such a night owl, someone who pottered about until the early hours – who had occasionally even run off to see her lover while Eira slept.

But she was now fast asleep on her back, snoring slightly with each breath.

Eira moved quietly to avoid waking her. Opened one of the blinds to let some light in.

She pulled the album down from the shelf, flicking past family photos and school portraits until she found it.

There was the grass, the beer bottles, the young people, faces raised to the sky or looking straight at the camera. And in the background: a scrap of the yellow wooden facade, horizontal boards, the distinctive criss-crossed railings.

Babelsberg.

There were no names written underneath, and Eira didn't recognise the boys sitting on either side of Kerstin. They looked a few years older than her, somewhere around twenty, with long hair and unbuttoned shirts.

One of them had his arm around Kerstin, had pulled her in close, but he wasn't the one that made Eira gasp.

The other boy. Dark hair down to his shoulders, his gaze fixed somewhere behind the camera.

Eira couldn't see a date, but Kerstin had been a librarian; being orderly was in her bones. She wasn't the kind of woman who would have just glued the pictures in at random. Eira turned a few pages, saw pictures of Kerstin and her friends in Stockholm. Of course, her mother had taken a sabbatical between the second and third years of senior high school. On the next page she was back in Ådalen, celebrating Christmas with her family and graduating in 1970 – without the usual white student caps, because the old traditions had been done away with in the name of equality.

Eira turned back to the photograph outside Babelsberg. Logically, it had probably been taken in the summer of 1968.

The dark-haired boy was holding a bottle of beer beneath his chin. Leaning forward.

And his eyes.

Eira turned on the light in the kitchenette and studied the picture in its glow.

Was she imagining things, or were his eyes blue?

She sat down on the edge of the bed and softly stroked her mother's cheek. Kerstin's snoring faded, but it was back with the next breath.

Her cheek was so warm.

'Mum, could you wake up for a moment?'

S hirin ben Hassan was at home on the outskirts of
Sundsvall, looking after her poorly child.

'You've had chickenpox, right?' she said as she opened
the door.

Eira had, one spring when she was fifteen or sixteen,
while the rest of her class went on a school trip to Berlin.

The poorly child in question was a seven-year-old boy
with itchy spots on his face, and he seemed thrilled to be
able to stay off school and watch YouTube clips of funny
cats in his room.

'My husband usually does this sort of thing,' said Shirin.
'I go stir crazy after a couple of days at home. I'm terrible
at playing, don't see the point of all these games. None of
them go anywhere. It always just ends in an argument
about the rules. As the adult, I'm supposed to be able to
explain why you can go there but not there, but it's all
completely illogical. Go straight to jail without passing go.
I mean, what's the point?'

Eira held out her phone to her colleague.

'Could this be him?'

The crime scene investigator's face and body language
both changed as she looked down at the snapshot from the
sixties. She took the phone from Eira's hand and zoomed in.

'Where did you find this?'

'In my mum's photo album.'

'You're kidding? Who is he?'

'I don't know,' said Eira.

She had managed to wake Kerstin the night before, got her to sit up and have a glass of water. Her mother had been confused, thought it was morning.

'Why do you want me to look at this?' she had asked. 'Which show is it?'

The words came out wrong sometimes, but still. Maybe she knew the pictures were from her own life, or maybe not.

'This is you, Mum,' Eira had said, pointing down at her younger self. 'But who are the others?'

A moment of reflection, or possibly confusion, and Kerstin began picking at the corners as though she wanted to remove the photo. Eira had gripped her hand.

'Do you remember, Mum? The summer after your second year of senior high school. You would have turned eighteen that autumn. Did you have a crush on one of them?'

'Would you mind passing me the umbrella?' Kerstin had asked, pointing to her handbag. 'I think I need to go somewhere.'

Eira had then followed her to the bathroom and back over to her bed. Closed the blinds, tucked her in.

Her mind had been whirring as she drove away, racking her memory for clues, for something her mother might have said. A story, an anecdote from her youth, but there was nothing there.

'Is it OK if I download this?'

'Of course.'

Shirin sat down at her computer in the part of the hallway

that seemed to be used as a home office, between the cleaning cupboard and an overloaded shoe rack.

She cropped the photograph so that only the dark-haired boy's face was in focus, and then positioned it alongside the computer-generated image. She lengthened the digital version's hair and gave him a similar shirt, several buttons open.

Shirin drew a few lines, measured the distance between his eyes, from his chin to the top of his head, the length of his nose.

'So, what do you think?'

'What do *you* think? asked Shirin.

Eira leaned back against the wall.

'They look alike.'

'They're more than alike. If this is right – and by that I mean if the technology isn't leading us on a wild goose chase, changing his features somehow – then I'd say we're looking at the same person.'

Eira had to go through to the kitchen to grab a chair, and she slumped down into it. It was dizzying, the idea that he had been here all along, in her mother's shrinking memory.

Shirin had zoomed in at the left edge of the image, on the pale greenery that revealed it was summer, petals.

'Are those roses?'

'Could be.' Eira thought she could make out a bush covered in white flowers. There was something similar in her own garden, her mother's pride and joy: the white Finnish rose, with its incredible scent. It was fairly common in Norrland, because it could withstand the cold and the elements – 'just like us', her mother had said when Eira was younger, when the buds began to open.

'If it's the Finnish rose, it only flowers for one week a year, in late June or early July. They call it the Midsummer rose in Finland.'

The realisation that they had found something was really starting to sink in, and Eira felt the rush as her investigative instincts took over.

'I wonder what this could be?' Shirin continued, zooming in on the man's chest. He was wearing a chain around his neck, a waistcoat over his shirt. The resolution was terrible, but she was able to adjust the contrast and increase the sharpness.

There was something on his waistcoat. A shape.

'Is that a star?'

The crime scene technician's fingers danced over the keys. Images appeared and disappeared, replacing one another. A lightning-quick search, and there it was.

A yellow star against a darker two-tone background. They couldn't see the colours on his waistcoat, but it should have been red and blue.

'The United NLF Groups,' said Shirin. 'Looks like our guy here wanted to stop the war in Vietnam.'

'Didn't everyone?'

There was a loud shout, followed by another, growing in volume. 'Muuum, come here!' Shirin headed upstairs, and Eira nipped into the toilet. She was starting to notice just how often she needed to pee at the moment.

She sat on the toilet for much longer than she needed to, racking her brain. Kerstin had never really talked about politics at home; that was more her father's area of interest. Both parents joined the International Workers' Day march on May 1, of course. It was a real occasion. A memory of a dinner party came back to Eira. They had guests over, and the political discussion got heated, Veine barking something about communist ideas, Kerstin growing quiet. Eira remembered a certain tension in the room that day, that was probably why it had stuck with her. A sense of danger, of a fault line between them.

'I've applied for a new job, a management position,' Shirin told her once she came back out. 'They've asked me to go for an interview.'

'That's great,' said Eira. 'I'll keep my fingers crossed for you.'

The crime scene technician's eyes drifted down to the reconstructed face, staring out at them with his empty eyes.

'I know I go too far sometimes,' she said. 'It's like they take over, like the dead people's will is stronger than my own. I know that sounds crazy.'

'You might want to phrase it another way in your interview.'

Eira laughed, but Shirin didn't join in.

She understood.

Acting on her own initiative, bending the rules governing use of a person's DNA.

'I'll have to talk to my boss about this,' said Eira.

'You will.'

'But I'm not sure I need to tell her everything,' she continued. It wasn't the first time she had grappled with something like this, when what was right and what was true seemed to be pulling in different directions. 'We knew he was of southern European descent and we also knew the year. I can say I came across a photograph of a young man with dark hair and blue eyes in my mum's photo album and realised it was the same year. We're always looking at old photographs together. What else are you supposed to do when you can't have a proper conversation any more?'

It was a distant time, a spring and summer that slowly began to come into focus. The ice had broken up in April that year, and the summer heat had arrived in May. In Paris, street brawls broke out and students occupied the Sorbonne. Workers went on general strike, and the number of protests against the war in Vietnam grew and grew.

Almost everything that caught Eira's eye had happened elsewhere, News Agency reports on the national and international pages. In the United States, anti-Vietnam protests took place alongside civil rights marches following the murder of Martin Luther King. American soldiers fled the war, and many of them were granted asylum in Sweden. President Lyndon B. Johnson was furious after Olof Palme appeared alongside the ambassador to North Vietnam at a protest in Moscow.

The librarian, Susanne, always asked after Kerstin, but she was fifteen years younger than Eira's mother and didn't know anything about those days. She had brought out the heavy bound newspapers, and Eira was now scouring the pages in search of words like *Vietnam* and *National Liberation Front*.

Even Kramfors had seen demonstrations, gatherings of several hundred people. Eira studied the faces in the photographs, jotting down any names.

In late May 1968, someone had painted *VIVA NLF* and *CRUSH U.S. IMPERIALISM* on the roof of the school building. Eira wasn't quite sure who that message had been aimed at. American spy planes flying low over Kramfors? Either way, the police had quickly managed to find the culprits by going to the only paint shop in town and asking who had bought the type of paint used. The shopkeeper knew exactly who they were, and the two boys – aged sixteen and seventeen – were ordered to pay 450 kronor towards the clean-up.

Eira reached early July, when the white Finnish rose should have been in bloom. Most of the articles were about auctions and industrial holidays, and she almost missed the short piece at the bottom of the page.

VIETNAM DESERTERS LEAVE TORSÅKER

In the image, several young men were pictured in front of a barn. The photograph had been taken in winter, and one of them was leaning against a snow shovel.

Torsåker was an old parish around twenty miles north of Kramfors, best known for the witch trials that took place there in the seventeenth century. Seventy women had been led up a hill and beheaded, their bodies burnt. But deserters from the Vietnam war? Eira couldn't remember ever having heard about that.

According to the article, a Christian textile manufacturer with roots in the area had opened up his empty family farm to the young deserters, hoping to offer them a healthy life away from the drugs and vices of the big city. It didn't go into any detail about what went wrong, but just five months later their stint in the countryside had apparently come to an end.

No names were given in the article, and none of the young men had spoken to the reporter. Eira googled the manufacturer and found an obituary.

She asked the librarian to see the newspapers from February 1968, the month when the deserters had first arrived in the area.

While she waited, Eira flicked back through the book in front of her and found a News Agency article she had skipped over because it had nothing to do with Kramfors. A number of deserters had arrived at Stockholm Arlanda airport, and a group of people had gathered to welcome them. They were celebrated as heroes in Sweden, but were unable to return home. The United States didn't recognise the war in Vietnam as a war, which meant they wouldn't be facing the death penalty, but they could almost certainly expect a long prison sentence. Sweden was the only country outside of the Eastern Bloc that was willing to offer them asylum.

In the picture, several men were standing in a line at the bottom of the boarding stairs. One was laughing, another looking down at the ground. Eira noticed how young they all were, around twenty if not younger, and some of the surnames mentioned didn't sound especially American. Picciano, Gallo – names that made her think of Italian mafia families, Robert de Niro and Al Pacino. She got up and immediately had to sit back down again. Damn low blood pressure.

Could that be the answer?

First- or second-generation immigrants to the United States obviously shared DNA with those who had stayed behind in places like Italy and Greece.

'Are you OK?' Susanne asked when she came back with

the heavy tome. 'You look a little pale. Can I get you something to drink?'

'Some water would be great, thanks.'

The librarian went away and returned with a cup, couldn't help but reach out and touch Eira's belly.

'To think that Kerstin will finally get to see you with a baby of your own. I just hope she has time to enjoy it.'

When the weather was nice, Eira liked to take her mother for a walk along the river, or to the new bookshop where they could have a coffee in a setting where Kerstin felt comfortable.

The hill up to Babelsberg was probably a little too steep, but Kerstin powered on. She had never been the sort of person to complain. Out of the two of them, it was Eira who was short of breath and needed to take a break, but the dull ache in her pelvis was nothing to moan about.

It was still early June, and the lilacs hadn't opened yet, never mind the bushes in the flowerbeds. Eira broke off a stem covered in small white buds.

'Are these roses?'

'They are.'

'Could they be Finnish roses?'

Kerstin rubbed a leaf between her fingers and seemed to forget Eira's question. Eira helped her to sit down on the steps, and she took out a couple of water bottles. At the bottom of the slope in front of them, they could see the railway tracks, apartment buildings.

'Do you remember coming here, Mum? When you were younger?'

'Of course I do. It was . . .'

The words were so hard to find.

'Dancing,' said Eira. 'Shake Time with Chepp Steppers.' She had googled the band and found a few articles reminiscing over those days. They had mostly played covers of other bands – the Beatles, of course, and their Swedish equivalent, Hep Stars. Eira searched for one of their biggest hits on Spotify.

'I bet they used to play this one, didn't they?'

Kerstin laughed and rocked from side to side, singing along with the tune, managing to get the right words in the right places. That was the incredible thing about music. But then she lost interest and started sweeping a few leaves away with her hand.

Eira asked her about the NLF movement.

'What was that again?'

She showed Kerstin the photograph of her teenage self and the two young men outside Babelsberg and tried to talk about the war.

'Uff, I don't want to think about that, nothing good'll come of that.'

They hadn't eaten, but Kerstin patted her stomach as though she was full. Even her movements had started to become irrational.

Eira had found an article from February 1968 that mentioned the names of two of the American deserters who had arrived in Torsåker. Neither of them looked like the young man in the photo, and neither had an Italian name, but she asked her mother all the same.

'Did you know them?'

'I knew lots of people, I did. Now then, where did I put those keys?' She started rummaging through her bag, anxiety rearing its head again.

Just say something real, for God's sake. That was what Eira felt like shouting, but she held her tongue. Her irritation seeped out all the same, and she snapped, 'Surely you must remember something?' She couldn't stand the way her mother now only seemed to exist on the surface. Her depths had vanished, the ability to let one thought lead to another. To occasionally say something wiser than what Eira had just said.

The realisation that she would never do that again left Eira with a feeling of emptiness.

Kerstin shifted anxiously.

'I think we should go now.'

Unni had been a constant presence in Eira's life while she was growing up, but their last conversation hadn't ended so well. It happened last autumn, before Kerstin moved to the care home, when Eira tried to share the address in the hope that her mother's friend would visit her there.

She remembered the awkward silence on the other end of the line.

'I know I should,' Unni had said. 'But I'm not sure I can handle seeing her like that. I want to remember her how she was.'

As though Kerstin's feelings didn't matter. As though she was already dead.

After a brief hesitation, Eira scrolled down to her number anyway.

Unni picked up after seven rings.

'Has something happened to your mum?' she shouted. The rest of her words were drowned out by the wind, and the call dropped.

'I'm somewhere south of Långsele,' Unni said when she phoned back a few minutes later, now safely parked on a side road. She was taking her new Jaguar for a spin, she told Eira a gift to herself. A cabriolet, which explained the background noise. It was finally warm enough to put the roof down.

'Don't tell me she's dead.'

'She's alive,' said Eira.

'And what about you? How are you?'

'I'm pregnant.'

They met a few hours later, with Unni breaking the speed limit through Bollstabruk and parking her expensive new toy across two bays outside the café.

She was planning to go for a drive later, along the country lanes through the forest first, then down to her old neck of the woods around Forsed.

Flipping the bird at the past.

The waitress set down two huge slices of Swiss roll in front of them.

'Are you happy?' asked Unni. 'Or are you leaning more the other way?'

'Somewhere in the middle, I guess.'

She had managed to get most of the story out of Eira before their coffee was even cool enough to drink, the mess she had got herself into.

'Christ, Ricken? I remember him. He was always hanging around your place, wasn't he? Incredibly charming, if I recall.'

'Mmm.'

'So which of them do you want it to be?'

'It doesn't matter what I want.'

Unni laughed. She had stopped dying her hair, which was now cropped and grey, and she had a pair of sunglasses perched on top of her head.

Laughter lines all over her face.

'You know, I just caught a glimpse of Kerstin in you.'

'What do you mean?'

Unni paused, thinking or hesitating. Perhaps even she realised that it wasn't so simple.

'I never really understood why she gave in to Veine. I know he was your dad, but she was never in love with him. All that really matters is the life *you* want to live.'

'No,' said Eira.

'Yes.'

'If this child is going to have a dad then it also depends where August wants to live. It depends on Ricken, who has never made any concessions to anyone. And I also have to be here for Mum, who isn't going to be much of a grandmother, and Magnus, who . . .'

'Who is where he is, yes.'

Eira felt her eyes welling up, and she had to swallow.

'What if I'm a shitty mother?'

'Nonsense, you can do this.' Unni gave her a fist bump, the way she always had. 'How hard can it be? I grew up with a couple of drunks for parents. There were times when we didn't have anything to eat, when I went to school in filthy clothes, but look at me. I turned out all right.'

She gestured out to her Jaguar, which had attracted a group of admiring older men. It stuck out in the middle of the drab square. The decline was more obvious in Bollstabruk than elsewhere; so many boarded-up windows and empty shops. The café was run by a local community initiative, which meant that the coffee cost next to nothing.

'I'm sorry I haven't been to see her,' said Unni.

'It's not me you should be apologising to.'

They had been friends since they were in nappies, that was what Kerstin always used to say; their fathers had worked together at the pulp mill in Väja. Until they got the boot, Unni liked to add. She had often come over to cry on their sofa when Eira was younger, loved up and then dumped. Eira remembered her and Kerstin drinking wine late into the night as she eavesdropped for as long as she could manage to stay awake. So many memories.

She took out her phone and brought up the image.

'Does this look familiar to you?'

Unni spent a long time studying the photograph, and Eira tried to read her reaction. She thought she could see a smile trying to break through, but it faded and disappeared.

'Crikey, Kerstin is so young here.'

'I think this must have been taken in the summer of 1968. Do you recognise the others?'

'Why are you asking about this all of a sudden?' Unni didn't look up at Eira; she could see straight through her, knew her all too well. 'Most people don't start digging into their parents' secrets until it's all over, once they're dead and buried.'

Eira weighed up the risk of saying too much, assessing how much damage it would do if word got out and people started speculating.

'I'd appreciate it if you wouldn't mention this to anyone else,' she said after a moment. 'We don't want things to start spreading before we know more.'

'You know me.' Unni trailed a hand over her mouth in a zippering motion.

'You might have heard,' Eira continued, 'that we found a body in the river by Lunde in April.'

Unni's cup paused halfway to her mouth, and she stared at Eira.

'What are you saying? Is it him? Did you find Steve?'

'Steve?'

'If Kerstin only knew.' Unni had slumped back and was looking up at the ceiling with her hand on her forehead.

'Would you mind telling me what you're talking about?' The noise from the kitchen seemed to fade, and Eira could no longer hear the sports report from the TV nearby. 'Who's Steve?'

'Have you mentioned any of this to Kerstin? Don't say anything. Or is it better for her to know the truth? God knows.'

'Unni . . .'

'Just give me a minute. Give me a chance to remember.'

She waved to the Eritrean woman who was busy clearing tables and asked for a glass of water, knocking it back in one go and then drying her mouth. She took a deep breath and pointed at the photograph.

'That one is Terry,' she said before moving her finger to the dark-haired man. 'And this one is . . . hang on, it's on the tip of my tongue. John!'

'You just said it was Steve?'

'No, no, it's John. There were three of them, but Steve isn't in the picture.'

'Three of what?'

It was hard work talking to someone whose mind seemed to dart about as much as her hands. Eira had always had the sense that only half of what Unni said was true. It wasn't that she deliberately told lies, but she bent the facts here and there, exaggerated things to make life just that little bit more exciting.

'Americans,' she said now. 'They'd all done a runner from the war in Vietnam. When can it have been . . .'

'1968.'

'That was it.'

'Why did you just ask if it was Steve we'd found?'

'Has your mother really never mentioned him?'

'No.'

'I don't know whether Kerstin would want me to tell you about any of this. It would be one thing if she was gone, but she trusted me, you know?'

'It's a police inquiry,' said Eira.

'Sorry, sweetie. I always forget you're police.'

Unni let out a brief laugh and folded her napkin, placed it on top of the slice of cake she hadn't finished.

They had come strolling across the square with a bag of beer one Saturday that spring. Unni herself hadn't been there that day. She had dropped out of school as soon as she could and found a job at the workers' mess hall in Sandslån, sharing a room with three others.

'But there were some pretty decent men there, too. Hundreds during the log-driving season. I remember one in particular, from Para . . .'

She didn't have time to hang around the square on Saturdays, in other words, but Kerstin had told her all about that day – repeatedly over the weeks that followed. How the world seemed to have both stopped spinning and sped up, a wind carrying new and exciting things.

Like so many others, Kerstin had joined the United NLF Groups that winter. She read Marx and Mao and started to understand the bigger picture, the way the world worked, how little she had known. They sold the *Vietnam Bulletin* and handed out pamphlets to shoppers. She had just made her first speech that day, knees like jelly as she told the residents of Kramfors that imperialism had to be crushed, people liberated. And then they had sung NLF songs: *Vietnam is close, right outside your window* and *Farmer in the jungle by Saigon, do you feel the support . . .*

And then, just like that, there they were. Kerstin was already slightly giddy after her speech, the ground swaying beneath her.

An American voice, saying: 'Feels kinda awkward to see that flag here, in the middle of nowhere . . .'

If there was such a thing as love at first sight, the kind of overpowering emotion you read about in magazines, then that was what Kerstin felt. Assuming she hadn't been exaggerating, of course, which she did sometimes.

Love had hit her like a thunderbolt, an ambush.

'I've never seen her so loved up,' said Unni. 'Forgive me for saying so, my dear, but your dad never came close.'

And then they discovered that the three young men had run away from the American army. The whole thing was incredible – to *Kramfors* of all places. Who wouldn't fall head over heels in love?

'They'd been living in a collective somewhere.'

'Torsåker?'

'Could have been, yes. The idea was that they'd do work

on the farm and that sort of thing, but I guess they didn't want to die of boredom up there in the woods.'

The whole thing had been hard to understand for someone like Unni, born and raised in Forsed, desperate to get away, but that's how it was back then. People wanted to get out into the countryside, to live in harmony with nature. To escape the temptations of the big city. To study Marx and Trotsky and free themselves of their egos.

As though someone kept rummaging through your brain, Steve had said to Kerstin as they lay among the sleeping bags and blankets in an abandoned loose box in Lunde.

He was from some blue-collar city in America, God knows which, though Philadelphia seemed to ring a bell. Terry's old man had a job at a steelworks somewhere, and John was from California. What did they know about hens and turnips, about the earth that had been frozen solid when they arrived?

The forest was creepy, he'd told her. Trees everywhere, no way of knowing if anyone was sneaking up on you – it was almost like being back in 'Nam.

They had been living in the collective for a couple of months when they decided to leave. Didn't bother telling anyone; they'd have been subjected to some sort of interrogation if they had. Instead they just hitched a ride to Kramfors, where they slept rough outside the station and spent the last of their money on bread and beer.

That was when they heard the music in the square, songs about Vietnam, and they realised that even in the middle of nowhere, there were people who could help them.

They found someone with a spare sofa, and another

knew of an empty barn on the outskirts of Lunde, a place where people stored furniture and bedding.

Finding work was never a problem: stacking and grading wood at one of the timberyards, loading and unloading the boats.

'I'm wondering whether Steve didn't find a job down at the docks in Lunde. I guess he did, given he was sleeping in a barn there,' said Unni. 'But I'm not sure, I really didn't spend much time with them.'

The staff had started to wipe down the tables, clearing the pastries from the counter. The café would be closing soon.

'Kerstin had other friends back then, people who talked about going to *university* and travelling to *Paris*.'

Unni had made out with the guy called Terry at a party once, that was all, in a cramped place in the centre of town where people went to smoke. A few weeks later, when she got a chance to come over from Sandslån again, she found him on a mattress in the corner with some final-year student from Nordingrå.

What she remembered most were fragments of things Kerstin had told her afterwards, once it was all over and she needed her old friend again.

'What happened?' asked Eira.

'The same thing that always happens,' said Unni. 'Steve dumped her, in the most cowardly of ways. Without a single word.'

They took shelter beneath the overhanging roof of an empty shop as a sudden downpour passed over Bollstabruk.

'One night they're screwing in the barn, and the next . . .

Poof! He's gone up in smoke. Bear in mind this was the first time Kerstin really fell in love. She hadn't realised these things could happen.'

On the other side of the street, a woman in a headscarf trudged by with a couple of heavy shopping bags. A gust of wind blew her umbrella inside out.

'She just couldn't understand it,' said Unni. 'She thought he might have done something stupid, went out looking for him along the riverbank and down by the wharf, back and forth every night.'

Eira shuddered as she thought back to the body being recovered from the river. Was there a chance there could be a second one down there? Part of her brain started thinking through the logical next steps, whether or not she would be able to get the divers to come out again, but another was focused on the impossibility of it all. The fact that the remains had been found by chance. She thought about the depth of the river, the currents, the fact that 500 cubic metres of water flowed out into the sea every single second. Searching for another body would be pointless.

'Kerstin was worried that he'd hurt himself somehow. Steve was always so jittery. I remember her telling me that he had shrapnel scars all over his back, from a grenade. Craters, like the moon. We didn't know anything about that sort of thing back then – anxiety and PTSD, that's what it'd be called now. Nightmares, shaking, screaming, the whole lot. He genuinely thought they were after him. You forget how young these boys were – no more than nineteen or twenty. It wouldn't surprise me if one of them had decided to take his own life.'

Eira hadn't said a word about murder. It had been in the papers and all over the internet, but that didn't mean Unni had seen it.

'Can you be any more specific about when Steve disappeared?'

'It was autumn,' Unni said with a frown, scratching her head. 'I know that because I remember it was dark in the evening on those days when I had time to come and look after Kerstin. It was freezing cold outside the barn, but she just sat there crying.'

'And what about John? What do you know about him?'

'Is that who you found?'

'It could be.'

'I can't remember ever talking to him. He was handsome, but he was harder to read. You know what I mean, when you can't tell whether a man is deep and brooding or just cocky? Not my type, basically. And don't ask me what happened to him. I was busy peeling potatoes until Kerstin called me in tears.'

John, thought Eira. That had to be one of the most common names in the English-speaking world. Steve too.

'Do you remember any of their surnames?'

Unni laughed.

'You expect far too much of me, Eira. I can barely remember the names of my own long-lost lovers.'

She held out a hand, palm upturned. The rain had eased off.

'Looks like the coast's finally clear to put the top down again.'

Allan Westin couldn't settle that evening. So much pacing about the damn house, getting up to pee, and then he was wide awake again.

The old rage had come back to him. The regret, too. The failure to be the man his wife needed him to be.

If he'd had any booze in the house, he would have turned to it now. To feel the burn in his throat and the lull that followed. Surely he would be able to sleep then.

He regretted that he hadn't kept Rabble this evening. There was something restful about having a living creature sleeping soundly beside you, squirming in his sleep and barking softly from time to time. Allan didn't claim to know much about what went on in the mind of a dog, but he imagined they must be simple dreams, possibly about the little dachshund bitch they'd seen earlier, over by Hyssbacken.

He should have forgotten all about taking the wretched pooch over to Eira's place. Left her to get on with whatever she was doing upstairs rather than start shouting for no reason. Asking how was she doing, whether everything was OK.

'Yeah, fine.'

'And the little one?'

'All good, they say. No problems.'

If only he'd said to hell with the pleasantries and the small talk, then she wouldn't have come down the stairs with her notepad and the stack of old letters in her arms.

'You busy cleaning?' he had asked. 'At this time of day?'

'I'm hoping I'll find something.'

Eira had dumped everything onto the kitchen table.

'Oh, I meant to ask,' she said. 'You used to work down at the docks, didn't you?'

'Yup, started off as a docker and then moved over to the shipyard. Why?'

'Do you remember any Americans around here in the late sixties? I think they probably worked down there too – I'm guessing that's where it was easiest to find a job? They'd run away from the war in Vietnam, were sleeping in a barn in Lunde . . . Hold on.'

She held out her phone and Allan had squinted down at the screen, thinking back to the strange image of the dead man's face she had already shown him. This was a real photograph, not something made on a computer; it showed real people. He stared until his eyes could no longer see. A haze of past and present, cataracts and vitreous now clouding his vision.

'What about them?'

'It could be one of them, the body we found in the river,' she had said.

The lass was police. He should have known she would work it out in the end. She'd inherited it from her father, this stubbornness.

'Didn't you say he was Greek or something?'

'A person can be several things,' said Eira. 'It's possible

125

he was Italian American. Damn it, I forgot to ask Unni about that.'

She had started typing something on her phone then, and Allan had explained that he didn't necessarily know the other dockers, that they were put into different teams.

'I might have seen them out and about, but it would've just been in passing.'

'Can you think of anyone else who was around then? Anyone who might know more?'

'From back then? Still alive? I'll have to have a think.'

Eira had slumped down into a chair then. She had a lot on her plate right now, getting big as she was. It wasn't good for her, he had said, working so late into the night.

'I'm not sure you could call it work,' said Eira. 'The investigation has basically been shelved, I'm the only one still looking into it. Did you see that it was Mum in that photo, by the way?'

'What? Was that Kerstin?'

'Did you know her back then?'

'I wouldn't say I *knew* her. She was a lot younger than me . . .'

They said goodnight and 'I'll come and get the dog in the morning.' The same things they always said. Allan had gripped the railing as he stepped down from the porch. There were gulls circling overhead, chasing the crows away in order to build their nests.

The wet grass had soaked through his slippers.

There were times when he was ashamed to be an old man. The way she looked at him with something bordering on love, but also as though he was feeble. As though all she expected of him was to get up in the morning and keep himself neat and tidy.

'It might come back to me later,' he had said before she closed the door. 'Once I've slept on it.'

S ilje had her hands full interviewing witnesses in a murder
  investigation all morning, but GG was in his office as she
passed. Eira knocked on the open door. He was on his phone,
but he waved her in and ended the call a little abruptly.

'Wow,' he said, looking down at her belly. 'You must be
getting close?'

'Two months to go.'

'And then everything changes.'

Eira always struggled to know how to respond to comments like that. She smiled.

'You know,' she said, 'the mystery man we found in the
river . . .'

'I knew it.'

'What?'

'It wouldn't be like you to drop a case when there are still
questions to be answered.'

His words made her feel warm inside. She remembered
all the times when GG had told her to do just that, that
sometimes even a police officer had to let go. He always
managed to say something that made her feel . . . seen.

He laughed.

'Sooner or later you always manage to find a neighbour
who has a cousin who slept with the guy sometime a
hundred years ago.'

128

'Wrong,' Eira said with a grin. 'It was fifty-five years ago, and it was his friend.'

He roared with laughter, and she joined in – at least until the baby got excited, and it felt like a boxing match in there. Eira slumped down onto the sofa. Despite no longer being in charge of the unit, GG had somehow been allowed to keep the big office.

'And it wasn't a neighbour's cousin,' she added, much more serious this time.

There was no need to mention Shirin's ethically dubious CGI face. Eira put a copy of the photograph down in front of him and explained who the woman in the middle was.

It wasn't technically a lie, more a shortcut that made her look a little smarter.

'I saw this photo in her album and realised it had been taken in 1968. That fits with what we know so far: a dark-haired man in his early twenties, of southern European descent. Mum's memory is pretty bad now, unfortunately, so she couldn't tell me anything about him, but I spoke to a friend of hers. It turns out Mum was together with someone who isn't in the picture. There were three of them, American deserters from the Vietnam war who ended up in Kramfors.'

'Are you kidding?' said GG, studying the image. 'Tell me you have a name.'

'John, that's all. He probably came from California.'

Eira told GG about the collective in Torsåker, that the three young men had been hanging around Kramfors all summer and that they might have found work at the dock in Lunde.

'Some of the deserters didn't dare tell their parents what

they'd done. That means they might not have known where their son was, or even that they'd disowned him, which could explain why we haven't been able to find him in any missing persons databases.'

She had spent half the night reading about the war and deserters, and her eyes were aching. The U.S. had launched its opening attacks on North Vietnamese targets in 1964, and the first ground troops arrived the very next year, aiming to wipe out the National Liberation Front guerrillas and stop the spread of communism. Many young American men had run the minute their draft card arrived, and some had burned them in public. Others were discovered to have gone AWOL from U.S. military bases in West Germany. Desertion from Vietnam itself was virtually impossible, but the soldiers occasionally flew to Japan while on leave. That enabled them to get in touch with Beheiren, an underground network that helped to smuggle them out of the country in fishing boats, sailing them over to the Soviet Union along the so-called 'Rising Sun Route.' Once they arrived in Moscow, they were paraded at press conferences where they publicly distanced themselves from America's unjust war, and most then moved on. Close to 1,000 deserters had eventually found sanctuary in Sweden.

Eira had managed to find a few called Steve, but none of them were from Philadelphia. She had paused when she came across the name Steve Kinnaman, thinking it sounded familiar, but as she kept reading she realised that was because his son had gone on to become a Hollywood star, long after he himself escaped to Sweden via the Thai jungles.

People had offered to host the deserters in their homes,

and lawyers had taken on their cases pro bono. The young men were able to collect eighty-five kronor a week from the social welfare office in Zinkensdamm, and some of them had supplemented that by fishing in central Stockholm until they found jobs as paper boys or at the brewery in Vårby.

Or until, alternatively, they were sent to a collective in Norrland.

'It seems to have been pretty chaotic with all the different political groups vying for their attention,' Eira continued. 'You had the NLF, who wanted armed revolution, plus a more social democratic group wanting peace. Then there were the Maoists and the Trotskyites. In the end, they formed the American Deserters Committee in order to speak for themselves.'

'Great stuff,' said GG. 'If you're right then it shouldn't be too hard for the police in the States to work out who he is.'

'There must be records here, too. They were granted asylum and received welfare payments.'

GG leaned back in his chair and gazed out through the window. Sundsvall was grey. The sky, the public-sector buildings. This might be the greyest area of town, thought Eira.

'Unless I'm mistaken,' he said, 'it was in January that year that the siege of Huế and the Tet Offensive took place – not to mention the Mỹ Lai massacre that spring. Just imagine escaping all that only to end up on the bottom of the Ångerman River. One of life's cruel ironies.'

He seemed to know far more about the war than she did. Eira hadn't memorised the dates of any of the battles, just the routes out of there.

'Have you talked to Silje about how to move forward with this?' he asked.

'I haven't had time, and she's not around today.' That sounded like an excuse, and it was. 'What would you have said, if you were still my boss?'

'That the Swedish police investigate murders even if the statute of limitations has run out. We want to know, the public wants to know – never mind his family, who could still be alive.'

'There's one more thing,' said Eira, hesitating briefly, possibly because this was all getting a little too close to Kerstin and, by association, her. 'One of the other deserters, Steve, also seems to have disappeared or left without warning. From one day to the next, sometime around the start of autumn. The murder took place in early September.'

'Sounds like a possible perpetrator.'

'Or another victim.'

'Interesting,' said GG. 'Just let me know if you need any help looking into it.'

Eira laughed.

'You really want to help me? On a case we can't even prosecute?' It was as touching as it was absurd, GG with his thirty-year career and various management positions behind him.

'And give up all this?' He gestured to his messy desk, files and papers everywhere. 'For every kingpin we arrest, another ten step forward with AK4s, shooting each other to take his place. The sixties, you said?'

Eira decided to pay Unni a visit on her way home, in one of the brick apartment blocks lining the hillside in Sundsvall.

Useless as ever at replying to messages, at remembering anything at all. No, nothing had come to her, she said after Eira turned down a glass of wine but kicked off her shoes and sat down for a while. The walls were covered in pictures, a vinyl spinning on the record player.

Eira had an investigation again.

Take a few days, that was what Silje had told her when Eira explained what she had. 'See if you can find anything else before we reach out to the Americans.'

There was no statute of limitations on murder in the United States.

Unni turned down the volume, a raspy voice singing the blues.

'The more I try,' she said, 'the less sure I am about what I really remember and what I'm just trying to remember to make you happy. The memory can't handle us going in with a magnifying glass. I'm not even a hundred per cent sure his name was John any more.'

No surname had popped up in her deceitful memory, but it could well be true that he had Italian roots.

Handsome, like she had said.

'For someone so young to decide he didn't want to live any more . . . it really is a shame.'

'He didn't kill himself,' said Eira.

Unni's eyes widened as she explained.

'Oh lordy, the things people do to each other . . . Here, this calls for more wine.'

Unni got up to fill her glass. She drank so fast, asking again whether Eira wanted any, despite her obvious bump. Eira thought back to what she had said about her childhood, that her parents' drinking had tainted everything. That her friend, Kerstin, had grown up in a teetotal house – not for religious reasons, but because her mother controlled the purse strings. Not a single öre on drink until everything else had been paid for, and there had rarely been any money left over.

Was that the main difference?

Or was it something else? Education, her grandparents' efforts to make Kerstin keep studying, their belief in brighter days to come?

Unni had brought the bottle back with her, and she set it down on the floor by her armchair.

'I'm sorry my memory's so bad,' she said. 'But none of this ever really mattered to me. I was never comfortable around that crowd, wore the wrong clothes and all that business. I used to get dolled up whenever I went into town – Kramfors was a big deal back then, you understand – but they'd all be sitting there in their fraying jeans . . . I felt so out of place, dressed up like a dog's dinner.'

'You did mention something about a girl who was older than you? From Nordingrå?'

'Right,' Unni hit herself on the head. 'That little bitch, she stole my man the minute my back was turned. Pretty and sweet, as I remember it, the kind of girl who makes you feel like an ogre. They were all so different to me, from the farming families over towards the coast. No matter how tough things got, they still had plenty of food on the table, a farm they would inherit one day. They were their own people.'

'You don't happen to remember her name, do you?'

The record got stuck, and Unni stood up and lifted the needle, carefully lowering it to the next track. She paused by the window, taking in the open view of the town, the sea beyond, the papermill on the other side of the bay.

'Could it have been Titti?' she asked, testing the name in her mouth. 'Or Kicki,' she thought aloud. 'Yes, I think it was Kicki.'

Eira sat quietly, not wanting to disturb the memory.

'You know,' Unni continued, 'no one had ever taught me how to be alluring, all those games girls play. I was too much; I frightened the life out of the boys with how horny I was. The men back then, they wanted to be the protector, but I was too scared to depend on anyone. I'd seen just how quickly that could all go to shit.'

'Kicki?'

'Yeah, that was it.'

Unni raised her glass in a toast to herself, a pleased look on her face.

'If Kicki was her nickname,' Eira continued, 'then she was probably called Kristina, right?'

'Yup, that's usually the way.'

'And you're sure she was in the last year of senior high school? That she would have graduated in 1969?'

'Hmm,' said Unni. 'Now I'm wondering just how sure I am.'

E ira delved straight into the drawers once she got home. She had gone through most of her mother's papers the night before. Paper dolls from the fifties, pictures of pretty items of clothing Kerstin had carefully cut out of fashion magazines when she was a girl. Exercise books from her school days, essays she had won prizes for, letters sorted into piles and tied with string. They were from her parents and friends, a whole stack in Veine's handwriting and from Eira while she was working in Stockholm, but nothing from Steve.

In the bottom drawer, she found a few school photographs in cardboard frames.

There had been three girls called Kristina in the class of 1968, but that was a worthless piece of information if Unni was right and 'Kicki' hadn't graduated until the next year. Eira lifted out textbook after textbook. Maths, geography, history. Why had her mother kept these things? Did she really think she would ever read them again?

She had been hoping to find a school yearbook, but there was nothing of the sort. The class lists must be saved somewhere – nothing was thrown away in bureaucracy-loving Sweden – but it was Friday night, an eternity until the various public bodies reopened on Monday morning.

Kristina, Kristina. It was such a common name, not least

among that generation, named after various queens and princesses. There were at least 709 Kristinas, she discovered after a quick search online, in Kramfors municipality alone.

What else could she do other than wait? All the women around her mother's age started flitting through her head, Facebook groups about absolutely everything. Eira herself had been invited to join *Ådalen School Class of 2006*.

The NLF groups, she suddenly realised. The demonstrations. People who had spoken out against U.S. imperialism in the papers, in *Tidningen Ångermanland* or *Nya Norrland*; people who painted slogans on rooftops. She took out her notes from the articles she had read.

A number of men's names cropped up, but only one girl.

Kristina Norberg.

Eira typed her name into the Facebook search bar, and her jaw dropped when she saw the results. She recognised one of the faces from the list of thumbnails at the left-hand side. It was probably one of the most recognisable faces in Kramfors municipality: that of its former leader.

Could it be?

There was no trace of the youthful sweetness Unni had described.

The woman was known professionally as Kristina Frånlund, but she must have taken her husband's surname. In a few places, she was referred to by her maiden name: Norberg.

Born Nordingrå, 1949.

It had been a few years since she withdrew from public life, but she still lived in Kramfors.

It had been a wretched year. The worst one of all, and Allan had a fair few under his belt. Eighty-two, to be precise.

Everything had been dredged up and come surging back to him. As he paced back and forth at night, sleep reduced to an hour here and there, he found himself thinking that the forgetfulness that had struck Kerstin next door, the fog that opened its jaws and gobbled up everything a person had been, would be a mercy.

His problem was that he remembered too damn much, especially from that summer. 1968.

The job down at the docks hadn't been so bad. The wood and the sharp metal edges had torn his hands to shreds, but the skin eventually toughened up. Like leather, she had said. During their first few times together, he had been worried about his roughness on her soft flesh, but Maarit hadn't minded.

It feels nice, she had said, that you're so gentle with me.

Someone had hurt her, and not just in the way that boys do – being careless and then running off to America without a word, like his own grandfather had. Really *hurt* her. Grabbed her hair and shoved her, forced themselves onto her and left her scared to be alone with a man for several years afterwards. That was his good fortune, because it meant she was there, available, even though they were both over twenty-five when they met at the fair in Lunde.

Allan would have killed the man with his own bare hands if he'd ever got the chance, but Maarit always refused to say the bastard's name.

I've forgotten it, she said, though he knew she was lying. *Forget I said anything. It's you and me now.*

He searched for the letters they had written to each other that winter, after Maarit went back to Luleå. She'd had to go – her job on the cold buffet in Kramfors was only ever seasonal – but that hadn't extinguished the love that had sparked to life between them. Allan couldn't work out where she might have put the letters, whether she had even kept them.

I'll come to Luleå, he had written. *I'll come to you.*

Where you are is where I want to be.

Showing bravery through the pen in his hand so that she would feel secure. He had no time for God, but he would have been willing to swear on Stalin's grave that he would never hurt her.

Once spring arrived, he would take the night train the three hundred miles or so to Luleå and try to find work, assuming she still wanted him.

There were docks in Norrbotten, after all.

The loving words she had written back. They weren't in any of the wardrobes, nor the drawers in the desk.

About her longing that winter.

Allan would never forget that day at the train station in Luleå. Her blue coat, her hair shorter than he remembered it. It was still cold, though the ice had started to break up, and the docks were recruiting left, right and centre.

He remembered her shyness as she drove him home in her second-hand Volvo Amazon. To her one-bed flat in Lövskatan, in the shadow of the huge ironworks.

This'll do for the time being.

The bed was too narrow for two, but Allan could do something about that. The minute he got his first pay cheque, on credit if necessary.

He had gone over to the office at the ore port the next day. He could still hear the roar of the plant, the conveyor belts transporting the ore high overhead, but not the exact words that were spoken.

The official had looked down at his papers, but Allan never found out what was written there. Was never given any reason.

Allan Westin, was it?

No, they didn't have any work for him.

He had cleared his throat and told the man about his experience at the docks in Lunde, the shipyard, that he had good references, but no.

It was the same story at the port of loading and the iron-works, despite the fact that Maarit's own father had told her they were looking for men. They'd even put out adverts through the job centre.

Not quite the type of experience we're looking for.

At the pub one evening, with Maarit's brothers and some of the others, after they'd had a few drinks and got to talking, someone had asked: 'Is it true you're a communist?'

'Damn right I'm a communist,' Allan had replied. It would never have occurred to him to claim otherwise.

He remembered a lowered voice, someone leaning in to him.

'You're not the only one who can't find work for that very reason.'

A cold wind blowing in from the 1930s, when several of their fathers had been affected. When the communists were rounded up and sent to camps in the far north, held prisoner there while the war raged and Sweden allowed goods trains full of German soldiers to pass through the country.

But after all that time, in the sixties? In the Social Democrats' Sweden? Wasn't this supposed to be a democracy, a place where everyone was entitled to their opinion?

Allan couldn't quite remember how that evening had ended.

He got drunk, that much was certain. Possibly an escort home to Maarit.

And after that: a goodbye on the platform, once all his promises had fallen like dominoes.

The journey home, alone.

He found the letters in the end, in a chest in the attic. Where they kept everything they had stashed away out of sight. Winter coats Maarit hadn't worn in years, a broken food processor. There was an old wasp's nest hanging beneath the eaves, cobwebs full of dead flies that caught the morning sun in the window.

Allan sat down on the blue wooden chair the children had always loved because of the secret compartment beneath the seat, and he rifled through the past.

Her letters from the months that followed.

The big words she wrote, emotions that hit him like a punch to the gut.

And then: that she was pregnant.

All the ways Maarit had tried to make it work. She was sure there were other jobs Allan could do, long lists of things she thought it might be worth applying for.

His point-blank refusal. Nothing she wrote could have made him get back on the train to Luleå.

He knew who he was down in Lunde; this was where he belonged.

We can get through this together, she wrote.

Allan had spent that summer fighting and getting drunk on his own. Oh, he had hated the world back then.

Was he supposed to just forget all the things he believed in? His conviction that the people had to rise up and seize power by force, because it would never be given to the poor and the downtrodden otherwise. Was he supposed to pretend he didn't know that?

To demean himself, beg.

'Like hell,' he swore to the comrades that summer. 'I'll be damned if I do that.'

But the baby? The woman?

He had no answers there.

Skarpåkern was a residential area spread across a hillside on the edge of Kramfors, old farming land at one point in time.

Eira parked by the kerb. She hadn't called ahead, hadn't wanted to risk having the former municipal leader assert her right to peace and quiet at the weekend.

Kicki Frånlund was hunched over a planter as Eira approached.

'Beans,' she said, straightening up. 'And this will be chard and spinach.' She used her arm to wipe the sweat from her brow. Her hair had gone grey. 'How can I help you?'

'I'd like to talk to you about a murder,' said Eira, holding up her ID.

'I beg your pardon?'

'I have reason to believe that you were acquainted with a man we found dead recently.'

Eira rarely used such formal language. People generally gave better answers when she spoke to them the way she would anyone else, but in her experience that didn't apply to those in positions of power. They had a tendency to swat her aside like a gnat, demanding to talk to the prosecutor – who, if she was really unlucky, also happened to be an old classmate.

'Who?' asked Kicki Frånlund. Her voice was gruff, almost as though she was barking an order. 'Who's dead?'

'I think it would be best if we sat down.'

She asked Eira to wait in the sun room, returning ten minutes later with clean hands and a thermos of coffee. There were cups and glasses already on the table, as though she never knew when she might have guests.

'OK, would you mind telling me what this is about now?' she said.

It had been some time since Kicki Frånlund had left her post as the chair of the local municipality, but she still had an air of authority, her gaze as sharp as it had been in her prime. During her time in office she had been instrumental in pushing for the expansion of the rail line, fighting to link trains and planes in the area. Her detractors had always said that she was more on the side of business and tourism than the people who actually lived in Kramfors.

'Your name cropped up in our inquiries into a murder we believe took place in 1968.'

'Wow, so long ago?'

Kicki Frånlund seemed to relax slightly.

'I understand you were active in the NLF movement in Kramfors at the time?'

'Yes, that's not something I'm ashamed of. You could say it was my political awakening. Vietnam was a terrible war, an unwarranted attack on a small nation. I wish we were seeing the same sort of engagement today, for Ukraine, but that was a different era. People are too busy writing cruel comments about each other online now. I'm not sure when that happened. Why is it so difficult to get people together to push for change?'

The ex-politician sounded like she was on some TV talk show, not having a chat with a police officer.

'We think the man may have been active in the same circles,' Eira continued. 'That he was a deserter from the U.S. army.'

Kicki Frånlund took a deep breath, palpably shaken.

'You can't be serious? Are you talking about Terry Anderson? It must be fifty years since I last saw him, so I'm not sure how much help I can be. Was it politically motivated? I can't say I'm surprised if it was. Hold on . . . didn't you say this person died in 1968? If so, it can't be Terry.'

'No, he wasn't the one I meant,' said Eira, making a note of the name Anderson. 'We think it could have been another American, John. You don't happen to know his surname, do you?'

The woman remembered them as though it was yesterday, possibly because she had helped them write various letters to the Swedish authorities.

John Aiello.

Steve Carrano.

Letters in her notepad. Names. They had them at last. Eira felt a sense of calm settle over her, of victory. It wasn't the intoxicating kind, but it was soft and reaffirming. A hand on her belly, as though to say: *we did it*.

'They sound like Italian names,' she said.

'Yes, but I suppose lots of Americans are the children of immigrants. You said you *think* it could be John. Does that mean you aren't sure?'

'That's why I'm here,' said Eira. 'To find out.'

Kicki Frånlund was quiet for a moment before she turned away.

It was a time of her life that stood out from all the rest. Kicki had rented a room from an old lady, and she had lost her virginity there during her first term in Kramfors, far from her parents in Nordingrå.

That area of the High Coast had been such a backwater back then, which was hard to believe when you saw the sheer numbers of tourists heading up to Skuleberget or Rotsidan these days. Kicki was proud of having contributed to that. But Kramfors . . . It was practically a metropolis. A town of thirty thousand people, almost twice as many as now. She remembered the huge senior high school where almost no one knew who she was, the dances at Folkets Park, the parties. Kicki occasionally got so drunk that she threw up in the toilets at the temperance house.

She had once found a bag that someone had left behind there and stolen everything inside. She had become a master shoplifter that spring term. Her best trick was to roll up a blouse and clamp it between her legs if she was wearing a skirt. No one would ever think to look there.

That was how she got hold of the kind of clothes almost no one else had.

Not that she told the young policewoman any of that.

'Uff,' she said instead. 'This brings back so many memories.'

There were rooms inside her that she had never let anyone see. Topics she had never mentioned during interviews, when they were trying to root about in her childhood and upbringing and the more private areas of her life.

That was my political awakening, she had said.

My time in high school opened my eyes to the world.

'Were you in a relationship with Terry Anderson?' Eira Sjödin asked without warning. She had put her mobile phone in the middle of the coffee table and started recording. 'Did you know him well?'

Kicki smiled, searching for the right words. This was another thing she had never talked about, possibly out of fear that someone would work out who he was. It was all so long ago, a blessed time without social media; there were no archives for them to scour.

All the mattresses on all those floors.

'It wasn't some great love affair,' she said. 'But it was exciting for a country girl like me. I'm sure you know what I mean. Americans, right here in little Kramfors. And it was flattering that he chose me. It probably had something to do with my need to take care of people. I think he woke those feelings in me.'

Had he chosen her? Or was it more that she had lowered her head to his lap one evening when the air was thick with smoke and there was American soul music playing on the stereo, in the seedy basement of one of the old wooden buildings that had long since been torn down.

That spring, Kicki had stolen clothes that were nothing like the things she had worn before; had walked up to one of the girls at school and said she wanted to do something for Vietnam. They all seemed so confident, like they didn't need to make concessions to anyone.

'And what about John Aiello? Did you know him?'

'I can't say I did, not really. He was always around, of course. The three of them were practically inseparable at first.'

John, with his thick, dark hair and eyes she barely dared meet. Kicki could still feel his presence in the cramped kitchen at that place in the centre of town, stacks of cups and bottles everywhere. She remembered the stench of mould, or maybe it was old food, as he pushed her away. John was the one she had taken an interest in first, but he had rejected her, right there in that tiny kitchen. His hands, she recalled from the few seconds she had held them, were softer than any she had ever felt before.

'John could lose his temper,' she said. 'He could really fly off the handle. I remember him throwing a cup once, smashing it against the wall. Steve Carrano had a bit of that in him, too. I didn't know anything about psychology at the time, but I understand it all a bit more now. They were working-class boys who joined the army – Steve had actually *volunteered* to join, I remember him cursing himself for that – and they had no idea what they were supposed to be doing on the other side of the world. Vietnam had never threatened America, and the Vietnamese people didn't see them as liberators. Back then, I don't think I realised just how young they were. I was even younger, so they seemed older, exciting . . . you know. John was twenty, and Steve was probably only nineteen. It's not really so surprising that they held it all in. But with Terry, it was different. He was more of a free soul. He'd been to protests back in the States, fallen out with his dad – a World War Two veteran who'd been involved in the Normandy landings.'

'Is there anything else you can tell me about John?'

It was strange to think that there were some voices you could still hear even after half a century had passed. The broken Swedish, English slipping in whenever John Aiello couldn't find the right words. She had thought he sounded like a poet, and though it was Terry's arm around her shoulders, it was John's voice she wanted to hear.

Freedom is just a dream, a breath in the wind.

It was the middle of the day, the sun blazing down on Öd's Wharf.

How did you manage to escape? Kicki had asked.

It was easy, the easiest thing ever.

John Aiello had been working as a medic at Ramstein Air Base in Germany. It wasn't so bad, definitely not the worst place to be, but it did mean he came face to face with the injured as they returned from Vietnam. None of them could understand why they had been sent over there; even the doctors on the base were against the war. The only ones who still supported it were the non-commissioned officers, who were convinced that everything the USA did was right and good.

John studied art history and literature two nights a week, courses organised by some American university. He hung around the library and met some of the locals, got involved in the anti-war movement. They held demonstrations, which was lawful in West Germany, and on one occasion they even marched around the base with placards reading *STOP THE*

WAR. They were apprehended, of course, but there hadn't been any repercussions. Not right away, in any case. John had been moved to a smaller medical facility, which was fine, but then he had started to hear about some of the others who had been involved in the protests. One of his friends was taken away in the middle of the night, shipped off to Vietnam.

He started having nightmares, trouble sleeping. All he could hear as he lay awake were the planes taking off, echoing through him.

That's going to happen to me too. Tomorrow? The day after that? Will they show up tonight?

One day, a friend of his – Ray, who had also been involved in the protests – said, 'Let's just go.' He had a desk post, which meant he could produce fake leave papers for them, and with those documents granting them two weeks' leave, they were free to travel around Europe. They stole two boxes of rations from the storeroom – cans, food for men out in the field – plus a tent. Ray also managed to get hold of a car, possibly from one of his friends in the peace movement, or maybe it was stolen; John didn't ask any questions.

It thundered the night they left, the rain torrential. At some point they had stopped to take a leak and he yelled into the rumbling, screaming out in victory. Nature's fireworks seemed to John to be a celebration of peace, and since that night, he always felt a sense of anticipation whenever the sky grew dark and stormy.

They made camp by an anthill, something they didn't realise until the next morning. Ray started jumping around, shouting and brushing off the ants, but John just sat calmly, studying them. The way they marched in line. He lifted one of them off to one side and watched as it hurried back into the fold as quickly as it could. Did an ant ever imagine it was free?

At a lake somewhere along the way, he had burnt everything that led back home. The picture of his parents, of the girl who had promised to wait for him.

Certain information had circulated on the base, smuggled copies of *Second Front Review*, a magazine published by deserters that provided information about where others could find safety. It was only once they had pitched their tent by the lake that they started talking about where they were heading. Their residence permit would only last a month in France, but if they went to Sweden they would be able to stay. There were no slums or starving people there, and the girls were pretty.

Their car broke down in Denmark, a NATO country, and so they dumped it and took the ferry to Malmö. They had a phone number, scribbled down on the inside of a matchbox, and they begged for change and then called it from a telephone kiosk.

An hour later, they were picked up by members of a Swedish committee that supported the armed resistance in Vietnam. There were a number of deserters in Malmö, but after a few months John got bored of them, claiming they were only interested in smoking weed and doing amphetamines, and he made his way to Stockholm. He spent a while sleeping here and there – on the sofa of an older woman, in an NLF office, at a barracks in Tantolunden – and the idea of heading north, to the countryside, felt like an appealing proposition. The fresh air, the freedom.

'Could there have been anyone who wanted to hurt him?' asked Eira.

The sun had climbed above the house, and was no longer shining straight in on them.

'Everyone,' said Kicki Frånlund. 'At least if you believed Terry and Steve. They were always talking about people trying to plant ideas in their heads, dark cars parked on the street at night, a clicking sound on the phone. They were convinced the CIA was watching them. The kid John travelled to Stockholm with vanished after going off to ring his mum.'

'The one called Ray?'

That was something she could look into, thought Eira. Or was it? She was struggling to tell what was relevant, felt unsettled that she kept catching glimpses of her mother in everything.

'Do you know what happened to the others? To Steve Carrano and Terry Anderson?'

'I have no idea about Steve.'

'I heard he left Kramfors that autumn. Did you see him? Do you know why he left?'

'I wasn't here then,' said Kicki. 'I had to go back to Nordingrå towards the end of that summer. My mum wasn't well and they needed help on the farm.'

'What about Terry?'

'He headed south before that. I guess he missed city life.'

'Was your relationship over by then?'

'It was never really anything serious.'

The former politician got up. Shook the thermos but didn't pour any more coffee. Eira waited. The glass in the windows looked handblown, uneven, a butterfly flapping against the inside of the pane. She had the sense that everything Kicki Frånlund had said was superficial, almost as though someone else had written the words.

'Have you heard from him since?'

'No, and if you'll forgive me I don't really see what that has to do with anything. You can turn that off now.' She looked down at the phone as though it was an insect crawling over her neat table.

Eira reached for it and stopped the recording. She had five messages, she saw as she said a quick 'thank you' and hurried out to the car. She had noticed the screen light up earlier, but she hadn't wanted to interrupt her conversation with Kicki.

Where are you?

Shit.

August's brief message was followed by another.

We've been waiting fifteen minutes.

Eira stepped on the accelerator. She had completely forgotten about their meeting.

Or maybe she had repressed it.

H er bump felt enormous as she made her way into NC Café and Johanna – slim as a reed – leapt up to give her a hug.

'God, you look fantastic. Is there anything more beautiful than a pregnant woman? It's so great that you're going to be a mum.'

August pulled out a chair for her, something he had never done before. That detail lingered in her mind as his fiancée wittered on and on about what Eira should be eating to make sure she got enough iron and protein, but without destroying the planet.

Did the father-to-be automatically transform into a protector, or was it all an act, a part he was trying to perfect?

Look at me, look how responsible I am.

It was nice that he wanted to be.

August got up to get a glass of water and asked what Eira wanted. Flapping about like a gull watching over its young.

'I think it's important that the two of you also have a relationship,' he said once he sat down again.

'Can I feel your bump?' asked Johanna. 'Is that OK?'

Eira couldn't think of any reason to say no. They could well end up raising this child together, after all. She had met August's girlfriend once before, but that was largely in her capacity as a police officer. Johanna had written a number of inappropriate comments on Facebook during an ongoing investigation. To her surprise, Eira had liked her. Her cheeriness, her naivety, her lust for life.

Johanna let out a slight whoop when she felt a kick, leaning in to August's shoulder and kissing him on the neck.

'You're going to be such a great dad.'

'I think so too,' Eira said with a smile. 'Assuming it's his.'

'I want you to know that none of this is a problem for me,' said Johanna. 'I'm not judging you.'

'Why would I think you were?'

'Maybe not you.' Johanna began to squirm, as though she was trying to escape her body, gesturing to the street outside. 'But this is, like, the countryside. We're in Norrland. I just mean that you might be used to other people judging you.'

'No, not really.'

Eira could have told her about all the illegitimate children in her own family, in the area round about. About Lunde, where sailors made a brief layover and then the single mothers got together to open a haberdashery, teaching their daughters to cope just like they had. She could have said that she had rarely heard anyone judge anyone else. Life was what it was. People were attracted to one another, and what happened happened. Yes, this was Norrland, as religious as it was rebellious and blasphemous, but above all it was a place where few had large estates to pass down through the generations. Having children outside of wedlock wasn't quite the threat it was in wealthier areas.

August stroked Eira's arm.

'We need to talk practicalities,' he said. 'I didn't get a

chance to tell you that I've been invited to an interview for a post in Stockholm.'

'Hey, that's great. Congratulations.'

'I haven't got it yet.'

'And we have a chance to switch to a bigger apartment,' Johanna spoke up. 'Which would be great if we're going to be parents half the time.'

She trailed off, realising what she had said.

'I mean, obviously it'll be full-time for you, honey,' she continued, turning briefly to August before meeting Eira's eye again. 'What do the two of you think?'

'About which part?' asked Eira, unsure whether Johanna was talking about where they might live or whether Eira and August would have a romantic future together.

'We haven't really talked about it yet,' said August.

'No, God, I'm just . . . Stockholm, you know. I get so sick of it sometimes. It feels like you always have to be three steps ahead of everyone else or you just don't stand a chance.'

Eira's salad arrived. That had felt like the easiest thing to order – something they could all agree was good and healthy, both for the baby and the planet. It also required a lot of chewing, which meant she could avoid having opinions for a while.

August and Johanna were talking about different areas of Hägersten and how close they were to Svandamm Park and the various nurseries and playgrounds, the amount of time it took to get into central Stockholm – it made a real difference whether it was twelve minutes or seventeen, apparently. All the difference.

Eira recognised much of what they were talking about from her years subletting a place in Västertorp. Nice area. Sculptures between the buildings, from an era when town planners still cared about that sort of thing; trees and grass and swimming pools.

'I'm not sure I ever mentioned it, but my parents got divorced when I was twelve,' said August. 'Dad moved to Denmark and us kids had to fly to Copenhagen one weekend every month. It wasn't exactly the dream.'

'There's no need to worry, honey,' said Johanna, stroking his arm. 'You're not going to be that kind of dad.'

'Sorry, things have just been a bit crazy lately,' said Eira. 'I haven't had time to think that far ahead.'

It struck her that she had stopped thinking about the future in general. And the present, for that matter. On the drive over to the café, she thought she had caught a glimpse of an NLF flag fluttering above a rally, and she found herself wondering which of all the modern buildings had replaced the spot where Unni had once made out with Terry Anderson. It was a strange realisation, that the new life twisting and turning inside her felt less real than that.

'It's good to have a strategy, at the very least,' said August. 'And if we do end up deciding on Stockholm, then we'll already have some idea of what's what. Since we're living in Johanna's flat, we could use the points I've built up in the housing queue . . . I've been in it for years, so we'd probably be able to wangle it if the baby does turn out to be mine . . .'

Living in Stockholm, Eira thought once they had parted ways as the best of friends and Johanna had made her promise she would reach out if she needed anything. *It was so good to meet face to face and talk everything over.*

Would that really be such a bad idea?

She wouldn't even need to make use of August's time in the housing queue. Like so many other Swedes, Eira had joined Stockholm's never-ending housing queue when she graduated from high school, as she started to think about what she wanted to do with her life. She hadn't logged in to check on it in a while, but as she got into her car she decided to do just that.

Fourteen years in the queue. That could be enough for something in a decent suburb, possibly even in Västertorp.

A place without any memories, where no one knew who she was, without any roots getting tangled in everything she did. She had a vision of freedom, an absence of everything. Plain walls where nothing had ever hung before, rooms that had never been used for anything.

. . . *a dream, a breath in the wind.*

There were traces and fragments of a person in so many things. An advert for trips to Vietnam, the scent of a particular tobacco. A report from the local housing committee on the development of the Öd's Wharf.

Which of them had made her think of Terry last winter, after all this time?

Kicki Frånlund had slumped down into her armchair and poured herself a whisky. Aged in Swedish oak, from their very own barrel at the distillery upriver. She savoured every drop of it, not just for the taste and the alcohol but because of the sense of pride she got from the label. They certainly knew their whisky, these local distillers.

Just because she was retired didn't mean she had left the party, that she was no longer engaged; she was still a part of everything, not some lonely woman who spent her time tracking down old flames on Facebook.

Kicki had been happily married to her second husband for years, thank God, but this was something other than a longing for the wildness of her youth.

An epoch.

So much bigger than her own personal story, and yet also utterly intertwined. It could be the seed of a book, if she ever got round to writing it all down. *A Country Girl Takes the Throne: Memories from a Life in Politics.*

Well, maybe not everything, and above all not the part involving Terry. That had become painfully clear when she found herself thinking about him last winter.

There were multiple Terry Andersons on Facebook, but judging by his age and the place where he was born Kicki had quickly worked out which one was him. She could see that he now lived in St. Petersburg, Florida, but most of his page was private. Kicki had poured herself a glass of whisky that evening, too – possibly a couple – and then she had sent him a friend request. A short message explaining who she was, that her surname had been different back then, not to mention her looks.

'I don't know if you remember me,' she wrote, attaching a photo of herself as a young woman. Hitting send had given her a flutter of excitement, a quick rush of heat. A brief moment in which she was still that girl, memories of something ground-breaking and physical. She hadn't been all that sexually experienced at the time, but looking back now she could see that what she'd had with Terry had been special. He went for it as though his life depended on it, without any declarations of love. For some reason she had found that liberating.

Terry had accepted her friend request, and with that the door to his world was flung open. It turned out to be a nightmare – a Mordor, as her son would probably put it – and she felt disgust at the thought of his hands on her body.

Despite that, Kicki had kept reading.

There were posts claiming that the CIA had a base on the moon, that vaccines were deadlier than the viruses they claimed to prevent. That a worldwide network was trying to brainwash people into becoming zombified armies, or to get them hooked on drugs. Queen Elizabeth was apparently one of the leaders of this conspiracy, controlling the drugs trade across the world.

Kicki's immediate impulse was to delete Terry before anyone noticed they knew each other, and yet she hadn't done that. It didn't matter that over half a century had passed, that she had been someone else back then. A person was forever bound to their past; it was inescapable. The person you were remained inside you.

And so she had entered his dark world, googling some of the things he had written in an attempt to understand. A quick search for *Terry Anderson* + *Florida* + a few key words threw up hundreds of hits. All Kicki could do then was pour herself another whisky, forgetting to add a few drops of water this time.

The conspiracy theories he shared stemmed from someone called Lyndon LaRouche, a political idiot who had founded a movement in the late sixties. The Swedish branch went by the name of the European Workers' Party.

She remembered them well. A combination of inverted class warfare and right-wing extremism, famous for their awful caricatures of Olof Palme. The party had only ever received a handful of votes in the parliamentary elections, but they had also featured in the investigation into Palme's murder. One of the early suspects, the so-called thirty-three-year-old, was found to have some of their materials at home. He was quickly released, but it was broadly agreed that their unreasonable hatred of the prime minister had played a part in what had happened.

Kicki's head had been spinning as she read on. How did this fit with Terry's left-wing beliefs from the sixties, with the twenty-year-old she thought she had known?

She had gone down a rabbit hole of Lyndon LaRouche interviews on YouTube that evening, many of which made her think of horror films. He claimed that everyone had been tortured by their mothers, that his devotees would be trained in martial arts and that a new human species would be created. She had also found a number of articles on the foundation of the European Workers' Party in Sweden. That was where Terry Anderson's name cropped up, along with a number of other deserters. He seemed to have returned to Stockholm after his time in Kramfors, joining the American Deserters Committee, which later splintered. The deserters had begun to get themselves a bad reputation. A few too many had been arrested for drugs offences, while others – Terry among them – wanted to see more political action and travelled down to Germany to infiltrate the American military bases there. At a political café in Frankfurt, they met LaRouche and found themselves a new sense of purpose.

How was that possible? Kicki had spent a long time sitting with her eyes shut that evening. She had even played music from those days in order to get a clear view of him. Had Terry really been so lost that he was willing to go along with anyone and anything just to find something to believe in?

Had all of this been in him back then? Something she hadn't seen or understood?

Two people's paths had crossed that summer. One ended up where Terry ended up and the other had become a politician in Kramfors. Kicki herself hadn't stayed on the far left for all that long; there were too many weighty theories and letters from the leadership in Stockholm. *You're lazy. Call a meeting and go through your shortcomings.* The Social Democrats were also the only party with any real power in Kramfors, and she didn't see the point in wasting her time.

It had been years since she was in the political fray. These days she spent most of the time with her plants, their scents bringing back memories from childhood. Her garden was well on its way to becoming the most beautiful in the area, with rockeries and English roses that weren't the easiest to grow this far north.

She had sent a reply to Terry when he wrote back to her. *So great to hear from you. Of course I remember.* But since then, things had been quiet between them. Kicki had muted him on Facebook and managed to forget about the whole thing – until the police officer knocked on her door.

She closed her eyes and felt everything start to spin, unsure whether that was because of the whisky or the world, time dragging everything out of joint.

There was a frantic tapping sound somewhere overhead. Probably a black woodpecker, she thought, on the wall beneath the eaves. Eira knew she wouldn't be able to get back to sleep, so she reached for her phone to google how to get rid of woodpeckers before they do any damage. As she did so, she was overcome by a sudden weariness.

Taking care of a house.

There was so much that could go wrong.

The facade would need a fresh coat of paint next year at the very latest, a couple of the windows too – at least on the south-facing side, where they got most sun. One of the planks was rotten on the veranda, and what about the chimney? When was the last time they'd had it swept? All these thoughts raced through her head as she reached for her phone, but then she saw that she had two messages and forgot all about them.

She clearly wasn't the only one struggling to sleep.

Kicki Frånlund.

Silje Andersson.

She opened Silje's message first.

'They've found him.'

The baby stirred, and a fist – or maybe it was a heel – made her stomach bulge. She pressed gently on her belly as she read.

The American police had acted quickly once they had the dead man's name. Silje evidently didn't switch off when she left the station, because their reply had arrived just before midnight. John Lorenzo Aiello, born 1948 in Long Beach, California.

There was a photograph of him attached to the email, from his army days. John's hair had been cropped short when he was conscripted, in May 1966, and the truth was that his face was more like the CGI image than the real one, the wilder one, from her mother's photo album.

That blank expression.

Just one year later, in September 1967, he had been reported missing from the U.S. military base at Kaiserslauten in West Germany.

His parents were both dead, but he had three brothers and two sisters. A couple of local officers would be visiting them to break the news in the morning.

Eira opened the second message.

'There's one more thing I didn't mention yesterday,' wrote Kicki Frånlund. 'Terry Anderson is alive and living in Florida. I don't want anything to do with him – I think you'll see why. I'd appreciate it if you wouldn't share this information.'

She had attached a number of screenshots from the man's Facebook page, and Eira immediately understood why the former politician wanted to distance herself from him. On the basis of what she read, Terry Anderson could easily have been one of those who stormed the Capitol after Donald Trump's election defeat. She kept scrolling through the posts, pausing when she reached the last screengrab, a thread of messages.

Kicki Frånlund had written to her ex-boyfriend late the night before. She hadn't mentioned anything about the Swedish police, which was probably wise. Considering the circles Terry Anderson seemed to move in, he likely wouldn't have responded if she had.

'You don't know what happened to Steve Carrano, do you?' she asked after a few general questions about how he was.

'No, sorry, haven't been in touch with him since the early seventies.'

Eira read that line again. So, Steve had been alive after 1968.

'What about the other guy? John, was it?'

'Sorry, no idea.'

There was a brief pause after that. Eira could see from the timestamps that his next message had taken a minute or so to arrive.

'I think he stayed up there,' the American wrote. 'Or it's possible the CIA lured him back. That happened to a few of us. From what I heard they ended up in prison in Morocco or at their former bases. Idiots didn't realize it was a trap.'

Their messages got longer and more rambling. Terry wrote that the three Americans hadn't had much in common other than their opposition to the war. John was a recluse and Steve was a bit of a basket case, always so uptight. *The guy did a load of drugs*, he said. *And all that sex and leftist crap too, you remember?*

'I do.' Kicki Frånlund had sent a few laughing emojis then. She knew what she was doing. 'So do you know if Steve is one of the guys who went back to the U.S.?'

'Like I said, I haven't heard from him since the seventies, but I think he went back up to Norrland, some collective there. They were super popular in those days. What was it called . . . Skog-something. That's one bit of Swedish I do remember. Man, you guys have so much forest up there. Skog everywhere . . .'

'Could it have been Skogsnäs?' asked Kicki.

'Yeah, think so.'

And with that, their conversation was over. At least in the screenshots Eira had been given.

The Norrland air. So crisp and fresh, full of oxygen. It smelled like pine and damp earth and the murky water where the algae formed a layer of green sludge.

Lina splashed her face, beneath her arms, between her legs. It was cold as hell and made her fingertips go numb, but as she had once told a man who wanted to warm her up: I was born frozen.

She crouched down to pee. The risk of being spotted out here was fairly low; the ratio of people to trees in Norrland was something like one to a hundred thousand. She used her foot to dig a hole for her tampon and toilet paper, her dirty knickers, then kicked dirt and twigs over the top.

Her new knickers were black, lacy at the back, stolen while the assistant went off to look for another size. She caught a whiff of sweat as she pulled her top back on and realised she would have to find somewhere she could stay a while.

Warm water.

Washing that actually dried.

Cash.

Life had been easy enough while she was living off men with Visa cards, but ever since Täby she had been drifting around without a plan. Northwards, that was her only thought, because of the forests and the solitude. Pitstops among the hopeless people living on the fringes, in tents, and caravans with broken wheels, tiny cabins or boats that were barely afloat, stuck in the ice. But that always came to an end whenever some jogger or dog owner called the authorities to report it; they didn't want to see the suffering first-hand.

She had only just made it out of the last place in time. Stood and watched as the police car pulled up between the trees. Hunting for people to haul in and lock up, checking ID and all that crap. Lina Stavred hadn't had any ID since she burnt it at a rest stop over twenty-five years ago.

No, she avoided society as far as she could. Whenever she needed to steal food or tampons, she preferred to stick to the medium-sized towns. They were less risky. People there didn't care as much; they didn't know everyone else.

There were also libraries with computers that anyone could use.

Free toilets and internet access.

She had spent two hours in the last one she had passed, made it a rule never to stay any longer than that. There were always old ladies who got curious in places like that. Who started asking questions, remembered her picture. Lina recognised the type from her childhood, at the library in Kramfors. Damn, hadn't Magnus's mum worked there? What was her name? The one who always used to pass her books with a smile and a whisper, as though Lina was carrying humanity's future inside her and only a librarian could coax it out. Virginia Woolf and Cora Sandel and Simone de Beauvoir. They all wrote about women who wanted to break free, who were meant for something bigger.

She'd probably been in the first year of senior high school when she started to see the pattern. The librarian wanted to mould Lina into the person she wished she could have been.

Kerstin, that was her name.

Old paper, weariness. All libraries smelled the same. The letters might as well have been carved into stone tablets in Mesopotamia. As stationary and unchanging as Kramfors itself – not to mention the hamlet where Lina had been forced to live, even after she started high school in town. And all because the Stavreds wanted to keep an eye on their daughter.

Sobriety. No boys or sex. A mouth that should keep quiet and which shouldn't do any of the other things it was made for. God forbid.

No one could climb out of a window as quietly as Lina, sneaking off to the crossroads where the boys were waiting, first on mopeds and later on motorbikes. And together they had done all the things her parents wanted to shield her from.

'I'm just a bit tired today,' she would say when her mother woke her up in the morning, not long after Lina had climbed back in. 'I think I'm getting a headache.'

She entered her own name in the search bar.

It had been a few weeks since she last found a computer to use, possibly even a month. Only idiots carried a phone around when the police might be looking for them.

She scrolled past one hit after another, headlines screaming her name. The photograph of the schoolgirl from years ago smiling out at her.

Lina rolled back in her chair and looked around. No one

was watching her. She made the window smaller and leaned in to the screen, preventing anyone who sneaked up behind her from seeing what she saw.

BODY FOUND IN LUNDE – IS IT MISSING LINA?

Didn't they get bored of this?

They had found some poor fucker on the bottom of the river and immediately assumed it must be her. Dredged that old story back up.

The one about Lina Stavred, who disappeared one night in July 1996, likely murdered. About the boy who was thought to be guilty, the body that was never found. A wound that wasn't allowed to heal, a darkness that lived on. People she didn't recognise saying they would never forget. But there was nothing about what happened in Täby, nothing about the fact that Lina was actually still alive.

Her mind started racing. She couldn't allow herself to be lulled into a false sense of security.

She had made mistakes at the villa in Täby, of course she had. Left evidence. The neighbours had seen her, said hello though she rarely replied. Lina had been living with that bastard for almost three months, calling herself Alberte, until one day he went too far. He thought he could control where she went and what she did, and all because he was the one paying the bills. Assumed that she would do what-ever he wanted. The police surely had her fingerprints and DNA. They might even be able to tell that she had been holding the knife, though she had tossed it into a lake as quickly as she could. Worst-case scenario, they were sitting on a match for her teenage fingerprints.

Who knows, they might even have planted this story to

lure her in. To make her think she was safe, only to pounce at the first traffic stop. Her eyes came to rest on a name in the text: Eira Sjödin, from the Violent Crimes unit.

That was when the penny dropped. Christ, Eira Sjödin, wasn't that Magnus's kid sister? The little brat had joined the damn police. Lina couldn't help but laugh at the thought that she had fucked the cop's brother. But then she remembered a woman called Sjödin who had been snooping around in Stockholm a few years earlier. She had left her card, but Lina had thought it said *Eva* Sjödin, crumpled it and thrown it away. There had to be millions of people with that surname, but she recognised the adult Eira in the photograph and stopped laughing. What did she know? What did she want?

Lina deleted her search history and went through to the toilets.

It wasn't often that she got to study herself in the mirror. Her hair was getting long. She had spent years dying it, trying to counteract any resemblance to the missing teenager, but she had decided to let her natural blonde grow back in.

Right now, it was more risky to look like the woman from Täby.

Maybe she was overplaying the risk. The police had more important cases to deal with. The politicians were always going on about fighting crime, but she wasn't who they meant. She wasn't the one they were chasing right now.

Another thought came to her as she left the toilets, and Lina sat down at another of the computers and searched her parents' names. For years, she had wiped out all memory of them.

A few old film clips came up, all from 1996, pleading with the public to help them find their daughter. The memorial. Their grief, the flowers. The lame school photo. No coffin. Classmates she had always hated in floods of tears. A town saying goodbye.

Just one year later, Lina Stavred had been declared dead.

They gave up so easily, she thought. Shouldn't they have been able to feel that I was still alive? It must've been nice for them. Personally, she felt nothing. Without photographs, faces disappear. People are nothing but atoms.

She didn't manage to find either of her parents, no current address. Lina searched for Geresta instead, the name of the hamlet where she grew up. What was the number of their house, the mailbox? She clicked on the map to bring up a satellite image, remembered the rolling meadows and the forest surrounding them, the mountain cows that used to graze there. Zoomed in as far as she could on the box in the middle of all the greenery, the house where they once lived. She remembered her room beneath the eaves, her grandmother's net curtains she almost managed to set alight while she was smoking. The roof looked dilapidated. The facade was now grey rather than red, and there was no car parked outside, but she thought the curtains looked the same as ever.

What was she supposed to do? Laugh? Her mother and father had gone up in smoke. They could have emigrated, they could have died, but the house was still there. It hadn't been deleted from the records, declared dead.

The damn thing was still standing where it always had.

Just north of Sollefteå, Eira turned off the main road and followed the Fax River deeper into the countryside. It was a landscape dominated by steep, sandy riverbanks, making the water less accessible. The mountains grew lower as she moved inland, the communities smaller and more scattered. Freeze-thaw damage had left the road a patchwork of repairs. Up ahead, a bus pulled in and an elderly lady emerged, waving to the driver before trudging off along a gravel track towards a lonely house.

The bus set off again, now empty.

Eira made a brief pitstop in Ramsele to use the toilet. The bus station was open there, and even had a small café. The last dozen or so miles took her straight through the forest. It was common knowledge that the residents of Skogsnäs had been forced to lay their own road; there hadn't been one when they first arrived in the area in the seventies.

Flashes of the Fjällsjö River glittered between the trees.

Eira had heard stories about when the first long-haired 'green wavers' turned up in Ramsele in the early 1970s. Some of the locals had been afraid. This was the era when the Baader-Meinhof Group were wreaking havoc, not to mention all the drugs – and the new arrivals certainly looked suspicious. Those fears had died down over the years, but whenever the residents of Skogsnäs were mentioned, it was often with a laugh or a shake of the head. Eira had never been there before, never had reason to be called out. She reached the small community and the landscape opened out onto fields and meadows, cows and goats grazing.

As she approached the end of the road, Eira recognised the description and pulled up.

She hadn't expected the houses to be so far apart, had assumed that the members of a collective would want to stay close.

The woman who answered the door smiled at Eira's reaction.

'The last thing we wanted was to be on top of one another,' she said with a slight English accent. 'We'd done that for several years, but we were sick of it. That's why we bought 300 hectares of forest, so we could build the houses with plenty of space between them.'

Her name was Sarah. She was pushing seventy, the daughter of a bookseller on Charing Cross Road in London, and one of those who had been around since the very beginning.

'So, how can I help you?'

There may have been a slight note of suspicion in her voice when Eira held up her ID, but no worse than usual. Eira hadn't called ahead, unsure how welcome she would be. The stereotypes had been circling through her since she was a girl, and she had imagined people in flowery skirts dancing in the fields, that sort of thing. Not something that looked like an old mountain homestead, built the traditional way using logs, but with the addition of a panoramic window here, a tower or unexpected angle there. The hallway behind the woman was painted in bright colours, pieces of broken china decorating the seams in the stone floor.

'I wanted to ask you about an American deserter,' said Eira. 'Steve Carrano. I was told he lived here at some point in the seventies.'

'Gosh,' the woman said in English, before quickly switching back to Swedish. 'Yes, we did actually have a couple of deserters here.' She stepped back to welcome Eira in. 'But I have no idea where they are now. The American authorities aren't looking for them, are they? I would have thought they'd have given up by now.'

She had a lamb stew bubbling away in the kitchen, where the walls were covered in decorative plates, testament to a life spent travelling the world.

Eira told Sarah about the dead man and the other desert-ers, choosing to be open about her mother's part in the story. There was no reason for her to be overly reserved and professional, especially not when a bowl of hot stew was set down on the table in front of her and there was moss and grass growing on the roof outside. The strict, laced-up world was miles away.

'I remember a Steve,' said Sarah, bringing over a glass and a carafe of water. 'He arrived with a Swedish girl, right in the early days. We bought the place in 1973, so it must have been the year after. Once word had spread about what we were doing here, people just started showing up. What did you say his surname was?'

'Carrano.'

'No, it was something much more common . . .'

She's wrong, thought Eira. The woman was getting older, and though her gaze was sharp she had been living out here for almost half a century. Skogsnäs was one of only a handful of seventies collectives that had survived this long, and countless people must have passed through over the years.

'They had to sleep in a construction trailer,' she continued. 'There was only one farmhouse back then, but we managed to buy a few unused trailers from a building firm. We'd just had our first child and didn't want to be so close to the others, and then they turned up. I remember he used to scream at night, he could still hear the helicopters . . . Larsson! That was it, Steve Larsson. His wife's name was Eva.'

'So they were married?'

'Newlyweds, as I recall. I suppose that was why they ended up out in the trailer. I wonder now whether it wasn't a honeymoon; they might have been driving their beat-up old car through Norrland's inland. Those were different times, you know. I think they had half a plan to stay with us here, but he changed his mind. Lots of people were disappointed when they finally got here. Being part of the community meant coming out into the forest and working with us – we'd had to sell some land for logging, even though it was the last thing we wanted to do. You quickly learn the realities of life living out here like this. No running water, a single television for watching the news or kids' TV, nothing to smoke. People thought we got high all the time, but we had no money for that, and you couldn't even buy anything to smoke in Ramsele.'

The lamb melted in Eira's mouth, Indian spices.

'Could Larsson have been her name?' asked Eira. 'Could he have taken her name when they got married?'

'Oh, of course. That was it!'

Steve Larsson. Was it really that simple? Eira thought about hiding places. If not in the forest, then in a new name. About as Swedish as you could possibly get.

'Do you remember where he was from?'

'Well, he was definitely working class, I know that much. He wasn't afraid of getting stuck in, and nor were we. I grew up in post-war England, we were used to rationing, and my husband is from a farming family. If you ask me, the reason most of the other collectives failed is because they were full of upper-class hippies who didn't realise just how much hard work it would be. There was a local man who taught us everything he knew, traditions that would have died out with him otherwise, because his children weren't interested. We used to take the timber down to the river by horse – there was still log driving in the area back then. I'm wondering if he wasn't from Philadelphia . . . I remember we talked about Billie Holiday. She was born there, wasn't she?'

A quick search, Eira skim-read the Wikipedia page. No, the legendary jazz singer had grown up in Baltimore. But wait – her mother had got pregnant as a teenager, and the family had sent her away to give birth, to Philadelphia.

'Let me see if I don't have a photograph somewhere. I've been trying to sort through everything.'

Eira followed her through the library, the shelves packed with inherited books from Charing Cross Road, into a sewing room with enormous windows that blurred the boundaries between inside and out.

'We got lucky,' Sarah explained. 'Bought them cheap from the owners of a house that was being torn down.'

As she rummaged through her boxes and folders, Eira took out her computer and searched an online database. There was one Steve Larsson registered in Gothenburg, and he would be seventy-five that September. She felt the baby start to twist and turn inside her.

She checked the other registers, too. Ones that weren't available to the general public. Steve Larsson was born in Philadelphia in 1947, a Swedish citizen since 1974. He had no children and was no longer married, but he ran a record store on Andra Långgatan in Gothenburg, Vinyl Records.

'I knew it!'

Sarah had spread photographs across the floor, many of them of young people with long hair and bare chests, and she was waving one of them in the air.

Written on the back: *Steve and Eva, July 1974.*

He looked just like the others, with his hair parted in the middle, spilling over his shoulders. Slim, with loose cotton trousers and an open shirt, squinting in the sun. The girl beside him had dark hair, and they were busy doing something, their hands in a bucket. Scrubbing potatoes?

'Is it OK if I take a picture of this?'

'Be my guest.'

Eira told Sarah she had found an address, that the couple had since divorced and that Steve Larsson now lived in Gothenburg.

'Oh, of course! We had a few people move up here in the eighties, punks who had occupied and saved a section of the old Haga district there. They couldn't afford to stay when the buildings were renovated, and so we told them to come up here. I remember now that they said hello from the deserter who had lived here once.'

Eira saw the punks' houses as she drove away, but she didn't bother stopping. *They built their houses much closer together – you'll see them when you leave. Their very own little neighbourhood, just like being back in Haga. That's probably what saved us, allowing people to do their own thing.*

She turned up the radio, loud music as she pulled out onto the main road.

She had found him. He was alive.

Selling records in Gothenburg.

S ilje asked her to close the door and then gestured to the low armchairs in the corner of the room. Eira had to brace herself on the armrests in order to sit down.

It was becoming a struggle just to tie her laces. She had to stuff pillows between her legs and beneath her belly in order to get comfortable in bed; not that it really worked, which meant she was also more tired than usual. There was probably some key nutrient she wasn't getting enough of – iron or protein or one of the other many things she should be thinking about – but for some reason none of that seemed to stick in her head. Unlike everything to do with the deserters from the Vietnam war. She still found herself reading about them whenever she realised there was no point trying to get back to sleep.

In 1974, President Gerald Ford had announced a partial amnesty for deserters. Not because they were forgiven, but because 'reconciliation calls for an act of mercy to bind the nation's wounds and to heal the scars of divisiveness'. Those who took the deal had to spend two years in alternative service to the nation, and they were then able to leave the army with a dishonourable discharge. A few years later, President Carter went one step further, granting a pardon to those who had evaded the draft, though this didn't fully apply to deserters.

'Terry didn't know whether John stayed in Sweden or went back to the U.S.,' said Eira. 'He must've taken up some sort of offer himself, but many others refused. They were convinced they had done the right thing by refusing to fight and wanted full amnesty without any caveats. Some of them remained in Sweden. Steve Carrano, for example.'

'Have you found him?' asked Silje.

'He left Kramfors at roughly the same time John Aiello vanished, and he ended up marrying a Swedish woman and taking her surname. He's called Larsson now, and he runs a record store in Gothenburg.'

Eira had called the shop, but in the brief pause before he picked up she had changed her mind. A man who had once thrown away his ID papers and fled across the Sea of Japan could easily do something similar again.

'Hi, I was wondering whether you had any copies of a record I'm looking for,' she had said when he eventually picked up. Old records, she thought, old heroes. Vinyl had fallen out of fashion around the time she was born, but it had enjoyed something of a renaissance lately. 'That one by the Beatles, what's it called . . . where they're crossing the street on the cover.'

'*Abbey Road*. Sorry, no chance.' He had a strong accent when he spoke Swedish, leaving no doubt at all as to which continent he was from. 'They always fly out whenever I manage to get one in. Assuming you mean the original press from 1969, that is.'

Silje had got up and moved over to her computer.

'I got an email from the police in Long Beach last night,'

she said. 'They've spoken to one of John Aiello's brothers. I'll forward it to you.'

'What about Gothenburg?'

'What about it?'

'I think I should go down there,' said Eira. 'Talk to him face to face. We don't know whether he was involved, whether he might try to run again.'

'You're right,' said Silje. 'I can call Gothenburg and ask them to send someone out. It would be great if you could summarise everything we know, prepare a few questions for them.'

'Wouldn't it be easier if I just went down there myself? I already know the case, and I can work on the train if there's anything else that needs doing.'

Silje's eyes drifted down to her bump, so big and impossible to ignore. Eira's face had also become more rounded lately, her breasts now a pair of alien organisms.

'You must be getting close, no?'

'I feel fine,' said Eira, forcing herself to keep calm. 'It's a normal, uncomplicated pregnancy. My grandmother drove a horse and sled and chopped wood until the very last minute.'

Silje smiled.

'OK,' she said, though she quickly grew serious again. A blink, a momentary wavering of her gaze that told Eira there was something else going on.

'So can I book the tickets?' she asked.

Silje didn't reply, brushing something invisible from the surface of her desk.

'When I took this job,' she said after a moment, 'they

made me go through the equality guidelines and the budget and the systematic work environment management stuff, but the bastards didn't say a word about how it would make me feel. Last autumn, when GG was . . . well, you know.'

It was as though she didn't want to come out and say it. Eira was struck by the fact that GG wasn't the only one who had been affected, that they had all been a part of it. Silje was the first person to have noticed that something wasn't quite right, when he stopped answering his phone.

'At least then it wasn't me who sent him out there,' she continued. 'It wasn't me who used my position to say: go there, do this.'

'I'm not planning to get hurt,' said Eira.

Silje pulled a face, possibly to conceal how she felt, and then turned back to her computer.

'Keep the costs down,' she said. 'And book a cheap hotel.'

Allan had worked until every muscle in his body ached that summer. Taking extra shifts at the dock, the minute the flag went up. He was going to be a father, after all.

In the evenings, once the working day was over and Lunde was quiet again, once the noise died down and other sounds took over, he had gone hard on the bottle. It wasn't just the loneliness that was eating away at him, his longing for Maarit now that he had felt her warmth, going deeper than he ever had before, falling asleep beside her. It was like a roar inside him, that longing. No, it was the betrayal, too.

The traitors' sly glances. Allan felt them on his back wherever he went, like mosquito bites, gnats. There was never anyone there when he turned around – or rather, only people he knew. Workmates, neighbours, the usual faces.

The more he thought about it, ranting and raving with his buddies as they sat under the bridge with their aquavit on the brightest of nights, on steel beams that shook as the cars drove overhead, watching the tugs float by with their long loads of timber, the more convinced he became that whoever had spread the word about him and his political beliefs had to be someone close to him.

Allan didn't have an official role within the party; he'd quit when they started fawning over the Social Democrats and the market, communists in name only, so what was this list where they'd found his name?

Who had even known he was going up to Luleå, other than the people around him?

He'd kept his fists busy too, that summer. Almost like he had in his youth, when he entered the ring as a light-weight for a few seasons. A real talent, that was what his coach had said, a man from Bollstabruk who got himself a proper speaking part in the film about the shootings in Ådalen that year.

Everyone had been involved in one way or another. Allan himself found work moving gravel. It paid well. Tonnes of the stuff had to be picked up and moved over to Gålån on the other side of the river, tipped out onto the tarmac to make it look like the old road between Frånö and Lunde where the real march had once taken place. Too much of Lunde had been torn down and changed since the thirties; it didn't look right on film.

And then, once it was all over, they had to clear the gravel away again, which meant more work.

Allan had also been an extra, in both the procession and the events the day before, when the workers stormed through the gates by the dock where the strike-breakers were hiding on a boat.

Once the film crew left, the tensions they had stirred up remained. The rage that had been forced beneath the surface when it was suffocated by unfair judgements, false words masking what really happened in 1931. Riots, according to the right. A tragedy, according to the Social Democrats. And the most spineless members of his own party had also bowed down and stopped calling the shootings in Ådalen what they really were: murder.

The whole thing seemed to mirror his own situation, because wasn't it just the same old persecution of communists – only more in secret now?

It was discussions along those lines that had led to most of the brawls he was involved in. Out drunk one evening, after a meeting at the People's House, he had lashed out at a union rep and his Social Democratic friends, accusing them of spreading their bile across the country.

Hadn't they gone after the communists the minute the smoke cleared after the shooting in Ådalen? Jumping into bed with the conservatives and the liberals, betraying and deceiving in the name of power – or consensus, as they called it in the non-socialist press?

Someone had wrestled him to the ground, told him that they'd let him off this once, but next time they would call the police.

Someone else had dragged him home to his mother, where Allan had been given a dressing-down and something cold to put on his eye. Didn't he realise he was a grown man now, about to become a father? Was this really how he wanted to carry on? God forbid. Becoming just like his own father, who had spent Allan's childhood staggering around town, eventually collapsing to the ground one bitterly cold night. He wasn't found until the postman did his rounds the next morning.

Yes, damn it, Allan wanted to snarl. *I'm going to keep going until I get my hands on the bastard who's been spreading this shit, forcing me to be stuck here like a bloody fool, a pathetic sod who can't even support his own child.*

A grown man wasn't supposed to live in his parents' home. That didn't help his rage a bit.

When the film premiered at the Bio Royal in Kramfors in May the next year, he had spotted himself in the crowd on screen. Maarit had come down to visit, and she was sitting beside Allan when he saw his own face on the screen, twisted, warped and roaring with hatred.

'You were so convincing,' she told him afterwards.

He would never tell her about the fear he had felt during the film, so bad that he had to grip the armrest of his seat and couldn't remember what happened next. Because the face she had caught a brief glimpse of was his true self.

T he sun was warm as Eira left the tram and cut across Järntorget towards Andra Långgatan. She had been seconded to Gothenburg a few times when she first joined the force, and she knew that the corner outside the 7-Eleven was one of the main hubs for the drug trade in the city. Her police officer's eye took in the cheap bars and nail salons with Vietnamese staff, a black doorway that no doubt led to a strip club. She had already passed two record stores by the time she reached the right one, at the end of the street, where the older buildings gave way to drab grey concrete boxes from the sixties, and her swollen breasts were sweaty after the short walk.

In the shop window, a couple of fibreboard sheets had been covered in record sleeves. The faulty strip light on the ceiling flickered as she opened the door.

Eira could hear guitars, a melancholy male voice. The air smelled like dust and something chemical, distant: vinyl and times gone by. She saw David Bowie's painted face, Tom Waits smoking a cigarette in a bar.

A new track started, and she noticed a movement towards the rear of the shop.

The man was tall, well over six foot, and it was as though he unfurled as he emerged through the low doorway. He definitely looked like he was in his seventies, with long grey hair tied back in a ponytail, sideburns but no beard. The semi-functional lighting gave everything a pale, dreary glow.

'Hello, are you looking for anything in particular?' Eira recognised his American accent from their phone call, as though he was swallowing the ends of his words.

There were so many ways she could open, and Eira had considered them all on the train south. All the things she wanted to ask, things that no police officer in Gothenburg would understand. She didn't doubt that they would be able to get Steve Larsson to talk, but no amount of contractions, heartburn or unwieldiness could have stopped her from taking the night train to see him herself.

The opportunity to stand face to face with this man, to see his reaction as she got straight to the point.

'I think you knew my mum,' she said.

'Really? Who is she?'

Eira said her own name and Kerstin's, mentioned the time and place, watching as his face creased in confusion and thought.

'Kerstin?' he said, forgetting himself for a moment and slipping into English: 'Are you kidding me?'

Wide eyes, a brief laugh, a slight shock as he did the maths. Eira read it all on his face, his skin furrowed yet transparent somehow.

'How old are you?' he asked. 'You're not . . .'

'No, no.' Eira laughed at his reaction. 'I'm thirty-five, so you don't need to worry.'

Steve Larsson laughed too, leaning back against one of the shelves behind him. The shop was cramped; not much room for manoeuvre between the shelves and the racks, crates on the floor.

'Sorry, I didn't really think you were that old. It would've made you, what . . . over fifty, huh? God. How is your mum?'

'Good,' said Eira, taking out her ID. 'But that's not actually why I'm here. I'm investigating the murder of an old friend of yours, John Aiello.'

'John? John Aiello?'

The record had ended, the music replaced by a low crackle over the speakers.

A few seconds of silence.

'When? How? Did you say murdered?'

He was so taken aback that he had switched to a mix of Swedish and English, and Eira could see his mind racing between the past and the present. The confusion. Regardless of whether or not he knew anything, her sudden appearance was clearly unsettling.

She took out her phone.

'I hope you don't mind me recording our chat? It's for your own benefit, too – legally speaking.'

'What happened to John?' He peered over the top of her head, at the row of rock stars on the wall, all frozen in time. 'I haven't seen him in . . . God, how long has it been? Over fifty years. I haven't given him a single thought since . . .'

His fingers brushed the stacks of records beside him.

K erstin.

He remembered her now. Her warmth under the blankets, her messy hair and soft fragrance, the feeling of wanting to stay. To cling on.

Steve couldn't picture her face, but there was something painful in there, and he tried to avoid anything that hurt. He'd become a master at getting hold of medication for that sort of thing, knew *exactly* what to tell the doctors. Trouble sleeping, various aches. Smoking a joint sometimes helped, but the woman in front of him was a police officer.

The shaking in his hands had gotten worse over the past year. Time didn't exist; it was a jester laughing in his face.

Did you really think we'd let you get away, Stevie boy? You dumb, dumb knucklehead, marching down the avenue. You're a pig, Carrano . . .

Knucklehead, dumbass, pig.

He had left that all behind, or so he thought. Vietnam, the politics, the sense of being followed that made him lock his door. He turned the *Back Soon* sign and showed Eira Sjödin through to the little kitchen behind the shop.

'Sorry, it's a bit cramped. I only have instant coffee.'

'That's fine.'

'The owner of the building wants to kick me out so they

can rent the place to a coffee-shop chain and double the rent, but they won't get rid of me that easily.'

He suddenly saw the place through her eyes. The burn marks on the waxcloth, the smell of old smoke. The crack in the mug he handed her.

Vinyl had surged in popularity lately. Young people had started buying record players, and they loved the sleeves, had rediscovered listening to music the way it was meant to be heard. They were happy to pay hundreds of kronor for Thin Lizzy and Dire Straits, several thousand for important first-press LPs. Steve enjoyed talking to them, putting on a track they hadn't heard before or introducing them to a classic guitar solo. Young guys with their entire lives ahead of them, the thrill when they found something they didn't realise they'd been looking for.

It was the year the Stones released 'Sympathy for the Devil', that was what came to him now.

1968.

The music brought back memories, one after another. A barn that still stank of livestock even though it had been empty for so long it was practically falling down. There were areas where the rain got in, and he remembered the sound of it dripping onto wood, into a metal bucket. People had brought them mattresses, firm things stuffed with black horsehair that poked out through the rough fabric and made them itch. Moonlight seeping in through cracks in the walls.

'This is my mum,' said Eira Sjödin, handing him her phone, a photograph. 'It was taken in June 1968. Was it you behind the camera?'

Three young people sitting on a blanket on the grass. Steve quickly put it down on the rickety table.

The police officer was heavily pregnant, and perhaps that was why he struggled to see her as the cop she claimed to be.

The daughter, too, of the young woman in the picture. He wanted to take her hand, stroke her belly, comfort her over something he couldn't even name. And yet . . . that image. Steve had to take another look. There was Terry, who obsessed over every chick he met, and there was John. Between them, the beautiful Kerstin. Laughing as she gazed up at the sun, at him. He remembered it now, that moment. Maybe it really was him who'd taken the picture.

'We found his body just over a month ago,' Eira Sjödin continued. 'But it took us a while to identify him. I'd be grateful for any information you might have about that summer.'

John.

The ambiguity on his face, his eyes meeting Steve's through the camera lens all those years ago.

Eira Sjödin was talking about water, saying that was where they'd found him. Was it the sea there or was it a river? They were one and the same, he remembered that now; the dizzying depths his workmates at the dock had talked about, the powerful currents. Steve had grown up in Philadelphia, between two rivers to the south of the city, but he had never learnt to swim. They had lived in a tiny apartment on the ground floor of what was basically a slum, eventually moving to the suburbs once his old man managed to work his way up to a job as foreman at the factory. His father, who was no longer welcome at the veterans' club as a result of his son's insanity, or was it cowardice? Same same. Their nice new neighbours had stopped inviting his mom over too, and the other wives had looked away whenever they saw her. Steve had tried to reach out to his parents a few times, to explain that Vietnam wasn't a real war, that they had been duped. *Your father doesn't want to talk to you. It's probably best you don't call again.*

Every once in a while, when Steve was alone in the shop, he would put on something by Bill Haley or Dizzy Gillespie, records from the discount crates, and then he would close his eyes and remember the din of the factories and the loud streets of South Philly – not to mention the time he got his hands on a rare single by Soul Survivors. They had climbed the charts the year he left the country.

'What did you say, Steve?'

Had he said something? About John?

'Sorry. Sorry, I just can't get my head around you finding him after all these years.'

Steve sat on his shaking hands. Every nerve in his body seemed to end there.

'How well did you know John Aiello?' she asked.

She sounded like a cop now, no doubt about it. If there was one thing he had learnt during his time on earth, it was that people had two sides to them. Smiling on the outside while they plotted away in secret, prepared to betray those closest to them at the drop of a hat.

'I'm not sure I really knew him at all.'

Eira Sjödin looked down at her notepad, flicked through

a few pages. The woman was clearly thorough. Notes and a recording. Everything he said would be preserved.

Studied, assessed.

'According to what I've been told, you met John in Stockholm in late 1967,' she said. 'The two of you shared a room at a barracks in Tantolunden, then moved to a farm in Torsåker for a few months. Once you left there, you both spent the summer in Kramfors and Lunde. How could you not know him?'

Steve leaned back, which was a mistake because the back of his chair was loose. He closed his eyes and felt the dizziness of the past. The realisation that you could never lower your guard, that there was no such thing as a safe haven.

'Hasn't that ever happened to you? You think you know a person,' he said after a moment or two. 'Someone you trust, who you believe to be your friend, only to find out they're someone entirely different?'

The warm fall of 1967, after he landed in Stockholm and was given a hero's welcome at the airport, was followed by stormy weather that saw snow in October.

Still, Steve was used to the cold. He remembered his mother using rags to plug the gaps around the windows as a boy.

The barracks in Tantolunden weren't exactly paradise, but that was all that was on offer. A roof over their heads, a bunk bed jammed into a narrow room, and a toilet and shower they shared with the men in the block next door. John had taken the top bunk, and he slept peacefully at night, but then again he'd never been to 'Nam. Felt safe, he said. Looking back, that should have been one of the first warning signs, but Steve hadn't understood that at the time. He assumed it was normal for someone who had been stationed in Germany, far from the jungles where the Vietcong hid among the trees, disappearing underground and then popping up again. Burrowing into the base to toss a grenade at you while you were sitting on the can.

John Aiello might have practised driving a bayonet through the gut of a straw man, but he had never actually crept into a village under cover of darkness, the enemy lurking all around – the Vietnamese loved digging damn tunnels. He'd never had a young woman throw herself at him, clutching a baby in her arms, until everything exploded around them and no one got out alive. She hadn't understood when Steve had hissed at her to run, clinging on to him in the belief that he could protect her, but his orders were clear: everyone had to die. The whole place had to be razed. Search and destroy.

He had watched the houses burn and he had run into the forest, where there was nowhere to hide – from either the enemy or his lieutenant, who kept screaming at him to kill. When Steve was finally granted leave, it had been obvious to him that he couldn't go back. He got drunk in a bar in Tokyo and started telling people he wanted to get out. Someone knew someone who knew how, and so he found himself setting sail one night, throwing up over the railing, making the leap into nothingness, onto a Soviet boat with the lights turned out. Things had been crazy in Moscow, so much vodka and so many women wanting to do things with them. He remembered running around a huge building with several other deserters, playing hide and seek among the statues of Lenin. And then they arrived in Sweden, where they were welcomed as heroes, but Steve wasn't a hero. He had thrown a burning torch into that village and left it in flames behind him, and then he had left his buddies in Hell. He was an embarrassment to his family and his country. In another time, another war, that would have been punishable by death.

At night in Tantolunden, where most of the others were construction workers from Norrland who spent their downtime drinking and singing and shouting, the worst of it came back to him. Moments when there were no enemies out there, just himself, alone in a bed that was too short for him, the voice in his head screaming for him to kill, John refusing to let him open the window when he broke out in a sweat.

Go back to sleep, for chrissakes. This is Sweden, man. No one's gonna get you.

The two faces of a person.

It was during their time in Stockholm that they had first realised the CIA was watching them – not that it came as much of a surprise. Did they really expect the most powerful organisation on earth just to stand by as soldiers threw off their uniforms and flipped them the bird, refused their phoney war?

Steve was convinced he had heard a click on the line when he used the phone, and others reported the same thing. A kid from Connecticut who was staying with a family in Bromma had seen a car parked on the street outside two nights in a row, men inside it who turned away when he walked past.

And then Ray had vanished. He and John had left the base in Germany together, but then they had fallen out, Steve couldn't remember why. Maybe it was over something political, if one of them was a Maoist and the other a believer in Trotsky's permanent revolution, or maybe one of them wasn't all that interested in politics and just wanted to be able to smoke in peace. Either way, Ray had been talked into going to the American embassy by some guy who made it seem like he'd bumped into him by chance, who swore he'd be allowed to walk free if he just turned himself in and distanced himself from everything he thought and felt.

God bless America.

They had tried to track him down, but Ray had disappeared without a trace. The worst part was that his family in Dayton, Ohio hadn't heard from him either, even though he'd told his buddies he was going out to call them that day.

And then there was the American journalist who came to interview them. She claimed to work for *Rolling Stone*, but the questions she asked just got weirder and weirder. Where exactly were you stationed, what were your duties there, who were your contacts during the weeks you spent in Moscow?

Steve had started looking over his shoulder everywhere he went. There often seemed to be someone watching him, someone who turned away when he spotted them. And so when one of the leaders of the American Deserters Committee mentioned moving to a farm in the north of Sweden, he had jumped at the chance. Away from the sleepless nights in the barracks, away from himself.

Ego-stripping, that was what they called it.

The idea was to liberate a person from their ego. One of the leaders of the ADC was obsessed with all that stuff, as were some of the other activists. You might spend hours being interrogated about why you thought this or that, and all to rid you of any non-socialist ideas.

You need to get out into the country, Steve. Away from the person you were. You need to stop only ever thinking about yourself.

The forest, when it closed in on them. The air, which felt so crisp and clean, the earth frozen solid. The lentil stews made by one of the other members of the collective, some kid who barely knew how to cook. The fear when he had to climb up onto the roof to clear last year's bird nests. What if there was still an egg in one of them? What if the ravens circling overhead decided to swoop down? Steve had seen Hitchcock's *The Birds* at the cinema in Philly, and he had visions of himself being chased by a screeching flock of them, flapping down the chimney, nowhere to hide.

They spent hour after hour chatting on the couches in the evening, because there was no TV there – TV was degenerative, it rotted the mind. They talked about everything they would do come spring. Growing vegetables, cabbage and potatoes, ploughing and renovating the barn, maybe even getting a few cows.

But Steve remembered that spring never seemed to arrive. He remembered the damp that made the roof bow and the paint peel, the fear that it might all come crashing down on them as they slept. The sense that the walls had eyes. There was actually a hole in the bedroom wall, and he was convinced he had seen an eye there a few times. Someone was constantly watching him in that house, ready to point the finger. *Do you support the revolution? Where's your heart, Steve?*

One night, one of those nights where the sky was a patchwork of bright spots and he could almost imagine the Milky Way as a single organism, a bridge rather than a collection of individual stars, he had become convinced that the whole thing was a trap. A way of isolating the United States' enemies somewhere remote in order to later get rid of them. There were thousands of possible ways – he'd been taught plenty of them back in 'Nam.

He had convinced John to escape with him the very next day. Terry overheard their conversation and immediately decided he would tag along; he was bored and wanted to meet some Swedish girls. Or had it been John's idea all along? Had he planted the seed in them? It would be a month or so before Steve started to think along those lines, that their latest move was just another way of getting at him.

He remembered the sun that greeted them in Kramfors, signalling that spring had arrived after all. There were people there, out running errands, all perfectly ordinary in their unzipped coats. Shopping for food or parking their cars, walking with strollers, stopping to push their kids on the swings; exchanging a few words with an acquaintance they'd bumped into.

Steve had enlisted in order to get away from a bleak future in one of Philly's many factories, but he felt a sudden pang of jealousy. This was precisely that kind of life. The time clock might well keep track of a person's hours, but it also signalled when they were free. It was a life where Saturday was really Saturday.

Then he had heard the music in the square. One part of him had wanted to run when he saw the NLF flag, the banner reading *USA OUT OF VIETNAM*, but Terry was already on his way over.

And that was when he saw her.

Fairly tall, wearing a short coat. Was it red? He thought it was red. Her fair hair kept blowing over her face, and the voice over the loudspeaker, it was hers, caressing the cobblestones and concrete. Maybe it was her voice above all else, as clear as a freshly washed window or a glass of water from the tap, with the sing-song Swedish melody, a kind of slow, halting be-bop, Steve thought, and he was determined to get to her before Terry.

'So why did you leave her?' asked Eira Sjödin. 'Why did you disappear from Kramfors?'

'I was scared.'

'Of what?'

'I don't remember how I found out. We knew the CIA had eyes on us, but it wasn't until late that summer that I started to realise it was him. That's how they do it: through someone who gets close to you.'

'Him?'

'John.'

'Are you telling me John Aiello was working for the CIA? That he was an infiltrator?' Eira Sjödin seemed sceptical, and he could understand that. Steve himself had found it hard to believe, but once the veil had been lifted from his eyes all the signs were there.

'We'd travelled together, slept in the same barn. We took turns cycling down to the docks every morning to see if the flag was up. If it was, that meant there was a boat needing to be loaded or unloaded. John made sure we were always together, and that's their MO.'

'Did you ever find any evidence that he worked for the CIA?'

'No, no, he wasn't an employee or anything. It doesn't work like that. They don't want to have to pay a wage or take responsibility if anything goes wrong. They must've made contact with him at some point, or maybe he reached out to them. That's what happens when people have something to offer. They say: I'm in such and such organisation, with this subversive enemy of the state, I can provide information. And then you get paid for whatever you hand over. That's the treacherous part of it. You never know who it is; it's someone who seems just like everyone else.'

'So what happened towards the end of that summer?' asked Eira Sjödin. 'Before you left?'

E ira studied him as he spoke. Steve Larsson had gripped one hand with the other, trying to hold it steady. She had noticed it shaking earlier, that it bothered him.

If John Aiello really had been working for the CIA when he was murdered on Swedish soil then that complicated things in ways she would rather not think about.

Two men had come to get John one evening, Steve explained. From the barn where they were staying in Lunde.

'It was dark, and I remember I was freezing. Fall was coming.'

'Could you be any more specific about when this was?' Eira placed a hand on her belly, either to calm the baby or to protect him or her from what was to come.

'September, maybe? Yeah, I guess that was it; the work had started to peter out. We couldn't stay in the barn, either – it was getting too cold at night.'

Steve had been on his way home, if you could call the barn home. They had borrowed a bicycle from someone, but John must have had it that night, because he'd gone off ahead. As a result, Steve was walking alone, taking the long route along the road rather than cutting through the trees the way they usually did, probably because it was so dark.

When he heard them coming out of the barn, Steve had

hidden among the trees, which meant he didn't see anything. Just heard their voices in the distance.

'And you think they were from the CIA?'

'Like I said, it was dark. I didn't see their faces.'

Eira felt confused, trying to bear in mind that this was during the Cold War, a time when the Soviet Union sent submarines into Swedish territory in the Baltic. It struck her that perhaps those days were coming back, but the CIA? In Lunde? Could she even believe a thing Steve Larsson said? Yes, he remembered her mother. He even remembered her coat – Eira recalled seeing that same red coat in an old photograph – but others had suggested that he had been traumatised by the war. That he was jittery, paranoid.

'What language were they speaking?'

'I've always thought of them as Swedes, but they could have been speaking English. I don't know.'

In order to avoid being spotted, Steve had crept away through the trees as though he was back in the jungle in Đăk Tô, moving without a sound. He didn't dare look back until he heard the voices fading away, their footsteps, swaying branches and a muttered expletive. That was when he thought he had caught a glimpse of John between two men, though it was dark and they were nothing but shapes in the faint moonlight.

'What did you think?'

'Nothing. Your mind goes blank. I just knew something was wrong – you get a feel for that sort of thing when you've been the places I have – so when I heard the shot I ran into the barn, grabbed my things and cleared off.'

'The shot?'

'From the woods, down towards the river. Not too far from the bridge. You learn how to listen, too. To gauge distances and directions.'

'Just one shot?'

'Just the one.'

'So who do you think they were?'

'Men sent to collect someone. That was all I needed to know.'

Steve had left Lunde that night, packing his things and setting off on foot. He had boarded a bus heading south the next morning.

'I checked the news everywhere I went, but I couldn't find anything about a gunshot. Nothing about John. I assumed that meant he must have gotten away, that it was just a warning shot, but I never mentioned him to anyone. Today is the first time I've heard his name since.'

Eira stopped the recording. She needed to use the toilet, but she didn't want to stay in his cramped shop. She wanted to get away.

'Why didn't you ever reach out to Kerstin?' she asked while Steve struggled with the lock on the door, hands shaking. It took him a while.

'I don't know,' he said. 'Guess I was scared. I mean, I could've called, but I don't know whether that ever even crossed my mind. What does anyone know when they're twenty?'

The key turned at last, and he opened the door onto the street.

'Do you want me to pass on a message to her?' asked Eira.

Steve Larsson squinted over to the tattoo parlour opposite, signs for extra cheap beer. Pigeons in a puddle.

'I don't know what to say.'

There was one more thing Eira wanted to do while she was in Gothenburg. She had two nephews there, boys she hadn't seen since their mother gave up on Magnus and moved south.

I'll never be the dad they need. They deserve someone better than me.

She got off the number nine tram in Hagen, the second-to-last stop, and made her way along the footpaths. The houses were like white sugar cubes on an idyllic hillside, children wobbling around on bikes. She found herself watching a couple of boys as they skidded and did wheelies, but after a moment or two she realised they were far too young.

Veronica was her name, dark-haired and beautiful as she opened the door to a jumble of shoes on the floor.

Big shoes. One of the boys was a teenager now.

'Come in,' she said. 'Sorry about the mess; I just got home from work.'

They had barely known each other while Veronica lived in Kramfors. She and Magnus were so much older, Eira practically still a kid at the time.

They had broken up by the time the second boy came along.

'Viktor's not home yet,' she said. 'But Axel's up in his room. I haven't told him who you are.'

'OK.'

The rest of their home was spotless, light and bright between the kitchen and the living room, a staircase leading to the bedrooms on the floor above.

The whole situation felt slightly awkward. An aunt the boys didn't know.

'I hope you don't mind me getting in touch,' said Eira.

'No, not at all.'

Veronica asked whether she would like anything, and Eira asked for a glass of water. She had grabbed a hot dog from the infamous 7-Eleven on the corner of Järntorget before getting onto the tram that would take her away from central Gothenburg.

'So, you're having a baby of your own?' Veronica said as she passed her the glass, studying Eira's bump with an expression that was hard to read. Perhaps she was thinking that Eira would be as useless a parent as Magnus had been, that it ran in the family. 'Lovely news, you must be so excited! I guess you're not so young any more either. Who's the dad?'

'Honestly, I'm not sure,' said Eira. 'It wasn't exactly planned.'

Veronica laughed.

'That's one thing I did know, at the very least,' she said. 'Though if there'd been someone else to choose from I would've done it in a flash.'

Eira held back what she really thought: that Veronica had chosen Magnus at one point in time.

'How are they?' she asked.

'Fine. I haven't told them where Magnus is, just so you know.'

Plates clattered together as Veronica unloaded the dishwasher. Eira saw pictures of the boys at different ages on the fridge.

Magnus had spent their early years drinking, rarely holding down a job for more than a few months at a time. In some ways, she could understand how Veronica felt, but in others she didn't understand her at all.

A parent wasn't something a person could choose, and the kids had the father they had. Magnus had given in and agreed to award her full custody, but they were still his children.

'What do they know about their dad?' Eira was aware this was dangerous territory, but if not now, when? She was carrying their cousin, after all. Magnus's sons were some of the closest relatives her baby would have. 'They must remember him?'

Veronica didn't stop what she was doing, loading things into cupboards with her back to Eira.

'You have no idea how happy I am that we live five hundred miles away,' she said over the noise. 'He writes to them sometimes, but I always read everything first. Says he misses them and loves them and that he'll take them to Liseberg to ride the rollercoasters, blah, blah, blah. Sometimes I don't even bother giving them to the boys, I just throw them away. I don't want them to know their dad killed someone, so I lie about his surname. I told Viktor he was wrong when he said his dad's name was Sjödin.'

'Magnus didn't do it.'

'Oh, come off it. I've read the judgement.'

'He lied.'

'I'm sorry, but that doesn't surprise me. Magnus has always lied. He might not have cheated on me when we first got together, I have no idea, but I know he did later. He lied about drinking, too. Do you want me to list everything he's lied about over the years?'

The bubbles tickled Eira's throat as she drained her glass, swallowing too much air. She stifled a burp.

'If you sit down, I'll tell you what really happened,' she said.

Veronica paused with a whisk and a couple of wooden spoons in her hand.

'I know you want to defend him,' she said, 'but maybe it's time you stopped. You're not a little kid any more.'

There were different ways to talk to a person. Eira's usual approach was to be calm, conversational, using a voice that rarely demanded attention or tried to overpower anyone else, but during her time as a police officer she had also developed another voice, one that she used to put an end to any nonsense.

'Sit down.'

Veronica sat down.

Eira then told her the whole story of what happened twenty-five years ago, without protecting either Magnus or herself.

About how, in a fit of jealousy, he had gone out to the old sawmill because he knew Lina Stavred was there with someone else. How he had misjudged the situation and attacked Kenneth Isaksson, got into a fight with him and come close to being strangled, until Lina hit the other man over the head with an iron pipe. They had worked together to bury the body beneath the remains of the old steamboat quay, and Magnus had then helped her to disappear from Ådalen, letting Lina flee on his motorbike. They let the world believe that she died that day, and an innocent fourteen-year-old boy had taken the blame. Eira explained that the whole thing had remained in paralysis until the boy, Olof Hagström, returned to Ådalen three years ago, and the police found Kenneth Isaksson's remains in Lockne.

'Magnus thinks it was all his fault, that's why he confessed to manslaughter. He gave up his life to protect her.'

'Why?'

'If he hadn't gone to Lockne, none of it would have happened. I think he thinks he ruined two lives that night, and that's not even considering his own, or Olof Hagström's.' Eira found her eyes drifting over to the photographs, from chubby little toddlers to gap-toothed grins and gangly bodies shooting up in height. 'It's hard to work out how many people are affected by a crime.'

'Hold on a second, I need to think.' Veronica moved her chair over to the extractor fan and took a pack of cigarettes from a cupboard. 'Let me get this straight. Magnus gave up his kids for some woman he hasn't seen since he was seventeen?'

'It's a bit more complicated than that.'

'What about you, then?' She lit the cigarette, turned on the fan. 'Your beloved big brother could tell you anything and you'd defend him no matter what.'

'This has nothing to do with me,' said Eira. She wanted to argue, to bat away Veronica's words, but she knew what she had just said was true.

'No, you're right. It's about Axel and Viktor, and I'm not going to let them grow up in your mess of a fucking family. I don't care what's true or not. I want my boys to be surrounded by people they can trust and who'll put them first, not some old girlfriend from years ago.'

Veronica smiled at her, possibly for the first time since Eira arrived.

'Did you know they both have Gothenburg accents now?'

The crack of a gunshot shattered the dawn silence, followed by the soft lapping of water as the shooter paddled ashore. Lina crouched down behind a tree. The hunter was no more than thirty metres away from her as he clambered out of his canoe. He waded through the shallows carrying a rod with a hook at one end, got hold of the limp animal and pulled it in.

A beaver, of course. Lina had seen the deep tooth marks on a few young trees nearby, the ingenious dam structure at the edge of the river.

Something made her creep closer. A certain reverence, the grubbiness of it all. The blood mixing with the water, the stench of death. The hunter was hunched over the animal with a knife, probably looking for castoreum. It was worth a fortune, wasn't it? She had a vague memory of a group of men talking about shooting beavers sometime in the past. Did they make booze out of it, or was it perfume? Or did it have something to do with sex?

The hunter was fairly overweight, and his trousers had slipped down to reveal his arse crack. He was breathing heavily, hadn't noticed her. Lina ducked behind a windblown tree. The beaver would almost certainly have been able to smell her, but there wasn't much it could do now it was dead. Too busy having its gut sliced open, hands rummaging around inside it.

He had put his gun down.

A rifle, the kind people used to shoot elk.

The blood was roaring in her ears. The beaver would no doubt have heard that, too.

Its flat tail sliced through the air as the man flipped it over, his forearms streaked with blood.

Once Lina started moving, it all happened very quickly. His reaction was slightly delayed when he heard her, but by then it was already too late.

'Christ alive, you scared me.'

He made the same mistake men often did: saw a woman and thought there was nothing to worry about. Lina brought the rock down on his head as he turned back around. Not too hard, not to kill him or anything, just enough to stun him and make him fall over. He struggled to get up from the ground, a kick to the arm keeping him down. She grabbed the rifle and ran.

'Hey, wait! What the fuck are you doing? Come back!'

The man's pathetic shouts grew fainter and fainter between the trees, and eventually all she could hear were her own footsteps thudding along the trail. When she noticed the sound of cars on a road nearby, she tucked the gun inside her jacket, took out a brush and neatened up her hair. A dishevelled woman emerging from the woods might evoke strange reactions, something ancient to do with trolls and spirits.

Lina paused by the edge of the road, her thumb in the air. She picked at something that was stuck between her teeth. If anyone pulled over, she would smile and say: 'Looks like there'll be plenty of berries this year.'

Y ou remember, Mum. I know you remember. It's in there somewhere. You have to help me. What can I say to get through to you?

Eira gripped her mother's hands, so slender and veiny these days, trying to catch and hold her attention. Kerstin's sharp golden-brown eyes had faded to a colour that reminded her of river water. Murkier, hard to define.

'I don't know what to say.'

Eira waited, but her mother didn't go on. She brought up the picture she had taken of the photograph in Skogsnäs. Steve had the same long hair he still had, brown rather than grey. A thin frame in an embroidered shirt.

'His name was Steve Carrano. The two of you were together for a few months. Did you love him?'

'That's not me.'

'Not in this picture, no.' Eira cursed herself and enlarged the image so that Steve's wife was no longer visible. 'But you knew him a few years before this. You thought he left because he didn't love you, but that wasn't why. He was scared. Do you hear that, Mum? It wasn't your fault. You did everything right.'

Kerstin patted her daughter's hand.

'Yes, yes, it'll be just fine,' she said, though her eyes seemed to be saying something else. Eira thought she could see a reaction, a memory that had taken the bait only to let go and disappear into the depths. A sadness that might stem from the grief of no longer knowing or from something she did actually remember.

'I don't forget anything.' Kerstin tapped her forehead. 'I won't let them think that.'

'Are you talking about Steve? What haven't you forgotten? What do you remember?'

Kerstin shook her head and gripped her cake fork again, stubbornly scraping the crumbs and cream from her near-empty plate.

'Am I talking to Police Investigator Shoe-din?'

The call from California had been prearranged, and Eira had closed the door to her office and started trying to think through the case in English terms.

'What you have to understand is that this came as such a shock to me,' said the man on the other end of the line. 'My parents told me John died in Vietnam. I was too young to process anything more than that.'

Frank Aiello was the youngest of John's five siblings – three brothers, two sisters. Just eight when his brother was conscripted, now in his sixties.

The American police had reached out to him at his home in Los Angeles to break the news, and Frank had taken his time trying to digest everything, but it was as though it just wouldn't sink in.

'"Sweden?" I said. Stood there like an idiot, told them they must have the wrong person. That's why I wanted to speak with you. I hope you don't mind.'

'Of course not,' said Eira. 'I'm glad you called. It hasn't been easy to find information about . . .' She came close to saying *the man in the river*. '. . . your brother.'

The word brother was far from simple. It encompassed grief and despair and a longing to put things right; it covered everything she knew about inadequacy.

'I'd love for you to tell me everything you can,' he said. 'And I mean everything. This might sound strange, but my parents never talked about John.'

Eira took a moment to search for the right words. She wasn't used to showing consideration in English, to switching from technical, police-like language to something that showed more compassion for a family member.

'I was there when we recovered your brother's body from the river,' she began. 'A group of divers found him. We believe he was shot from behind, most likely in early September 1968.'

There was no need to tell him that there had been an explosion in Sundsvall yesterday, yet another showdown in the criminal underworld that was taking up most of their focus right now; that solving his brother's murder had slipped even further down their list of priorities.

'I'm sorry to say that the statute of limitations has passed, which means that even if we do manage to work out what happened, no one will go to jail.'

Frank Aiello cleared his throat. When he next spoke, he did so slowly, his voice sincere, as though every word was of great importance.

'I've known that my brother is dead for a long time, but as for who he was, what he believed, what is true and what is lies . . . that's all I can think about now.'

Eira flicked through her notes, conversations with those who had been there.

'What I've found out goes back to June 1967,' she said. 'When John decided to leave the military base in Germany.'

She told Frank about his brother's escape, the thunderstorm, the barracks in Tantolunden and the construction workers from Norrland; the steady stream of deserters arriving in Sweden, the farm in Torsåker where they were meant to be growing turnips, what John had said about freedom.

. . . just a dream, a breath in the wind.

Eira heard Frank's breathing down the line, slightly strained and unsteady, as though he was trying to hold something back. Tears, perhaps.

'Sorry,' he said. 'It's just that I've always thought I was the only rebel, the only one who didn't fit in. The black sheep of the family, if you like.'

He had very few memories of his big brother. Nothing but fragments; snapshots from a party, or the time John got a pair of boxing gloves. *I'm gonna teach you, little tiger. Don't ever let them get to you.* Another came from the day John took him to The Pike, the amusement park in Long Beach. Just him, no one else, his last memory before his brother joined the army. The boardwalk down to the sea was known as the walk of a thousand lights, with carousels and the most amazing rollercoaster anyone had ever seen. Frank had been left with the impression that John was kinder than his other siblings, though he couldn't know for sure. Perhaps that was just something he had told himself in hindsight, because his brother was dead. He never got a chance to see him with grown-up eyes, and what does an eight-year-old really know? Childhood memories have to be shared and compared, that's what siblings are for, but John became a ghost who was never mentioned by name. They didn't even have any pictures of him around the house.

Frank had been taught that this was what grief looked like; you don't talk about the dead.

Looking back now, he realised that something else had been at play. A truth that had to be hushed up, an unbearable shame.

A deserter in the family. To his parents, that must have felt like Satan himself had crept into their house in Long Beach. Or maybe it was God, trying to test their faith – as unmoving as a mountain.

'Their reaction when they found out . . . I can only imagine it must've been worse than the big earthquake in '33, that it shook the foundations of everything they believed in.'

His family belonged to the Christian Anti-Communist Crusade, which was headquartered in Long Beach. An evangelical movement that existed solely to fight the Red Threat, organising rallies and broadcasting on TV, working with the military in countries like El Salvador and boasting supporters like Ronald Reagan and John Wayne.

Frank had called his eldest sister after the police got in touch, though they rarely spoke nowadays.

'At first, Catherine didn't say a single word, and that's when I realised she already knew, that she'd known all along. Not that John ended up in Sweden – that was news to all of us – but that he was a deserter.'

His sister had been at home when the military called in December 1967, had snuck downstairs to eavesdrop though her parents had sent them all to their rooms.

'She heard our mom crying, and then they said that John was no longer their son, that he was an enemy of America.

Catherine never questioned the lies they told. I have almost no contact with any of my siblings now, but she still gets in touch from time to time to try to lead me back onto the righteous path. According to her, none of them want anything to do with this. They've talked, apparently, and decided that whatever happened back then was God's will, John's punishment for betraying his country.'

'I'm sorry,' said Eira.

'Thank you. That means a lot.'

The pause that followed felt like a minute's silence for someone who had just died, and she waited for Frank to speak.

'If John ever reached out to Mom and Dad,' he said, 'then I'm sure they would have hung up and prayed extra hard. They probably burned his letters.'

'That would explain why no one ever reported him missing.'

'Yeah. To them he was already dead.'

Eira debated whether to mention the men who had come to get John. It was the sort of detail they would usually hold back in order to maintain the integrity of their investigation, and she felt a certain reluctance to share uncorroborated information.

'I'd like to bring my brother home,' said Frank Aiello.

'Of course. I'm sorry it's taken so long. His body is in a city called Umeå, a little further north of here. You're welcome to come whenever you like.'

'I'm just glad you managed to identify him. I wanted to thank you for that.'

'There's one more thing.'

He seemed to sense her hesitation.

'You can tell me, however difficult it might be,' he said. 'I was a journalist, I've followed police investigations in LA, which means I've already seen most things – even if it was a while ago.'

'I have a witness who thinks your brother could have been reporting to the CIA.'

'Excuse me?'

Eira repeated what she had just said. Frank didn't speak.

She noticed that seven new emails had arrived during their conversation, all relating to the explosion, trails leading back to one of the criminal gangs in Stockholm. Eira had been roped into the investigation like everyone else, helping out with jobs that could be done from her desk.

'That sounds weird,' Frank Aiello said after a moment. 'Why would he desert his post and distance himself from the war only to switch sides? Could they have forced him into it?'

'Maybe they promised him a lesser sentence if he ever returned to the U.S.'

She heard a slight laugh from the far side of the Atlantic.

'Considering what was waiting for John if he got home, part of me wonders whether a court martial might have been preferable.'

'Like I said, this is just something I heard.'

'If that was the case,' said Frank, 'then my parents didn't know anything about it. They would've turned the portrait of John into a shrine if they did, surrounded by candles.'

When he first heard the whispers after a few drinks one evening, Allan had assumed it was just the usual rubbish.

Gossip, bullshit.

Haven't you heard? That one's working for the CIA. Yup, I got that from a trusted source . . .

American spies in Lunde? It sounded like a bad joke, like people were messing with him and his convictions. Laughing at him when he failed to see it.

If he passed it on, people would think he really had lost his mind. They'd lock him up and throw away the key, force him into a strait jacket.

Allan had already gone off the rails several times that summer – especially after he'd been drinking. But for God's sake, he had sobbed one evening in his buddy's garden, *this is my fiancée we're talking about, my child. The life we were meant to be living.*

They told him to pull himself together.

That it was all in his head, that all this boozing and making accusations left, right and centre wasn't going to help Maarit and the little one.

So I'm supposed to bend over, am I? Allan had asked. *Keep my trap shut? Give up my beliefs like everyone else now that they've got food on the table? Like C.-H.*

Hermansson and all those other part-time socialists who trim their sails to every wind?

Am I meant to be grateful they haven't sent me to an internment camp up in Storsien?

Huh?

Huh?

Tell me the truth, are your bellies full now too?

How in hell were they ever supposed to bring about revolution if the very foundations, the party, was taking in water like a leaky old boat?

He had made contact with a number of people who still wanted revolution that summer. There was talk, hushed but stubborn, that the Soviet Union had promised to support those who wanted to guide the party back onto the right track, a group with a name that wouldn't raise any suspicions.

The Welfare Committee.

Who would suspect a thing behind such a bland name?

A new era would dawn, Allan had thought as he wallowed in his hangover. Waiting for the flag to be raised down at the dock, signalling that there was work to go round. They had made cutbacks at the shipyard during late summer. Knowing his luck, it would probably shut down completely. There was less and less traffic on the river, and one sawmill after another was going under. There was even a rumour – however unlikely it seemed – that the great Marieberg Mill was next.

Allan had grabbed a pen and tried to find the right words, but he didn't have them in him, not like Maarit, who could produce the most beautiful sentences, poetry flowing from her fingers. He then heard a whistle and looked up, saw that the flag had been raised and ran out to his bicycle instead, his dad's rusty old thing. He had crashed his own bike into the ditch while drunk.

Allan ended up last in line and got no work, spent his time drifting around instead. It was on one of those days, late that summer, when he had first heard about the American. Allan knew who they were, of course, deserters who had fled Vietnam and turned up in Lunde. Straight from the war. It was impressive, no denying that, but he had since heard that at least two of them had done a runner before they were even sent to Asia. If Allan had known more than a few words of English he might have asked them about it, but they had never been put in the same team at work. Someone had told him they understood a little Swedish now, but still. They looked like the hippies and middle-class revolutionaries you saw on TV, people who hadn't done a hard day's work in their lives.

Allan had been restless from the lack of work that day, and had swung by the People's House where the Social Democrats and a few union men were sitting on the steps, acting important.

Words were exchanged, like always. Raised voices, telling them a thing or two. They were the traitors, curled up in the employers' laps, agreeing to cutbacks and redundancies. Who knows, maybe it was one of them who had been shouting about who was a communist?

He remembered being shushed, that someone he knew had beckoned him over and hissed in his ear.

Haven't you heard about the American? One of the

228

*deserters, the dark-haired one, the one that looks like an
Italian. He's not who he claims to be.*

They'd got it from a trusted source.

Allan had laughed at first, but as the strange, perhaps even
likely truth of it sank in after a few pilsners and sausages, he
stopped laughing.

A man couldn't turn his damn back on anyone.

President Johnson's lackeys, practically on his own
doorstep.

His finger had been shaking as he dialled the number
that evening, one of only a handful of times he had made a
long-distance call.

Eira managed to catch Shirin ben Hassan as she was eating her packed lunch in the canteen on the ground floor.

She microwaved her plastic tub of goulash and they sat down at a table in the corner. Shirin had just sent off all the forensic evidence from yesterday's bombing to the lab in Linköping and had begged them to let her cut straight to the front of the line.

'Otherwise someone will manage to take revenge for this first bombing, and then the others will take revenge for that, and whoever planted the bomb will be in bits on the tarmac.'

The explosives had been left in the doorway of a block of flats, and an eleven-year-old girl who had been taking the family dog out for a walk was now in intensive care. A former member of a motorcycle gang was registered as living in the same building, but he was likely just a small cog in the machine. There were links to a number of shootings in Stockholm, conflict over who ran the drugs trade in Sundsvall. As the competition grew in the big cities, prices went down, meaning that Norrland had become increasingly valuable to the criminal gangs.

'I spoke to John Aiello's little brother,' said Eira. 'He couldn't thank us enough for everything I told him.'

'So it was worth it, then.'

Eira smiled.

'It was worth it,' she said.

There were violations, there were missteps, but she didn't count putting in a little too much effort as either.

'So, how's it going?' asked Shirin. 'Is there any chance of us solving this thing?'

Eira tried to spear a piece of meat in her soup, but all she managed to find were soggy vegetables. Her overriding sense was that she was going around in circles. She kept discovering new details about her mother, about that time and the war, but the question was whether that had brought her any closer to finding a perpetrator. Sometimes it felt as though the whole thing was a private matter rather than a murder investigation.

'I don't know,' she said. 'I'm glad we've managed to identify him, but maybe that's as far as we'll get.'

'I didn't think it was your style to give up.'

After eating half her soup, Eira pushed it away. Tasteless, over-boiled potatoes, a carton she'd bought from the supermarket. She had stopped cooking and freezing the leftovers the minute her mother moved to the care home. That was just another item to add to the long list of things she should do better: remembering that she was no longer alone.

'Coffee?'

'I'll get them,' said Shirin, moving to get up.

'No, I can go.'

When she got back with the two mugs of coffee – hers diluted with oat milk, because black coffee had started to make her feel queasy and cows' milk was apparently considered unhealthy now – Shirin asked her to go through everything they knew.

'Do you have time?'

'No, but by law I'm entitled to another fifteen minutes.'

Reeling off the facts didn't take long when Eira skipped over all the emotional, personal aspects, and she quickly got to the evening when a couple of unnamed men had been seen taking John Aiello into the woods.

The shot Steve had heard.

'And how far is it from there to the harbour?' asked Shirin. 'Assuming your mum's lover boy is right and is telling the truth.'

'Not far at all.' Eira pictured the scene: the gravel track on that side of the Sandö Bridge, past the houses beyond the Bethania Chapel, where the forest took over. 'Maybe a hundred metres, two hundred at most. But you'd have to walk past several houses, so it doesn't seem likely that they would have carried him there.'

'Is it accessible by boat?'

'Yeah, or pretty close, anyway.'

'OK, so they got hold of a boat,' Shirin mused. 'Maybe they already had one, or maybe they borrowed one. Did people even bother locking their boats up back then?'

It wasn't hard to imagine how events might have unfolded. Eira pictured the two men carrying John Aiello's body down to the shore. It was September, the night dark. At some point along the way, or once they were already out on the water – likely rowing, so they wouldn't be heard – they had realised they needed something to weigh the body down. They broke into the shipyard, which was simple enough. It was open and unmanned, easy to blend in among the boats, taking cover beneath the tall cranes. Eira remembered the black-and-white pictures of those she had seen in an exhibition at the People's House in Lunde.

'They must have been familiar with the shipyard,' she said. 'They knew which boats were in for repairs, exactly what they needed. It feels too long-winded and risky for them to have gone there with no real plan – especially if they had a murder to cover up. Why take that risk, you know?'

'So one of them was local?'

'At least.'

Shirin's phone screen started flashing; she couldn't stretch out her lunch break any longer. They both got up, throwing away their rubbish and heading for the stairs.

'I went back through the pathologist's report and everything you wrote,' said Eira, trying to keep up with Shirin, breathing heavily. She was used to gruelling workouts, and hadn't quite been able to bring herself to make the transition to gentle pregnancy sessions. 'Is there anything I should know that I haven't noticed? Anything you've been thinking about?'

Shirin paused by the secure doors on their floor, her key card in her hand.

'I've been thinking about the angle of the bullet,' she said. 'The one you called a shot to the back of the head. That's technically correct, of course: the bullet hit the top of his neck, between the first and second vertebrae, to be precise. But I wonder if it might also be a little misleading.'

'What do you mean?'

233

'What was your immediate thought when you said shot to the back of the head?'

'An execution,' said Eira. 'According to the forensic report the bullet entered diagonally from above. I imagined him on his knees with the gun to the base of his skull.'

'Exactly,' said Shirin. 'And we haven't really discussed this, since the focus was on identifying the victim. But if he had been trying to escape, for example, then that angle could also have been achieved if he was running down a slope – or if the shooter was much taller than him . . .'

'John Aiello was five foot nine.'

'The shooter could have been highly skilled, or they could have hit him purely by chance, shooting in desperation. These things happen.'

Shirin opened the door and Eira followed her in, towards the forensic technicians' department at the very back of the building.

The crime scene investigator was right that they hadn't discussed the case the way they usually would, going through the forensic evidence, the details. The murder itself had fallen slightly by the wayside. In summaries and in talking to Silje, it had become a brief report at most. There had been no real discussion, no bouncing of ideas; there was no time for that when organised gangs kept setting off bombs in the community. Eira hadn't wanted to take up people's time with a cold, possibly even hopeless murder investigation. She had been determined to handle the whole damn thing on her own now that they refused to use her for anything else.

'A nine-millimetre bullet,' she said. 'What do you make of that?'

John Aiello's vertebrae had been too damaged for any real analysis, but they had managed to determine the size of the bullet from the nick on his breastbone, where it had exited his body.

'That the weapon could have been military,' said Shirin. 'Though not necessarily.'

'American?'

'Possibly. The entire police force over there uses nine-millimetre ammunition, as does the Swedish military. The Germans were first, with the Luger. Did you know that the army panic-bought a load of them from the Nazis in 1939, when it looked like war was coming? The Finns developed their own version, and the Russians came up with Makarov ammunition at the start of the Cold War. If only I had a bullet or a casing, then . . .'

It was a trail Eira had walked along many times before. The glade was now overgrown, but her father had brought her here, shown her a special tree with thick roots that rose up out of the ground, forming gates to the underworld.

She always heard his voice when she came to places like this; rocks and sticks and remnants of old sawmills that carried meaning and stories not visible to the naked eye.

The church had tried its best to wipe out folklore and superstition during the witch trials of the seventeenth century, but it had failed. As late as the 1930s, people continued to turn to those with the gift, figures like the old Finn-Nyberg woman in Lunde, to have their children pulled beneath the exposed roots of a tree. By passing a newborn beneath the roots of a particular tree and uttering the words that had been handed down through the generations, the child would be protected against illness and death.

Eira's grandfather was one of the last to have been 'pulled' through the roots of the tree in the glade in front of her, but that hadn't stopped him from contracting polio and being left with a limp, nor from nearly dying of scarlet fever. She wasn't sure exactly which tree it was; the area was too overgrown, and it wasn't a memory she had made the effort to preserve, old traditions jostling for space alongside more recent knowledge, like the fact that there were lots of bilberries there.

Eira unclipped Rabble from his lead, letting him roam the damp terrain as she tried to get her bearings. The barn where the deserters had once slept, where could it have been? She followed various trails until the first houses appeared beyond the trees. It had probably been torn down, but she might be able to find the foundations if she dug beneath everything that had grown over the top – providing it hadn't been turned into an artist's studio or a B&B for the summer.

Coming here had given her a good sense of the distances involved, in any case, a feel for the scene of the crime. The men who came to get John Aiello wouldn't have needed to go far before they were completely swallowed up by the trees and the autumn darkness. The closest house was only around a hundred metres away, a hundred and fifty metres at most; that was how small the woods were. If anyone else had heard the shot, what would they have thought, in a community where practically every other person owned a gun? They probably hadn't even reacted, especially not in early September, when the annual elk hunt had begun.

Eira paused by the steep slope down to the gravel track that ran parallel to the river. If Shirin's theory was correct, was this where he had tried to escape? Where he had broken free, if they were holding him, scrambling downwards and aiming for the houses not far away. It wouldn't have been *completely* dark at that time of year, not when there were so many more people living in the area. There must have been lamps in their windows, possibly even a streetlamp to carve out his silhouette.

She found a slightly less steep path down the slope and called to Rabble, who came barrelling out of the grass and scrub. Her trainers were soaked through. As she walked along the gravel track, she paused beneath the arch of the bridge. It had always given her a dizzying feeling. She remembered her teens, when they had competed to see who dared to climb the struts. It would have been easy enough to moor a boat without being seen at the water's edge below it, taking that route to the docks. It wasn't far at all, and they could have rowed in the dark. Hauled the anchor onboard.

Who would react to a small boat like that crossing the river? It was nothing out of the ordinary, just a fisherman or a suitor heading home to Sandö.

She let Rabble splash about in the water for a while, the way he always did, and watched the evening soften as the sun dipped towards the horizon.

It could have happened just like that. It was a perfectly plausible scenario, right up to the point where John Aiello's body was sunk in the shimmering blue light.

The question was why?

Who? And how many of them?

The thought made her head spin as she approached the politics of the era, global superpowers at the height of the Cold War. But here? In Lunde?

Eira had only walked a short distance, but she felt the familiar dull ache in her pelvis.

Someone, or several people, had rowed back over the river, or to another beach. She pictured them fading like clouds, like fog. As the years passed, they must have grown confident they had got away with it. Perhaps they were still alive.

It had been years since they demolished The Pike and covered the beach by the old amusement park with land-fill. By the time Frank Aiello turned nine, the enormous rollercoaster was a thing of the past.

Back then, he hadn't understood why something like that had been allowed to happen. People said that the Cyclone Racer had to make way for roads and other amenities after the *Queen Mary*, a younger and more powerful version of the *Titanic*, was permanently moored and made into a hotel. That had been kind of exciting, given the size of the ship and the iceberg and the number of people who had died, but it wasn't the *real Titanic*, and it wasn't the Cyclone.

With two tracks running parallel to each other, riding it had felt like a race, the hills so steep they seemed to stretch straight up into the sky. The butterflies that came from screaming at the top of your lungs, the way you never got to otherwise.

It was silly, but at sixty-three years of age he still missed it. The old rollercoaster had been a masterpiece of engineer-ing with its wooden structure and smooth curves. He understood that now, as an adult, years after it disappeared. He also understood that the opening of Disneyland twenty-five miles away had out-competed more deprived places like The Pike, where everyone was welcome – whether they had money or not. Even a big brother who wanted to sneak out and show his kid brother the world.

Frank remembered John's big hand gripping his as they got into the rollercoaster car. He had spent the past few days crying like a baby over the loss of his brother. John must have taken him there in secret, he realised now. It was evening when they visited, because John had wanted to show him why The Pike was called the walk of a thousand lights. The bulbs were all different colours, and they seemed to linger when you closed your eyes. He remembered the music and the shouting. Their mom would never have allowed them to go there. Everyone knew the type of people who went to the amusement area at night – card sharks and strippers and tattoo artists. If Satan were to land in Long Beach, he would feel right at home at The Pike.

Frank drove by the huge container terminal, mile after mile of metal boxes stacked one on top of another, eventually turning off onto Queensway Drive. He got out of the car in an attempt to conjure up more memories, something else John might have had said, how he had felt, whether he was excited, scared, had he already thought about escaping?

The candyfloss and popcorn were long gone, but the smell of oil was still there, the sea, tears blurring his view of the *Queen Mary* so much that it was like the twinkling lights were back, the colours, his little hand in John's.

The second of the Aiello brothers, Mike, had taken over the house on Gundry Avenue, and time seemed to do a somersault as Frank pulled up on the other side of the street. It was as though nothing had changed there. No, there was a new sign about an alarm, a security gate. The house itself was still the same pale yellow colour, though the panelling must have been repainted at some point. The trees were taller than he remembered them, of course, the bushes as neatly pruned as ever.

Through his sister, Mike had let Frank know that any talk of organising a funeral was out of the question. He's angry, Catherine had said. Mike had always been so proud of his brother for fighting the communists in Vietnam, and he'd had a minor stroke last year. Just leave him be.

Not a word about the family plot, either.

You have no right. I have the papers, we all agreed. He isn't going to be laid to rest there.

The front door opened and an older woman came out. For a split second, Frank thought it was his mother, heading over to the church or the store, but he quickly realised she must be Mike's wife. Sylvia glanced in his direction and Frank started the engine, pulling away from Gundry Avenue, away from the memories of John skidding onto the driveway on his bike.

He had somewhere to be, an appointment with an old acquaintance in Venice Beach.

They had arranged to meet at one of the Cuban joints down by the beachfront, and Frank was desperate for a beer.

It struck him now, as he tried to spot his old mentor outside the restaurant, that Venice Beach had something of The Pike about it, in the grubbiness and the bright colours, the cheery lawbreaking. The fresh air, the idiots and the skateboarders, all the downtrodden but still-alive hippies, the graffiti-covered palms and the signs offering prescription marijuana for medical use. Perhaps that was why he had always felt so comfortable here.

'Frank Aiello?'

Jesus Christ, he really had aged. Richard Evans had been his guest lecturer and mentor back when Frank still had ambitions to become an investigative reporter in the vein of Woodward or Bernstein, uncovering corruption and lies and publishing the barefaced truth. But while Evans had moved back to the east coast and the big papers out there, Frank had stayed put in California with his self-doubt and his job as an English teacher in El Segundo.

'It's been a minute.'

The two men shook hands. Frank had too much respect for Evans to give him a hug; they had never been that close.

It was a little uncomfortable to see just how much his old mentor's shoulders had begun to hunch, the weight dropping off him and making his suit baggy – though it still looked expensive, screamed East Coast intellectual. Richard Evans was one of the big names within American journalism, and Frank had been fully prepared to fly to New York in order to speak to him, but when he looked up his details he had discovered that Evans was living just a few miles away, by one of the canals in Venice.

'Sitting here like an ageing cliché, trying to write The Book. It's all about my life in the service of the truth. You think I can use that in the blurb? Will anyone remember what that used to mean?'

Evans had always had a slightly grandiose way of talking,

with a hint of sarcasm that meant you could never be sure whether he was being serious or not.

They sat down at a table behind a couple of European tourists drinking tequila shots with their lunch.

'I'm sorry about your brother,' said Evans. 'Though I do have to admit that I got a kick out of reaching out to a few old contacts. One of them's in a care home now and can't even remember what he was ordered to forget.'

Frank waved to the waiter and ordered a beer and a plate of ropa vieja. Evans asked for the same, but with red wine instead.

'Old clothes, huh? Trust the Cubans to pick a name like that for something so delicious.' He leaned back in his chair. His pale blue gaze was as sharp as ever, making Frank feel ashamed about everything he had given up. Fragments of lectures came back to him, tumbling down from the shelves at the back of his mind where he had stuffed them. *The most powerful weapon a journalist can have is stubbornness. Perseverance. Even if it takes you twenty years, you'll get to the truth – because it's out there somewhere. It's always there. So go that extra mile. Ask another question. Make the next call, and then the one after that. There's always something else you can do.*

'So you suspect your brother was CIA?'

'Not me,' said Frank. 'The Swedish police. The detective I spoke to described it as a rumour, from someone who was around back then. I'm not sure they're really looking into it, to be honest. The statute of limitations for murder was twenty-five years at the time. I'm not judging anyone; I just want to know who he was.'

'And who killed him. And why.'

'Yeah, that too.'

Richard Evans smiled as their drinks arrived.

'You're right that I used to have a few contacts at Langley,' he said. 'And I did actually get a tip-off about a guy who was in the Vault back then. He's a beekeeper in Arkansas these days.'

'The Vault?'

'A department in the basement. He said it was like day and night didn't exist down there. No one was allowed to know what they were up to.'

'Which was?'

'Working on an operation that was never meant to exist. Even if your brother was part of it, you'll never find his name there. Any documentation that could reveal the informants' identities was destroyed. The beekeeper claims he can still remember the smell of burning tape. Recorded calls, printouts, names of handlers – it all went up in flames.'

Richard Evans paused for a moment to allow the waitress to set their plates down. She spoke to them in Spanish, wishing them *buen provecho,* but it was probably instinct or sheer habit that made him wait until she was out of earshot before he went on.

'Are the Swedish police sure he was murdered?' Evans asked, lifting a forkful of shredded meat to his mouth.

'Shot from behind,' said Frank. He managed to keep his voice steady; he was no longer an eight-year-old boy. 'Theoretically, I guess it could have been an accident – pretty much every Swede goes hunting at that time of year, but not with nine-millimetre rounds. And an accident doesn't seem too likely given how they disposed of his body.'

That was one of the worst parts of the whole mess: the way his brother had been so thoroughly consigned to oblivion, almost more violent than his death.

'It was called Operation Chaos,' said Richard Evans.

There was a young woman sitting outside the door to Kerstin's room. Short, white-blonde hair, straight posture. She looked up from her phone.

'Hi! Are you here to visit Kerstin too?'

Eira paused, confused. Her mother rarely had any other visitors. Friends disappeared, relatives died. Kerstin had never been one for surrounding herself with other people. Had fallen out with them sometimes, in fact.

'I'm her daughter,' she said.

'Oh, of course!' The woman's face broke into a delighted, dazzling smile. She couldn't be much older than her late twenties. 'Magnus has told me all about you. It's great to meet you at last.'

She held out a hand and the penny finally dropped. The closed door, the low murmur of voices inside. A prison officer, of course. Supervised day release, civilian clothing. The officer probably said her name, but Eira was no longer listening. She felt her clammy hand on the door handle, a draught from a window as she pushed the door open.

Her mother's laugh. Kerstin was in her armchair, dressed up for the occasion. Flowers in a vase. Eira didn't know why that made her so angry.

All she could see of Magnus was the back of his head. His hair had grown since they last met. He wheeled around, had probably learned to always keep one eye on what was going on behind him.

'Oh, hey,' he said. 'Good to see you.'

It was the first time Eira had seen him outside of prison, in the free world, in two and a half years. During her last visit, over the winter, she had tried to convince him to take back his confession yet again.

She put down the box of pastries she was carrying.

'I only got two,' she said. 'I didn't realise you'd be here.'

'Gosh, how lovely, everyone is here now,' said Kerstin. The glimmer in her eye, that joy, things Eira rarely got to experience any more.

Eira closed the door behind her. *Forget about the officer sitting outside, forget everything else.*

'Jesus Christ, sis, you're so big!'

Eira cut the pastries into smaller pieces and heated the coffee, and Magnus started telling anecdotes that made their mother laugh.

About the time he went over the handlebars on his bike, or when he brought home a lost baby gull. You must remember that, he said, and the miracle was that she did. Reality seemed to flow through Kerstin's brain, clearing the blockage like a log jam in the river.

Eira knew it might not happen again, so once she sat down she mentioned her trip to Gothenburg. The grandkids first, talking to Kerstin, telling her she had been to see the boys' mother, that they were doing well, lived in a nice place. She felt Magnus tense beside her.

'I'll buy them train tickets as soon as I get paid,' he said, turning to face Kerstin. 'They're old enough now, they can come up here on their own. I'll take them out on the river in the summer, we'll go fishing. And up to Skuleberget, to the caves where the robbers used to hide. Do you remember the time I hid up there? You spent hours looking for me.'

'You pretended you were an outlaw,' said Kerstin, laughing again.

'I also bumped into an old friend of yours,' Eira spoke up once they had been through a few stories about escapades on the mountain. 'Steve Carrano. He fled the Vietnam war and ended up in Kramfors. The two of you met at a protest in the square. Do you remember me talking about him?'

She held up the photograph from Skogsnäs, Steve's then-wife now cropped out of it.

'Oh,' Kerstin said as she studied the image. 'Oh, oh, oh.' She clapped a hand to her mouth and blushed.

'Tell me more,' said Magnus. 'This sounds exciting.'

'No, I can't.'

'Why not?' asked Eira. 'It was so long ago. We don't know anything about your life back then.'

Eira had once read a description of dementia as a forest where a person gets lost and can't tell one trail from another. Time and space fade away, and though the person might lose their bearings, their memories linger, robbed of context, a bit like trees once they're chopped down and transported downriver.

'It was what it was,' said Kerstin. The stern look on her face was the same one that had always made Eira try to be that little bit better. Tidying, smoothing over, organising. Kerstin gripped Magnus's hand and held it tight. 'To think you came back.'

For a moment, it was unclear whether she even knew who he was, but then Eira saw her drift back into the present and the man beside her became her son once again, and she was patting his hand to comfort and protect him.

'Would someone mind telling me what's going on here?' he asked.

Eira glanced over to the closed door. Supervised day leave came with strict conditions.

'How much time do you have?'

'Enough.'

As Allan remembered it, the fog had crept in from the river that morning. He was wearing his thick jumper, had to wipe down his bike saddle.

'Are you Allan Westin?' The man had been standing on the other side of the road, dressed in a way that confused Allan. A work coat with smart trousers underneath, dress shoes.

'Yeah, I s'pose I am.'

It occurred to Allan that the man could be from the police.

The undercover, dangerous kind.

'I've got to get down to the docks,' he said. 'They're allocating work for the day.'

The whistle sounded in the distance.

'I'll walk with you,' said the man.

Allan set off, pushing his bicycle, and knew he would be last in line.

The stranger had told him his name, Erik Johansson, and he remembered thinking it was the kind of name that was so common you'd never be able to track him down again.

His dialect was different somehow, a hint of Finnish or somewhere up towards the border, hard to pinpoint exactly where he was from.

An alias, Allan thought as the man explained why he had

come to Lunde. It was to do with the phone call, the one Allan had made, to the secret number belonging to those who were still fighting for the revolution. A comrade in Kramfors had given it to him, someone else who was frustrated by the direction the party was going in, who had whispered that the true believers were starting to organise.

His heart had been racing as they walked down towards the docks that morning.

Finally, Allan had thought. This is it.

Johansson had talked about the hunt for communists that was taking place in secret all over the country, said that Allan's tip had been so interesting that he – someone with close ties to the revolutionary forces, to the KGB itself – had thought it was worth paying a visit to Lunde.

He hadn't said any of the part about who sent him, of course. That was all in Allan's mind, which began whirring as they reached the brow of the hill and saw the small community stretching out in front of them.

The Lunde that had once risen up and then withered away as a result of collaboration between the unions, the Social Democrats and the conservatives; the red Ådalen that had faded to pink, teeming with fellow travellers and hobby socialists. That was how Allan described it, hoping to make the stranger realise he was on the right side.

The man had put a hand on his shoulder when they reached the docks.

'Could you point out this person they claim is the American spy?'

There was already a queue outside the office. Only one boat had arrived, which meant there wouldn't be enough work to go around. Allan felt a sting of disappointment for the income he had lost, but then he saw them coming out, the Americans, in their jeans and their donated clothing. The air had begun to quiver then, as though an electric current was passing through it. He didn't dare whisper until they had walked by.

That it was him, the one with the dark hair.

'And how sure are you?'

Allan searched for something to say as the workers boarded the boat that would take them to the sawmill, to the loading area, what he knew and didn't know; everything was such a muddle inside him back then. It felt ridiculous just to stand there, vacillating like an idiot. He'd heard the rumour from the union blokes, and why would they lie about something like that?

'I'm sure there's something in it,' he said. 'I heard it from a trusted source.'

The stranger had invited him to his room at the back of Wästerlund's Café that evening, closing the door, shaking out a cigarette and offering it to Allan before handing him a glass of vodka.

They toasted in Russian – *za zdorovye!* – and slammed their glasses down on the wooden table.

'Before long, the CIA will have infiltrated every place of work in this country,' said the man who called himself Johansson. 'Everyone knows the Social Democrats have been negotiating with the Americans and NATO about national defence. Any claims of neutrality are a myth and have been since the fifties. Believe me, our Soviet comrades know.'

Afterwards, it was as though the meeting had never taken place. Had he really gone to the room behind the café and talked as though the revolution was nigh? About the fact that Sweden was on the verge of being taken over by the United States, in a much more elaborate way than by force. About the fact that they all had a responsibility to act before the country became a vassal state.

Their brotherland in the east expected it.

In exchange, they would be supported in the work that had to be done on home turf, in taking back power from the weaklings in the party.

To show the Soviet Union just how faithful they were.

'*Za zdorovye!*'

E ira hurried to finish what she was doing in the bath-room, but even the most basic of functions had become unbelievably awkward now.

It was rare for anyone to knock on the door. Allan had already brought Rabble over for the evening, but maybe it was someone dropping off more baby stuff? Stina had said something about a crib and a pram, which meant that Eira hadn't bought either. An excuse, perhaps, because she still couldn't bring herself to think about what a baby actually needed.

The fact of the matter was that she hadn't even unpacked any of the bags people had already given her. Embarrassingly, they were still standing in the hallway.

'Hi, what are you doing here?' Eira instinctively ran a hand through her hair, which probably didn't make much difference.

GG had backed away from the door, and was standing below the porch. He looked pale in the hazy evening light.

'Sorry, it was stupid just to turn up like this,' he said. 'I'm bothering you, of course I am. I didn't even think about the time.'

'Has something happened?'

Eira noticed the weeds that had popped up between the

paving slabs, the dandelion leaves by his polished shoes. Some primal part of her was ashamed of that.

'No, I wouldn't say that.' His eyes darted off to both sides, beyond her, everywhere but Eira herself. It felt strange to be looking down on him.

'Come in,' she said.

The kitchen table was covered in notes and documents. Eira had turned her attention to phone lists over the past few days, tracing calls from one criminal to the next, requesting yet more records and finding yet more numbers. She had drawn a chart in order to fully understand how several networks were linked and did business with one another, a tangle of circles and lines. There hadn't been time to think about how to move forward with the murder of John Aiello. Only at night, occasionally, when she pictured the scene in the woods as he ran for his life, trees and roots, faces hidden in the darkness.

GG had paused by her chart, which looked like it could have come from the mind of some manic artist. He was in charge of the original investigation, after all – the drugs case – and though Silje had taken the lead on the bombings, he was still involved.

'I can give you a summary if you like?'

'That's not why I came.'

He seemed unsure of himself, which was unlike him.

'Can I get you anything? Tea?'

'I'm thinking of quitting,' he said.

GG wanted to go through to the living room, where he didn't have to see any police work and could slump back on the sofa. Eira found the courage to sit right beside him. The room seemed shabbier with him there, gaps on the walls where the pictures she had taken to the care home once hung. Why hadn't she put anything else up? It was so gloomy, so drab and dark.

She could smell dust, him.

'You shouldn't quit,' said Eira. 'You *can't*. You're so much better than everyone else.'

'I've become a crappy police officer. No, don't try to argue with me. You know it's true, you've seen me. I thought it would pass, but it hasn't.'

GG ran his hands through his hair, so thick and grey. Eira had stroked it once, but he had been unconscious at the time. She sat perfectly still, her own hands on the sofa rather than her belly. She wanted to forget all about that for a while.

'Does this have something to do with what happened at the lighthouse?' she asked hesitantly, immediately regretting her words. GG had spent days locked in that damn root cellar; she couldn't even imagine how frightened and power- less he must have felt before he lost consciousness. It warped the balance between them, belonged in silence. Something they shared but which didn't really exist.

'I'm so scared nowadays,' he said.

'Of what?'

'If I knew that I'd be able to do something about it. It happens without warning, there's no logic to it.'

Like that afternoon. That was why he had jumped into the car and driven over to Lunde.

'I wanted to talk to someone who doesn't look at me like I need fixing or locking up.'

'I don't,' said Eira, swallowing and putting a hand on his back. It was warm and damp. 'I don't see you like that.'

'I know,' GG said with a weak smile in her direction.

He had been walking across the square in Sundsvall after leaving work, couldn't remember where he was going. Running an errand, nothing important. To the pharmacy, maybe, to pick up the prescription the doctor had given him. He'd walked that way thousands of times before, in a city where he knew everything and everyone. He remembered hearing a voice behind him, a loud clang from something hard, a sudden movement. All the sounds and sensations were blown out of proportion, a moment of panic as he stopped dead and lashed out.

'I didn't have time to see who it was. I thought I'd already seen what was going to happen before I even turned around. I'd seen a weapon, thought I'd heard it, so I just went for it.'

And then he noticed the young man sprawled on the ground, an older woman shrinking back. GG had seen the fear in her eyes. People had stopped all around them, phones raised. A girl shouted, 'What the fuck are you doing?'

'There was no weapon. The kid was only thirteen, not some gang member. He just got too close to me while he was talking on the phone, that's it.'

'You're probably just burnt out,' said Eira. 'You've been working on this case for months . . .'

'I can't deal with being scared any more.'

She didn't speak, considering her words carefully, but all that went through her head were platitudes. That he was the victim of a serious crime, that he had come close to death. That he felt guilty, convinced it was his own fault. That it was complicated to be both a police officer and a victim, as though he didn't know that already.

'I'd miss you,' she said, swallowing hard.

'No chance,' said GG. 'You'll have your hands full.'

He grazed her bump with the back of his hand.

It was hardly the first time someone had touched it. Eira occasionally found herself getting annoyed that her body seemed to have become common property, and there were times when she felt moved for the same reason: because children were everyone's business. But she had never been aroused by it before, not even when the person touching her was one of the possible fathers, men she actually had feelings for.

Not like now, so powerfully that she had to grip his hand. She never wanted to let it go. Fuck, she thought, it wasn't over. It had always been this way.

She felt rough fabric as she leaned in to his chest, a silence so dense it was hard to breathe.

The scent of smoke and man and something softly perfumed.

'It was stupid of me to come over.' His voice sounded different, as though there was something getting in the way. 'I don't want you to . . .'

There was no end to that sentence. No response. Eira couldn't look at him, and nor could she look at the rug or the scratched coffee table or any of the other things that were so worn and tired after years of faithful service in the Sjödin home, all hissing that she should live her life, not get pregnant unnecessarily, not throw her opportunities away. Eira closed her eyes and felt his chest rising and falling. The top two buttons on his shirt were undone, an invitation to come closer. She had been there before, her lips searching his throat for a pulse. It had been weak and resigned back then, but today it was racing, hard and fast.

'Eira, Eira.'

He trailed off as she approached his mouth, his hands on her face. Was he pushing her away?

'What would he say?' GG mumbled.

'Who?'

'This little one's dad.'

His hand was heavy on her belly, life so relentlessly complicated yet again.

'That doesn't matter.' Eira gripped his hand and pushed it down, away from her bump, in beneath her baggy maternity pants. There was no way in hell she was planning to stop now. She hadn't had sex with anyone in almost six months, not since her pregnancy became an unignorable complication and she'd had to distance herself from both of her lovers. Finding someone else hadn't exactly been a priority, given the circumstances. But she didn't want anyone else, she didn't want anything but this.

'Please just forget about it,' she whispered, and then his mouth was back on hers and there was nothing wrong about that. If she twisted to one side she would be able to reach him better, swing one leg over his. She struggled with his buttons, groaning loudly when her phone started ringing. Christ, it had been so long.

Somehow it all came to an end. Maybe it was him, the impossibility of it all, or maybe it was the damn phone that had started ringing again.

GG leaned back on the sofa. She hadn't quite managed to undo his trousers.

Two missed calls from a private number. They would just have to call again. Eira slumped into his arms, closing her eyes. She could feel his damp chest against her cheek, had managed to undo his shirt, if nothing else. GG stroked her hair.

'I shouldn't have let that happen.'

'It didn't,' said Eira.

'Jesus, you only have a few weeks to go. I don't know what I was thinking.'

'I think you'll find it was me who started it,' said Eira.

His laugh sounded different, completely stripped of all arrogance. It was soft, like something a person might bury their face in if they needed comforting.

'I know plenty of men who've done this sort of thing,' he said. 'My own brother, for example. His wife was practically in labour at the time. So, in the name of equality . . .'

'I'm not in a relationship with the father.'

'OK.'

'I don't even know whose baby it is.'

'That sounds interesting,' said GG, still stroking her neck, playing with her hair. 'Tell me more.'

And so Eira told him the truth, that there were two possible candidates. That one would never leave his legally questionable kingdom on the far side of the river and that the other would likely be moving to Stockholm, but that both were willing to be involved.

'So which of the two options would you prefer?'

This one, she wanted to say. *I'd prefer you.*

'I don't know,' she said. 'It feels like I'm stuck in the middle of the motorway with traffic racing in both directions on either side of me, and I can't move. Because once I turn one way, I might have to turn back, and then it'll be even worse.'

'Running against the traffic?'

'I don't feel anything,' she said.

'For the fathers?'

'For the baby.' She spoke so quietly that he might not have heard her, almost hoped that was the case. There was her shame, rustling like mice under cupboards and doorways. What did it matter who the dad was when the poor child had a mother who couldn't manage the most basic of things? She was supposed to love them to the moon and back, never any less. 'I wanted to have this baby, and I still do, but it's like I can't access my feelings – if they're even there.'

'They'll come, believe me.'

'And if they don't?'

'With a newborn the way you feel is less important than what you *do*. Just make sure they're safe and fed, and that'll go a long way.'

Eira lingered in the sense of calm for a while, in the rhythm of his heart. Then her phone started ringing again, howling like a siren. Her cheek wanted to stay on his chest, but she lifted her head to pick it up. As she did so, all the other sounds came back to her: the hum of wood splitters and lawnmowers outside, people's reluctance to be idle.

There was a woman's voice on the other end of the line.

'Sorry, who is this? I didn't catch your name.'

'Jenna Taubert. We met this afternoon.'

This afternoon?

'At the old people's home. I work for the prison service in Umeå.'

Eira wrapped a blanket around her half-naked upper body and got to her feet. Of course, the prison officer outside Kerstin's room.

The baby started boxing furiously.

'What's going on?' she asked.

'It's Magnus.'

'Yes, I got that, but what exactly has happened?'

'He's gone.'

'What?' Eira had to leave the living room, had to be alone before she could process the woman's words.

'It was only for a minute,' the prison officer continued. 'He just wanted to say hello to an old friend before we headed back to Umeå.'

And you couldn't say no to him, thought Eira, drinking half a glass of water. She'd had a hunch of something by the door to her mother's room, from the slightly overfamiliar tone of the officer's greeting that didn't quite sit right, the simmering danger in the way she said Magnus's name.

'I dropped him off so he could go in, at a house in a small hamlet, with loads of old cars in the garden . . .'

'I know the one you mean.'

'Magnus went inside and I waited in the car. We had almost two hours to spare, so we would have been able to make it back no trouble.'

Around half an hour later, she had started to suspect that something might be wrong.

She got out of the car and went over to the house, knocked on the door. His friend had answered.

'And you didn't check to see whether Rickard Strindlund had a record before you took him there?' Without thinking, Eira found herself touching her bump. Petty theft, assault. Nothing too serious, but still.

'It didn't feel great when I saw the junk cars, but by then I'd already agreed. I know, it was stupid, but it was only supposed to be for a few minutes.'

Ricken had said that Magnus was in the toilet, and the woman had waited another ten minutes. The prison system was in crisis, and while the politicians liked to shout about longer, stricter sentences, it wasn't easy to find sensible, intelligent people to work ten-hour shifts for a low wage. Clearly they had to hire anyone they could get.

When Jenna Taubert eventually realised that her client wasn't in the bathroom, she had searched the house and run around the garden shouting for him, but he was nowhere to be found.

'It's not like he has a phone I can ring. He wouldn't pick up even if he did.'

'And I take it his friend had no idea where he might be?' said Eira, feeling an icy sensation settle over her. That idiot, she would give him hell.

'I don't know what to do,' the woman continued, possibly in tears. 'I'm supposed to call this in right away, but there'll be consequences if I do that. I don't want Magnus to jeopardise his privileges. He might even be risking being granted parole next year. That's why I called you.'

Because you love him, thought Eira. Because, deep down,

you're hoping you'll be able to keep seeing him once he's a free man, grateful for everything you've done for him. From the corner of her eye, she saw that GG had sat up and buttoned his shirt. Who was she to have any opinions on love?

'Where are you?' she asked.

'In the car outside an old school a few hundred metres from the house. There's a blue container full of scrap metal here. I've looked everywhere, but I can't find him.'

'I'll call you back,' said Eira.

The hardest part was convincing GG to let her go. A single kiss – several, really, telling her dizzying things about how he felt – had transformed him into her knight and protector.

'I'll drive you,' he said.

'It's OK,' Eira replied as she struggled to put on her shoes. Not the easiest of jobs when she couldn't find the damn shoehorn. 'It's my brother, not a callout or anything. Believe me, there are no violent thugs waiting out there.'

'But you don't know where he is. It could take all night,' said GG. 'And it's not like I've got anything better to do.'

Eira grappled with her shoe and her longing to give in to him, to let him take care of her.

'You don't know my brother. If I find him and he sees that I've got a cop with me, that'll be it. Magnus will never listen to me then.'

She pushed her feet into her boots instead, grabbing the keys and a jacket, unable to handle any more concern. His body was so big and powerful, and it was in her way, making her want to crawl into his arms and never be alone again.

'I can't let him ruin his life for a second time.'

He remembered the sunlight filtering through the blinds, growing weaker as evening approached. The man who called himself Johansson hadn't bothered turning on any lights, and there was a certain dimness to the room, a soft glow from the streetlamp outside, though maybe that was just the haziness of memory talking.

Allan hadn't seen a weapon, had he? Would he really have tagged along if he had, when the man said it was time?

He had needed to use the toilet then, he remembered that much. Spent a while in there as his stomach cramped and his bowels emptied.

'Where are we going?' he must have asked.

He didn't remember the response, just the September gloom as they left the streetlights behind and made their way in among the trees, dark as the grave.

No stars, no moonlight.

A torch in Johansson's hand.

No, wait, it must have been Allan who took the lead, because the stranger didn't know where the hell Svedberg's old barn was.

It was no secret that that was where the deserters were staying.

The barn had been empty since the last of the cows went

to slaughter and the property was sold off to a rich farmer who wanted the land.

There wasn't another soul in sight when they arrived, the taste of vodka as rough as sandpaper in his mouth. Allan probably wasn't quite sober, but nor was he drunk. They had crept inside and crouched down in an old pen, and Allan had whispered a question about what they were going to do when the Americans showed up, but the other man didn't answer.

He remembered the wood creaking as the door opened. A torch came on at the other side of the barn, and they heard the strike of a match. That was how quiet it was, even though Allan's heart was pounding. His throat was full of phlegm, and he tried hard not to cough.

The lamp flickered to life over in the corner, casting its light across a sleeping bag and a small table. It was the one with the dark hair, and he was alone.

'Don't move!'

The man who called himself Johansson had straightened up and stepped out of the pen, and the American had wheeled around and held up a hand, blinded by the torch beam.

'Who are you? What do you want?'

Simple words that Allan understood, despite his limited English. He could sense the American's fear, too. As Johansson moved forward, he spotted the gun in his hand.

Everything became a silhouette in the glow of the lamp.

He didn't understand what was said after that. The American's voice grew shrill, the other's harder, and Johansson eventually switched to Swedish and shouted for Allan to follow him.

'Come on, take the torch.'

Had he backed up against the wall of the pen? Questioned whether it was right, this thing that was about to happen? Did he think about Maarit and the baby?

Allan wasn't sure. All he remembered was feeling like a power line was surging through him as he led them into the woods, a red-hot anger towards all those who had ruined his life.

E ira took the Gålå bends at a dangerous speed, stepping on the accelerator on the straight stretches. The map was a part of her, the roads etched into her body. She knew the tree-clad hills and the low-lying meadows like the back of her hand.

Without slowing down at the junction in Strinne, she turned off. She cast a quick glance to the left as she passed the old school, saw a lone car parked outside, then continued down towards the bay.

The gravel clattered against the underside of the car as she drove along Ricken's driveway, slamming on the brakes as she reached the porch and blasting the horn.

'Seriously, I'm sorry, I didn't know he was planning to run off.'

Ricken clearly hadn't been expecting any more visitors that evening, or had he? Was the whole drowsy, underpants-wearing act just all a charade, a way of saying: *see how innocent I am?*

'You know damn well that he's risking having to serve the rest of his sentence for this,' said Eira. 'Another four years. But if he goes back tonight, he might be OK.'

'I really don't know where he is.' Ricken shrugged and held out his hands, the familiar nonchalance she had once fallen head over heels in love with.

Her anger came from somewhere in the distant past.

'Just stop, just fucking stop,' Eira screamed right in his face, flecks of saliva flying. He took a step back.

'Whoa.'

'Either you tell me where Magnus is or you can forget about having anything to do with this kid. I hope to God it isn't yours.'

'Jesus, calm down,' said Ricken. 'I'm telling you I don't know. I'm not lying, Eira. I'd never do that.'

'Bullshit. You're protecting Magnus, just like you always have. You didn't even dare be with me because you were so scared of him.'

'What are you talking about?'

Ricken tried to squeeze her shoulder, but Eira shook him off. She wrapped her arms around her belly, hoping the adrenaline and rage pumping through her hadn't reached the baby. They can hear and feel everything in there, so take it easy and sing some pretty songs, play a bit of Mozart for the little one.

'What did you do? Did you give him a car, a boat, your quad bike? Where was he going?'

'That's not why I broke up with you,' Ricken said quietly, as though that was important, as though it had anything to do with what was happening now. 'You were so much better than me. You deserved someone else, someone good. I couldn't let you get stuck with a guy like me.'

Eira was taken aback. The core of everything she thought she knew about love was bound up in this. The risk of being rejected, of never coming first; that was how the world worked.

'What do you mean,' she managed to stutter, 'with someone like you?'

'I let him take the boat,' said Ricken.

'Idiot. Why the hell did you do that?'

Eira marched around the corner of the house, between a couple of old rust buckets. To the rear of the property, the grass sloped down towards Strinnefjärden. There was a jetty there. She heard soft footsteps, right behind her.

'Which boat?' she asked.

'*Gerda.*'

'Does it have a motor, oars, a sail? I don't know what your fucking boats are called.'

'I've only got one, my grandpa's old rowing boat. I don't like motors out on the river, you know that.'

'I don't know everything about you.'

She gazed out across the narrow bay. The sky had painted everything a drab shade of blue, the colour of melancholy, giving her a sense that it was too late. Even if Magnus was rowing, he could have made it some distance by now, particularly if he went with the current, down towards the sea. He might have crossed over to Kramfors, hitched a ride there, caught the train.

'He wasn't planning to run,' said Ricken. 'He just wanted some time to himself.'

The thought came to Eira as she was looking out at the water. It wasn't far in a boat, straight across to the other shore. Could that be what he was thinking?

It was much further by car. She first had to drive back down to the main road and then make her way around the bay, turning off towards Lockne along the gravel track. Sleepy farms, their barns greying and tired, memories of an agricultural past; an old school, a sawmill. Forest that grew increasingly dense as she approached the tip of the cape. Back when the river was still a busy, working waterway, the sawmill had been centrally located, but these days few people would know where to find the remains. It wasn't possible to drive right up to it, so she parked the car by a grand little house one of the forestry magnates had built himself at some point in time. There was garden furniture outside, but she couldn't see any cars, no guests for the summer. Someone had made the effort to keep the trail down to the river clear, in any case, so she continued on foot. Her phone began buzzing in her pocket as she walked, the prison officer again, but Eira ignored it. She had already replied twice, brief messages. *Just stay where you are, I'll call soon.*

The blackflies were always worst in July, fat and persistent, huge swarms of them. Eira tried to swat them away at first, but she quickly realised it was futile; let them feast. The ground around her feet was blue with forget-me-nots. After a few minutes she spotted the old forge and boiler house between the trees, the remains of the tiled roof, the place where everything started.

Three years ago, the place had been crawling with crime scene investigators after a body was found in the clay beneath the old jetty. A murder to which her brother had subsequently confessed, the reason he was currently serving a prison sentence.

She instinctively slowed down, moving as quietly as she

could. Despite that, twigs broke and the ground squelched underfoot. Who the hell could tiptoe with a freeloader in their belly, with the extra thirteen kilos she had put on?

She called his name once she was close.

'Magnus? It's me, it's Eira. I'm alone.'

No response. No sound other than the midges and the birds in the trees. Once nature started to take over, the war was lost. The decay had really accelerated over the past few years. By the entrance to the old forge, there was a gaping hole. The door was hanging at an angle, and roofing tiles had fallen to the ground all around it. Eira had heard the building would be torn down sometime soon, possibly next year, when they began work to decontaminate the ground.

She spotted him through the doorway. The evening sun was shining in through the broken wall, filling the space with golden light. He was leaning against the old furnace, beneath the roof that might come crashing down at any moment.

'Magnus, it's just me.'

'I see that.'

'Can't you come out? It's dangerous in there.'

'Don't come in, then.'

Eira peered around the overgrown landscape. Scrub and hops had taken over, blurring the boundary between manmade structure and nature. She sat down on a small pile of old bricks someone had stacked up outside, presumably with the intention of coming back for them later.

To build themselves a barbecue, for example.

'How'd you know I was here?' asked Magnus.

'I didn't.'

Eira could no longer see him, but she could hear the noise he was making, the echo of his movements in the empty room. Remembered every inch of the place from when she and her colleagues had scoured it as a crime scene. She had followed her brother's thinking just like he had with Lina that evening so long ago. Lina, who had also arrived in a rowing boat.

A trickle of water between then and now.

'It was solid back then, the roof and the walls,' said Magnus. 'We used to hang out here, smoking and drinking beer, fucking, camping for the night. We actually fantasised about moving in. No one cared about this place, it was just here.'

Eira watched as three mosquitoes sucked blood from the back of her hand. It was better to let them finish, she knew. She remembered the scraps of a sleeping bag they had found, condoms covered in her brother's DNA.

'Why did you run away?' she asked. 'Why did you come out here?'

Magnus appeared in the doorway, leaning against the unsteady outer wall. Eira looked up at the roof above him, at the angular holes.

'Mum didn't recognise me when I got there today,' he said. 'It took her a few minutes. What's the point in anything if it's all just going to be forgotten?'

'So why didn't you just keep rowing? You could have been halfway to Härnösand by now. They might never have found you.'

'Like Lina.'

'You're the one who chose to take the blame.' Eira

slapped the back of her hand, despite everything. 'Can't you ever just face up to the fucking consequences of your actions? No, you have to flirt with your prison officer, go on a rowing trip down memory lane while the alarm starts ringing up in Umeå. What do you think will happen to Jenna now? She'll be transferred, you'll ruin her career. Great job, Magnus. Congrats.'

Three squashed mosquitoes.

Blood smeared across her skin.

'Sorry,' he mumbled.

'For which part?'

'Mum. For leaving you alone to deal with that.'

Eira tried to get up, but the stack of bricks was too low. Her hand slipped, and she came close to falling flat on her face, down in the grass and the mud and the poisoned earth, just like the memories, like everything they had to say to each other.

She would have to leave if she didn't want to start crying.

'Stay here and wallow if you want to,' she said, 'but help me get up, for God's sake.'

He moved towards her at last, away from the perilous building, holding out an arm. Muscular, he must have been working out in prison.

Eira wiped the mud and dioxins from her hands and started walking. There was just too much she wanted to say, no end to it.

'Wait,' said Magnus.

He hadn't had a clear plan as they drove out of Kramfors. It was more a sense of not being ready. Magnus just couldn't stop thinking about the emptiness he had seen in his mother's eyes during the first few minutes of his visit. Her joy once she realised who he was, the photographs they had looked at together, the story Eira had told him, about love affairs and deserters from the Vietnam war. It was dizzying stuff, but none of it could compare to that emptiness.

If we vanish from each other's consciousness, do we even exist?

Panic had gripped him. He couldn't be locked up again, not yet. He needed to talk to someone else who really understood who he was.

And no, he wouldn't have minded having a bit of fun with the pretty prison officer; things had been going well between them on the drive down. Christ, he'd been locked up for almost two and a half years, and she had a certain way of moving. Self-confident.

She probably had an Instagram account where she uploaded pictures of herself. Magnus couldn't check, of course, but he could easily imagine the hot screw wearing far less.

He had convinced her to take the long route via Träsk, and as they approached Bjärtrå he got her to turn the wrong way. A brief pitstop, that was all, to say hello to an old buddy. As they pulled up outside Ricken's house, he had hesitantly touched her arm.

'You're one of the good ones, you know. Not like the others. You're not afraid to show your human side.'

For a few seconds, their faces had come a little too close. Magnus had resisted the urge to kiss her, suspected she got off on it precisely because it was taboo.

Surely he deserved a bit of credit for getting out of the car instead?

For getting out into the wind, which was carrying a chill down from the mountains even though it was a warm evening, just like back then, the light the same pale shade of blue as it had been when he was so damn young and everything fell apart.

He hadn't even had the energy to talk to Ricken, just marched straight down to the rowing boat. Old *Gerda*, they'd been out fishing in her thousands of times before. Ricken said it would be dumb to run now, but Magnus said he wasn't planning to run, he just wanted some time alone.

The feeling of pushing the boat out and climbing in, the creaking of the oars; it was the epitome of calm to him.

On the far side of the bay, bathed in the glow of the late sun, dragonflies danced through the air, darting away as his oars broke the surface of the water.

Magnus had tied the boat to one of the piles still protruding from the water where the jetty had once stood, and leapt ashore. It was the first time he had been back since that night years ago.

The steep shore was the same. He remembered struggling

in the clay, with the body in the water. The guy's clothes kept floating back up and he'd had to drag more of the wood on top of him.

What about Lina?

She couldn't touch a dead body, she had said.

What the hell did you have to come over here for, she had asked.

You're the one who'll go down for this. Who do you think they're going to believe, you or me?

She had hurled the metal pole out into the river, and Magnus had watched the water close in on it. No one would ever know, she said.

Magnus had then kept walking, up the trail to the old forge. So much time had passed, but the past felt so present. Time was just a way of organising the world in a way people could understand.

'It's not too late,' Eira had said when she found him, his irritating little sister who could never just leave people be.

A plan had eventually taken shape as he sat alone in there, on the edge of the big furnace. The images of Lina had begun to change. What he had seen back then wasn't the truth; it was his own warped version of it. She was there to fuck the guy because she *wanted* to, not because he had forced her. Lina had left Magnus long before that. He had seen someone he loved, but that wasn't who she was, and then a person had died and everything had turned to nothing. The wall in front of him was proof of that. Of life's transience. All people are like grass, as they sing in church.

And now she had killed again. The sentence he was

serving, which he had given himself, was worthless. Guilt dragged him back to the past, and there was no way out.

Magnus had seen the widening cracks in the roof above him, the tiles hanging loose, and he had reached for a couple of the heavy iron poles still littering the floor, weighed them in his hands. Could he climb on top of the furnace to hit and pry at the roof, or would he have to throw one of the poles up there? How much force would it take?

Would they find him under the rubble?

Then he had heard her voice. He wasn't sure if it was all in his mind or whether it had reached him from the distant reality outside, at the end of the road.

'Magnus, it's just me.'

M agnus insisted on touching her bump once they were in the car. Said he wasn't going anywhere with her otherwise.

The baby was calm, not a ripple on the surface.

'Call me Uncle,' he whispered to Eira's belly. 'And make sure you don't turn out like me.'

She had told him that Ricken might be the father, and Magnus was less surprised than she had expected. Perhaps he had known all along.

'I'll kill him if he doesn't pull his weight,' he said. 'Staying home when the kid's sick, that sort of thing.'

'I'm not moving to Strinne, if that's what you're thinking.'

Her brother's palm felt warm through her shirt. The moment would be over the minute she started the engine. Magnus had let her call the prison officer, spoken to her himself. They had arranged to meet by the crossroads in ten minutes, and it was high time they got going.

'You're not going to try this again, are you?' Eira asked, her hand on the ignition.

'What?'

'Running off. Thinking about killing yourself. I can't drive all the way up to Umeå and start looking for you there.'

He shook his head, not especially convincingly. Eira thought about his sons in Gothenburg, about the fact that Lina had killed again, that Magnus had let her get away with it the first time. She didn't know where to start, just wanted to sit quietly. To watch the night come and go.

'I've been thinking about Mum,' Magnus began. 'What you said about the deserter, about her being so in love. Why didn't she ever say anything? I can understand keeping it from Dad, but why not tell us, once we were older?'

'Maybe it was too painful. I guess people don't tell their kids everything.'

'I used to hear them arguing a lot.' Magnus didn't show any sign of being in a hurry, of course not. A few more minutes, that was all he had.

'I don't remember much of that.'

'Maybe they'd stopped by the time you were old enough to notice. I think she gave up trying to change him. I heard her screaming that she'd never loved him once. He was accusing her of something. Not enough sex, I think. Said she never wanted it, that she was frigid. I crept downstairs and looked up the word once they were asleep.'

'She wasn't,' said Eira. 'We know she used to sneak out to have an affair.'

'She probably stayed with him for the sense of security,' said Magnus. 'Some people will do anything for that.'

Eira gazed out at the rocks and the moss, the scrubby forest on the hillside. Their parents hadn't divorced until Eira was thirteen, Magnus in his twenties. If she remembered anything from before then, it was a strange muteness between them. Perhaps she had thought that was how it was meant to be. People who circled one another without ever pausing or meeting. Irritation as a constant low hum, like the droning of a refrigerator.

Images flickered by, of herself at Ricken's inherited place in Strinne, a baby in her arms. In an anonymous Stockholm apartment, waiting for August to come back from a night with Johanna.

She knew she should start the car; ten minutes had already passed.

'How did he stand it?' she asked, thinking about her father, about his calmness, his squareness. 'How can a person spend half a lifetime with someone who doesn't even love them?'

'You and I didn't turn out so great at love either,' said Magnus.

After a layover in Amsterdam, Frank Aiello caught a direct flight to Gothenburg. With a stiff back and a dull ache behind his eyes, he then made his way across the city on the various tram lines.

Järntorget.

There was an app on his new phone that provided instant translations when he held the camera up to the text.

The Iron Square.

It was his first time on this side of the Atlantic. He'd once had dreams of visiting Paris and Rome, maybe even Egypt, but it was as though he was missing a vital cog, the link between dreams and action. Maybe it was down to a fear of the unknown, though ironically it was the people around him who had caused him the most distress. His family, the way they had driven him away, left him unable to be himself around them.

A kind Swede helped him download the right app to buy a ticket for the tram, and it turned out they were heading in the same direction. Frank was amazed at his luck in bumping into someone who both spoke excellent English and was getting off at the same stop. During their brief tram ride together, the man told him that he was a psychologist, that he was currently on leave to finish writing his novel. The conversation turned to John and the fact that he wasn't who Frank had thought he was, which had led Frank to ask questions about himself. Were we really the people we thought we were, or was there another being inside each of us, the person we were supposed to be?

The man walked with him once they got off the tram, said he lived on the corner of Andra Långgatan and knew all the shops selling old records there.

'Good luck with everything,' he said as they parted ways.

The heat felt oppressive, as though it was building to a storm, yet there were almost no clouds in the sky. Frank had read that it often rained in Gothenburg – the high terrain meant that weather fronts from the British Isles were forced upwards, cooling rapidly to form rain clouds – but here he was sweating in his blazer; he hadn't expected such high temperatures in a country at the same latitude as Alaska. The stuffy air followed him into the shop, and he found it difficult to breathe when he spotted the owner hunched over a record, studying the scratches and dust.

The man was in his seventies, grey hair tied back in a ponytail.

'Steve Larsson?'

'Are you American?' the man asked, instinctively responding in English.

Frank said his name and who his brother had been, causing the old deserter to slump down onto a chair. It had wheels and very nearly rolled out beneath him, and he had to grab the counter to avoid falling flat.

'Oh, God. I'm sorry. I'm so sorry.'

Steve Larsson stuttered slightly as he apologised, explaining that he had just found out himself, that he would have made contact with the family otherwise, if he had suspected anything back then.

Frank didn't believe half of what he said. There was too much nervousness and guilt on his face, his smile too superficial.

'Is there somewhere we can sit down?'

The air conditioning was broken, but maybe they could go outside? Steve Larsson locked the door but forgot to turn the closed sign. He had a long stride, almost as though he was trying to get away, and he kept chatting incoherently. About a barracks in Stockholm and a collective where they were supposed to be growing turnips, saying that despite everything they had been through it was as though he had never really gotten to know John.

'He withdrew into his shell, if you get what I mean. He was the kind of guy who kept himself to himself, not one to start shouting on the street. To be really honest with you, I wonder whether he had any political convictions at all. He spent more time talking about what he wanted to be, about his dreams and stuff like that.'

'What did he want to be?' Frank asked when they reached the end of the street. For some reason, the simplest words were the hardest to get out; it was far easier to talk about the war and the protests.

'He used to talk about art, about painting and that kind of thing. Poetry. Always said it wasn't something a man did where he came from. I understood that. I mean, I grew up in South Philly.'

Frank's response was drowned out by the noise of a refuse truck driving by. In a family where boys became factory workers and engineers, he had been ashamed when he showed off his essays, never talked about the authors he'd read.

'Did he tell you anything else about his family?'

'He said they were very religious, patriots.'

'And what about John? Did he have faith?'

It was an important question, one that would shape how his brother would be buried.

'I didn't get the sense he was especially religious, no,' said Steve. 'We were rebelling against pretty much everything, but what did we know – we were only twenty. I don't think we ever talked about it much. No, that's not right. We said that if there was a god then he was *everyone's* god, even the Vietnamese.'

They sat down in a café by the square. The best coffee in town, according to Steve. Frank had too many questions. Did John have time to fall for anyone? Did he ever experience love? Had he been happy during the brief period he felt like he was free? If only there were answers to them all, if only those answers would have helped.

In the seating area outside the café, young people were crammed onto crates with cushions, but there was almost no one else inside. The two men were sitting at a bar counter by the window, and Frank watched as the city flowed by outside, on a wave of sweat and summer joy, shorts and thin dresses. Thank god for air conditioning, he thought.

From his brief career as a journalist, he knew that there were some questions it was best to deploy without warning. A person's reaction could often reveal far more than their words.

'How did you know my brother was reporting to the CIA?'

Steve flinched, spilling coffee onto his tatty jeans. Frank handed him a paper napkin, and the older man crumpled it in his hand.

'Who have you talked to about this?' He seemed to have forgotten what the napkin was for, and the coffee began dripping from the edge of the table. 'I don't know what you think, but I didn't have anything to do with John's death.'

'I'm not saying you did,' Frank replied calmly.

'What was I meant to do? A couple of men turned up for him, took him out into the woods, and I heard a shot. Should I have run after them? Who do you think I was? I'd fled halfway across the world to get away from that crap. I didn't want to die.'

Frank studied him quietly for a moment, saw the man's foot bouncing against the base of his chair, the napkin in his clenched fist. Steve reminded him of his students when they hadn't done their homework but refused to admit it.

With Richard Evans's help, he had spent a week delving into the dark world of covert 1960s espionage, the sort of thing the CIA had relegated to the basement because it went against all of the organisation's own rules.

Infiltrating the anti-war movement, not to mention the Black Power movement, anywhere that might be harbouring pro-communist sentiment and therefore pose a threat to the nation's security. Of course they had also targeted deserters abroad. There were strong suspicions that a number of them were under the influence of the Soviet Union, sending military secrets east.

A journalist from the *New York Times* had uncovered the operation in December 1974. It had already been shut down by that point, all documentation destroyed – itself known as Operation Destruction – but there was no doubt that the organisation's tentacles had stretched all the way to neutral Sweden. According to anonymous sources, the CIA had access to knowledge that could only have come from the deserters' own ranks.

'When did you realise that John wasn't who you thought he was?' Frank asked, rephrasing his question.

'It wasn't something that happened suddenly,' Steve said with a frown, making a real effort to think back. 'It was more that I noticed things here and there. Acting strangely, withdrawing. Disappearing in the evenings. I don't know what he was up to. He claimed he just went on walks, but . . . man, who goes walking in the forest? There were bears there, that's all I'll say. He was your brother, so don't take this the wrong way, but John used to stare at people sometimes. It gave me the creeps. I started to get suspicious right after we left the collective. Before then, I'd always thought agents were people in dark cars, that a friend was a friend and an enemy an enemy, you know what I mean? I didn't think they could be one and the same, but then I realised they could've been right there all along, one of the people closest to you. That's the smart way to do it, no?'

Frank felt a powerful urge to grab Steve by the scruff of his neck, more powerful than he had ever had before. To shake the skinny, slightly hunched man who was frantically stirring his coffee, destroying the artful design in the foam.

'So you didn't know,' he said after a moment. 'It was just something you *felt*?'

'The only thing you can trust,' Steve replied, tapping his chest, 'is what's in here. My gut got me out of Vietnam and it brought me here. I'm still alive, aren't I? I didn't go home and atone for my sins like some of the others. I've always stood up for what I did, because in that moment, when I got onto the fishing boat on the outskirts of Tokyo in the middle of the night, I was being true to myself.'

Frank's hand was clammy as he clenched it in his pocket. He was a high-school teacher from a poor area of Los Angeles. It wasn't about being right about proving a theory; this was the kind of thing he liked to discuss with his students. There was no such thing as the absolute truth.

'They said the Army would make us into men,' Steve continued. 'And they called us cowards when we ran. We were seen as traitors *and* heroes. Everyone wanted a piece of us here, because a real man stands up for what's right – no matter what. Do you understand what I mean? We were both the scum of the earth and its saviours. Jeez, man. I was only twenty, like I said.'

'Who did you tell?' asked Frank.

'That John was working for the CIA? No one. People would've thought I was crazy, or they would have sent more agents after me. It wasn't the kind of thing you could talk about, surely you can see that?'

'But it must have been hard,' said Frank. 'Keeping something as big as that to yourself, I mean. Like you say, you were just a kid.'

Not much older than my students, he thought. Just twenty years of age. Who had he been then? A confused young man on the run from his family, alcohol and weed and rough mornings between filthy sheets as damnation caught up with him.

'I got lucky, I met a girl up there,' said Steve, wiping the sweat from his neck with the napkin. 'But I didn't breathe a word to anyone else.'

She managed to find an old Ford she could hotwire in the end, just north of Timrå. It had been a long time since Lina last did anything like that, but her hands remembered what to do. She felt a sense of triumph as the engine roared to life. The boys in Kramfors had taught her a thing or two after all.

Magnus had always been quicker than the rest, but he rarely stole them for long. He couldn't exactly go cruising around Kramfors in a car everyone recognised, not when they all knew his parents. He just took them for a quick spin, wiped his prints and then dumped them somewhere. They had forced open the gate to the old sawmill area in Marieberg once, driven right out onto the concrete quay, put the car into neutral and pushed it over the edge. *Something* had to happen, Lina had made him realise that. 'Otherwise you'll turn into your old man,' she'd told him. 'Watch out – the trap will snap shut; it won't be long.'

She remembered the waves, the bubbles, the vortex as the car vanished. Next time, she had said, she wanted to be inside when it hit the water. Accelerate off the edge of the quay, fly through the air and then escape. You just had to wait until it had sunk to get out, or so she'd heard.

You're crazy, he told her. The river's thirty metres deep.

Then Kenny had turned up and she had given Magnus

the boot; she was bored of him. A wimp, in many ways. Kenny was the kind of guy who would drive her straight over the edge if she asked him to, she could see it in his eyes, in the way he fucked her: he had no limits.

But then he died.

He actually went and died.

The High Coast's steep hillsides rose up in front of her now, and there was the river, or was it the sea? Who cared where one ended and the other began. A whole fucking load of water either way, exactly how she remembered it. Lina drove out onto a bridge where the pillars looked like huge erect dicks straining up into the sky. That hadn't been here back then.

It was late July, the sky still bright. She had almost forgotten about the midnight sun, the way it made sleeping impossible. There were no other cars on the bridge, so she stopped in the middle of the carriageway and got out. To the north, she could see the river twisting away like a shimmering snake among the dark trees.

So, she thought. This was where she had supposedly died. Where she sank thirty metres to the bottom or drifted out to sea, tumbling around in the current.

She had read all the newspapers she could get her hands on back then, following the events around her own disappearance and suspected death. All the people crying over what a great friend and student and daughter Lina Stavred had been, those hypocrites.

A car horn sounded, and she pressed back against the railing. She felt a rush of danger, of being alive.

E ira spotted him walking along the edge of the road and immediately knew who he was. Frank Aiello.

A blazer and smart shoes weren't exactly common summer attire in Lunde. This was a man with something other than digging in the garden or doing a bit of DIY on his mind, the sort of thing that kept life going and the worst worries at bay.

He must have got off the bus that stopped up on the main road, a kilometre away.

The American wiped the sweat from his brow and kept squinting down at the map on his phone, despite the fact that the road led straight to Wästerlund's Café.

Just to be on the safe side, Eira had described the striking neon sign on the roof and its position just before the Sandö Bridge, plus the fact that she was a few weeks off giving birth. She had grown used to her new body, or it to her, and no longer felt any aches and pains. Nothing but a slight weariness in her pelvis and mind.

Frank Aiello gave her a warm smile and a long handshake as they said their hellos. His gratitude left Eira feeling slightly ashamed. She should have been able to do more.

'So is this where it happened?'

They gazed out at the river, the sun glittering on the water. There were a couple of tourists in colourful wetsuits on paddleboards, white sails approaching from the High Coast. Eira pointed out various locations. That's where we recovered your brother's body, that's where we brought him ashore, over there in the forest is where we think he died.

'I know the police don't usually share thoughts and theories,' the American said after a long pause, 'but do you have any idea who could have done it?'

'Shall we sit down?'

They found a table inside, away from the bright sunshine. The décor was the same as it had always been: green and brown, drably egalitarian.

The selection on offer was broadly in line with that, though the latest owners had also added a number of Thai dishes to the menu. Frank Aiello spent a long time deliberating between a punsch roll and a Parisian waffle cookie, but that seemed to be where he finally ran out of steam. The summer temp behind the counter tried to remember the English for arrack and marzipan, and in the end he settled on a cinnamon bun.

'You should know that we don't have much evidence,' Eira began. 'I've tried to trace your brother's movements and talked to the people who knew him, piecing together everything we've got – the anchor, the shot that likely killed him. A picture has begun to emerge from that, but I can't guarantee it's one hundred per cent true.'

'However little you know, it's still more truth than I've ever had before.' Frank brushed the sugar from his fingers. The heat had made everything sticky.

'I think it could have started with the rumours about the CIA,' said Eira. 'The idea that your brother might have been a double agent. Political tensions were running so high back then, during the Cold War. The answers might be out there somewhere, but I don't know whether I'm the right person to find them. I'm not someone who likes to speculate and come up with elaborate theories; I prefer to work with facts, to put the pieces together.'

'Go on.'

Eira described the sequence of events as it logically might have unfolded, telling him all about the boat being rowed out onto the dark water, how easily the killers could have disappeared or returned to their normal lives. She explained that there were likely at least two of them, given the body and the anchor; it was too much for one person to manage. That at least one of them must have been familiar with Lunde, too. With the shipyard, the river and its depths.

'If there was any evidence, it probably washed away a long time ago. The only hope would be for someone to step forward – assuming anyone involved is still alive.'

Frank Aiello didn't speak, his gaze fixed somewhere on the other side of the window. A tourist bus pulled up outside, blocking their view, the passengers' cameras pointing at the bridge, the café, the neon sign on the roof. At the next table, a couple of Germans were chatting. They had read about how the café popped up without planning permission one night, hidden inside a barn because Wästerlund hadn't managed to get the right permits in time for the opening of the bridge. It was just one story among many, all reinforcing the idea that people weren't so fussy about obeying the law around here, rebellious Lunde. It seemed to Eira that tourism was largely about being duped. Everything these people travelled around to see had already passed – protests and neon signs, monuments and vinyl armchairs – while the present carried on in the background.

'I asked around a little,' said Frank Aiello. 'I hope you don't mind.'

'What about?'

'Operation Chaos.'

Eira waited as Frank Aiello pushed his half-eaten bun away and wiped his mouth.

'They called it The Vault,' he continued. 'The basement at Langley where they secretly gathered this kind of information.'

'The CIA, you mean?'

He nodded.

'The president at the time, Lyndon B. Johnson, was convinced the deserters were being controlled by Moscow, but despite all their surveillance they didn't find a shred of evidence proving Soviet involvement.'

'What about your brother?' said Eira. 'Did you find out anything about him?'

'Not as such. John could have been an infiltrator, willingly or not. Or maybe he wasn't. They destroyed all documents that might have proved anything either way.'

'I'm sorry.' How many times had she said that now? They weren't just empty words, something you were supposed to say; she really was sorry. If it hadn't been for her bump getting in the way she might have reached out and taken Frank Aiello's hand. He looked like he needed it.

'John's old deserter buddy seems pretty convinced, at

least,' he continued, telling her about his meeting with Steve in Gothenburg. 'But when I pressed him on that, he couldn't say how he knew. No one ever told him, and he didn't see John hand anything over. You know, the sort of thing you might expect someone to do if they were on the CIA payroll.'

'What do you make of that?'

'Steve escaped from the war; he was traumatised. And we know that the CIA *was* keeping an eye on them. It wouldn't be so strange for someone like that to start seeing things that weren't really there. One of Operation Chaos's strategies was to infiltrate, confuse, divide and disrupt, so there could well have been people who caused all sorts of trouble for that very reason.'

'You don't believe it, in other words?' Eira took a sip of water and leaned back in her chair, searching for John in his brother's face.

'I don't know,' he said. 'But if we're looking for a motive for killing my brother, whether it's true or not might not really matter. How many people act on what they only *believe* to be true?'

Frank Aiello paused and seemed to be studying her in a new way. A slight shift, as though he was now the police officer and Eira his witness, his tone different when he went on.

'I asked Steve who he might have told. No one, he said. No one but his girlfriend.'

'Kerstin? My mum?'

'I'm afraid so.'

It took a moment before Eira managed to say anything. Mumbling, as the baby pressed on her lungs and made it difficult to breathe, that it was too late to ask, that her mother didn't seem to remember anything from that time.

'But sometimes I wonder whether she does remember after all.'

'Could she have told anyone else?'

'No. No, I don't think so. Why would she have done that?' Eira realised how upset the question had left her – didn't it sound a little like an accusation? 'Mum never said a word about Steve or any of this. She knew how to keep quiet. Why would she have shared his secrets?'

'To help him? To get the suspect out of the way?'

'No,' Eira said again. 'No, there's no way.'

Allan Westin opened the door to let Rabble into the house next door. The dog could sense that something wasn't right, fussing and whining and prodding Allan with his nose, making him feel all warm inside.

'You'll be happy here,' he whispered. 'Eira will be home more once the little one arrives, she'll take care of you.'

Everything he had said was true, but his heart still ached as he turned and headed home. Locked the door from the inside, something he rarely did.

He did a loop of the kitchen and the sitting room, everything that had been theirs. Would Maarit even want any of this once he was gone? Would the kids? What was there to save? To come back to. Would anyone really show the grandkids around, telling them about all the evil that had happened over the years? *This is where Eira Söderberg died in May 1931, and that's the old toll house where Erik Bergström bled out on the sofa. The woman who lived there scraped up all the blood the next day and buried it at the spot where he'd fallen. Shot during a time of peace, you understand. A Swedish worker. Don't you forget his name. And you see over there? That's the Sandö Bridge, but beneath the surface, down in the depths, its dark shadow lives on. Eighteen people died when it collapsed.* And so on.

Death and bloodshed and grieving for generations to come.

No one would take his grandchildren and their children by the hand and lead them up into the woods behind Wästerlund's Café, at the very least. No one would point and say: *There! That's where your ancestor, Allan Westin, once stood and watched a man be shot.*

Without lifting a finger. Scared out of his wits, so bad that his pants were damp.

It had been dark that evening, so perhaps he saw less than he thought he had looking back, but he had definitely heard the young man make a break for it, heard the other man shout. Allan had understood every word of it even though it was in English – *Stop! Stay where you are!* – and he'd heard the shot that rang out, echoing between the trees, across the river, through the mountains and crevices and out to sea in the bitter Ådalen Valley of his youth.

The cry from further down the slope, right there in the woods.

Twenty, that was how old the American was, not that Allan had known it at the time. But he knew now. He'd seen it in the paper, printed right there in black and white, practically a child. He had also learned that there was a brother, Eira Sjödin had told him that, and that the brother had come to take the dead man home.

His remains, that was. The bones Allan had seen being lifted out of the river as the ground shook and swayed beneath him. It was like an earthquake, an explosion, the violence of the spring floods. He should have done this right there and then.

Gone home and grabbed anything flammable he could get his hands on, spread it out around the stove. Maybe it would look like an ember had escaped; these things happened sometimes. An accident. That way the insurance company might pay out however little the place was worth to those he left behind.

He had seen the American's brother earlier that day, walking to meet Eira Sjödin outside Wästerlund's Café.

His mind lingered on the words 'left behind' as he lit a fire in the stove. He would close the damper once it was burning nicely. An old man's forgetfulness or carelessness, that's what it would look like. Allan knew the carbon dioxide would knock him out – that and the vodka he'd taken the bus over to Kramfors to buy.

He swigged another few mouthfuls, bringing himself closer to the dizziness and fog as the flames licked at the logs.

Left behind was what he was too, ever since that day in 1968. Someone who kept living though the life had been sucked out of him, like his breath that night when he ran down to the shipyard to find something to sink the dead American.

The other man had stood guard by the body that they'd lugged down to the shore while Allan crept onboard the *Åbord* to take its anchor.

He remembered the sound of oar strokes, a torch beam glittering on the water. They had found the rowing boat dragged up on the beach, Allan didn't know whose it was. No one had kicked up a fuss about it over the days that followed, in any case; boats were often forgotten when people moved or died. He had hacked it to pieces afterwards, watched as the current carried it off towards the sea. The mountain brooks did their part from the other side, a never-ending flow over the depths downstream of Lunde's shipyard. Allan had wanted to row further, but he hadn't been the one in charge.

He remembered the weight that came close to tipping the boat as they pushed the body and the anchor overboard.

Like a fish breaking the surface and then diving again.

Rings that grew and then vanished. The silence afterwards.

Allan blew on the flames and added more wood, as much as the stove would hold, waiting until it was crackling away. He took another few swigs of vodka and nudged a burning log out onto the floor, saw the fire take hold of the clutter he had dumped there. He then turned his back on it all. Coughing and unsteady from the booze and the smoke, he slowly made his way up the stairs, bottle still in hand.

Eira woke with a jolt, claws scratching at her legs. Rabble was already on his way down the stairs as she sat up in bed, and when he reached the back door he started growling and barking.

'Oh, come on,' she muttered into the covers. 'What is it? A hare, a deer? Stop pretending you're a hunting dog.'

But Rabble's barking only grew more insistent, and he began leaping around like a creature possessed down there. Getting out of bed was a real effort – especially when there was no good reason for it, and in the middle of the night at that.

'Calm down, buddy,' Eira said as she made her way down the stairs. She stroked and patted him when she reached the door, but Rabble bared his teeth and pulled away. 'What is it? There's nothing there.'

That was when she smelled the smoke. Was that why he wanted out? His keen nose, a sense of danger? Eira did a loop of the kitchen, the living room. She hadn't used the stove or lit any candles, but she knew that phone chargers were a common cause of house fires, all electrical appliances were.

There was nothing to see, nothing but the smell.

Just to be on the safe side, she attached Rabble's lead before she opened the door, but he bolted out with such force that she lost her balance and had to let go to avoid falling. The dog shot off like a dark flash.

There was definitely a fire somewhere nearby.

Right as she saw the smoke billowing out of the house next door, Eira realised that her phone was still upstairs. Allan. Shit. Should she run over there or head back upstairs? Neither would be particularly fast. Calling the fire service had to come first, she decided, turning back inside. She climbed the stairs on all fours in order to get up there as quickly as she could, dialling 112 as she shuffled back down. Eira grabbed the fire blanket and the extinguisher from the wall in the hallway, forever grateful that she had insisted her mother buy all these things over the years.

'How quickly can you get an ambulance here?' she asked the operator. 'Do you have one in Kramfors?'

She remembered the hosepipe as she ran over the lawn and the smoke grew thicker, enveloping her. The tap was on this side of the house, but when had she last done any watering? Months ago. Where was the bucket?

At least the dog's howling would be loud enough to wake the rest of the neighbours, she thought. Darting back and forth by the front door. Lovely, ugly little dog. You knew he needed you, you understood.

The front door was locked, of course, and Eira cursed herself for not grabbing the key on her way out. She broke the window instead, reaching in and turning the bolt from the inside, crying out in pain as she burnt herself on the hot metal. She could have done with some damp rags to cover her mouth, she realised, and she tore the fire blanket out of its box and wrapped it around her nose and mouth instead, heading in, crouched low.

Calling his name.

She saw the raging fire in the kitchen at the end of the hallway. It seemed to be concentrated there, hadn't spread yet. Eira knew she shouldn't go upstairs, that the fire brigade would be here soon; there were full-time firefighters in Kramfors, just six miles away. They would be here any minute now and the police officer in her was screaming that she shouldn't go any further.

That voice got louder as she started climbing the stairs the same way she just had at home. There was an emergency fire ladder on the outside wall, she knew. She could use that. She had seen Allan use it once, after the gulls built a nest on the roof, perched perilously on the top rung with a broom in his hand.

The smoke was thick and poisonous, and Eira kept her breathing shallow, trying not to fill her lungs, to stop it from getting to the baby.

The door to his bedroom was wide open, and she quickly spotted his slippers on the floor by the bed. There he was, flat out on his back, fast asleep.

'Allan! Wake up! Wake up, for God's sake!' She shook him and shouted in his ear, but he didn't move. His hands were limp. Eira lowered her ear to his mouth and caught a whiff of alcohol. The old man was still alive. She opened the window and took a deep breath, tried to gauge the distance to the ladder, to the ground. She might be able to clamber over there, even in her current state, and if she fell it shouldn't be fatal. Not for her, anyway, but what about the baby? She had acted on instinct, without thinking, but what choice did she have?

Eira grabbed Allan's lifeless body and pulled him out of bed, finding a reserve of strength she didn't know she had. Then again, he had lost weight over the past few months, had never been a big man. She managed to drag him across the floor, but she quickly realised she would never be able to get him all the way down the stairs and out into the porch – assuming she even had time for that before the fire spread. The house was wooden, it could go up in a flash. Were those sirens she could hear, or was it just the damn birds?

There was no time to waste.

Two more metres to the window.

Legs first, that was better than his head. He might break a few bones, or worse. The garden outside was sloped, the bushes thick. Better odds than leaving him here, surely.

With a roar, she hauled him up and over the window frame.

There was a thud as he landed, but it sounded soft. In the currant bushes, the berries bright and red. It had rained earlier, which meant the ground had some give; he might be just fine after all.

Eira reached for the ladder and realised that she had probably been over-optimistic. Yes, she could reach it, but how the hell was she meant to actually get out to it? Her balance, the uneven distribution of weight. She had been taught how to fall properly, but while pregnant? How big a risk was it to land on her belly? She spent a few seconds weighing up her options, then wrapped the fire blanket around her face again, grabbed the extinguisher and made her way out into the thick smoke, descending the stairs backwards.

The fire had reached the hallway now, climbing up the walls and eating everything in its path. She sprayed an arc of foam in front of her and hauled herself out into the porch, stumbling among the shoes and the junk, but there it was at last. Fresh air.

She could hear the dog barking, and Eira crawled the last few metres outside and down from the porch, her legs numb. She needed to get onto her feet, away from the fire.

Around the corner of the house, towards the currant bushes.

Allan was awake, thank God. He was sitting up, calmly watching his house burn.

'Allan, you need to get back!' she hissed. The smoke had done something to her voice. She grabbed him by the arm. 'Are you hurt?'

The sirens were now howling in the distance.

'Have you broken anything? Can you walk?'

He coughed, a sound from deep inside him.

'I saw him die,' he croaked, avoiding her eye. 'He died right there in the woods, over by the Bethania Chapel. It was all my fault.'

'What are you talking about, Allan? Come on!' Eira yanked at his arm. She would drag him by force if she had to, though all her strength had drained away.

'The bloke you pulled out of the river, the American. I'm telling you, it was me.' Allan swung his arms, trying to pull away, accidentally hitting her in the chest. Not hard, but it hurt. 'Just leave me be.'

'I got you out, Allan. You'd be dead otherwise.'

'It would've been better that way.'

He clutched his hip, moaning, must have broken something after all.

'No, it wouldn't. Come on, you can lean on me.'

Allan made no effort to help as she pulled on his arm. The man was clearly in shock, just sitting there despite the fact that the heat was becoming unbearable. Parts of the house might start to collapse soon, and it dawned on Eira, as he started coughing so hard that he threw up, that he had started the fire himself. The thought came on suddenly. Hadn't he given up the booze? Why had he got so drunk? Was that why he had been so careless with the stove, or wasn't it carelessness at all? All this talk about the American, too. It was just too much to take in. Rabble was still darting around them, and she desperately needed to get them all away from the fire.

'Your old man would've been happy to get rid of the lot of us, let me tell you.'

'What does my dad have to do with anything, Allan? You're in shock. Can you get up?'

'I didn't understand at the time, but then I heard a thing or two.' He attempted to get up on his own, didn't want her help. 'Christ, if I'd known then . . . none of it would've happened.'

He was still blind drunk, of course, but nothing seemed broken. Eira had the alcohol to thank for that, for loosening up his joints.

Allan let her hold his arm in the end, and they limped over the grass together.

The heat eased off a little, but the smoke was still swirling around them.

The fire engines arrived at last, and a number of neighbours had gathered on the road. After what felt like an eternity, they managed to get the water flowing, and Eira felt the spray on her face as she guided Allan down onto the garden bench. She knew she should get him something to drink, but it was just too much effort, so she slumped down onto the seat beside him instead, breathing, breathing. The ambulance would be here any minute now.

'What do you mean you saw him die?' she stuttered. 'The American? Were you there when he was shot?'

Allan coughed and wiped his hand on his pyjama bottoms before he managed to speak, his spit black with soot. The press hadn't reported that John Aiello was killed in the woods, she was pretty sure of that. She hadn't mentioned it either.

The whole story came flooding out of him now, incoherent fragments about the hunt for communists and someone who had said the American was spying for the CIA, one thing leading to another and a stranger arriving from up north or wherever he was from, he was the one with the pistol. Hadn't meant to shoot him, just wanted to get the American to stop when he started running; it was so dark, a real stroke of bad luck. Who bloody knows. And as for the anchor, Allan had taken that from the *Åbord*, the tug in the shipyard, but none of it would have happened if he'd just been able to move up to Luleå to be with Maarit.

Eira didn't understand what his wife had to do with anything, nor various other parts of the tangled story. She had half an eye on the road, where the ambulance had just arrived, watching as the paramedics unloaded the stretcher.

'A pistol, you said? Do you know what kind it was?'

'A real-life Makarov, he kept boasting about that.'

Her police officer's mind started whirring. Makarov. That meant nine millimetre.

'Who was he, the man who shot John?'

'I don't know. It was all my fault; I'm the one who made the call and said we had a traitor who was reporting to the Americans – probably the Swedish Security Service too, they were one and the same, don't kid yourself otherwise. All that talk about neutrality? The PM could shove that up his arse.'

'Who did you ring? Why?'

'The comrades. A number. I assume they were in touch with the USSR, too.'

'Are you telling me the Soviet Union was involved in the murder of John Aiello?'

'No idea. The bloke came from up north somewhere, maybe even Finland. Called himself Johansson, but there's no point trying to track him down. It wasn't his real name.'

Eira took a deep breath in an attempt to clear her mind, to calm both the racing hearts inside her.

All those times she had talked to her neighbour about the investigation, never suspecting or imagining that he might be involved. It must have been there all along, from the moment he followed the divers into her kitchen. Was that why he had brought them to her, because he thought he could dupe her? What was it her father had always called him? *Comrade Stalin next door.* She had forgotten that. All she and Allan ever usually talked about were dog food, walks and the weather.

'So you were lying when you said you didn't know the deserters?'

'I didn't know them.'

'But you knew that John Aiello worked for the CIA?'

'I didn't *know*. I just heard it from someone.'

'Who, Allan? Who told you? Was it my mum?'

'What? Kerstin? I barely knew who she was back then.'

'So who was it?'

Allan looked up at her, meeting her eye for the first time. Eira saw something bottomless in his gaze. His eyes were watering, stinging from all the smoke, and he kept blinking firmly.

Then the voices drew closer, all around them. The paramedics had arrived.

'Allan Westin? How are you feeling? Are you breathing OK? Could you tell us your personal ID number? Are you in any pain? We're going to take you to Sundsvall now, are you able to get up?'

Eira told them what had happened, reassured them that she was fine. All she wanted was a glass of water, they were welcome to go in and get one for her; she had left the door wide open when she ran out earlier.

They wrapped a blood-pressure cuff around her arm and checked her oxygen levels, both normal, then listened to the baby. Eira could have told them that he or she was also doing just fine judging by the way they were dancing and squirming away in there.

'We'd still like to take you in, just as a precaution.'

'I'm OK,' said Eira. 'You don't need to worry about me. I should be here when the police arrive, I need to give them my statement.'

They seemed concerned, but what could they do?

Rabble ran after them as they loaded his owner into the ambulance and closed the doors, then turned around with his tail between his legs.

Eira buried her face in his coat and thanked him, promising him all sorts of treats.

The fire was finally under control.

The patrol car came skidding onto the driveway, and she realised it was August before he leapt out and came running towards her.

'Are you OK? I recognised the address, but we were already halfway to fucking Junsele.'

He hugged her tight.

'I don't know what I would've done if—'

'It's OK,' Eira whispered, leaning into his chest, as close as she could get. The adrenaline that had made her feel invincible earlier had now faded, and she was tired and light-headed, frightened by what she had done. If she looked up, she could see the fire ladder. The gable end of the house was blackened but intact, a few metres from the bottom rung down to the ground.

If she hadn't managed to get out, if the fire had spread more quickly . . . No, all those ifs were just too much for her right now.

'It was all fine in the end.' She drank from the bottle of water that had appeared in her hand – had he given it to her? 'Allan, my neighbour, is on his way to hospital. He nearly didn't make it.'

'What about you? I heard you went in? You're crazy, you know.'

'I was the only one here.'

'Eira . . .'

She pushed him back to get some air.

'There was no one else. He would have burnt to death in there.'

'Shall we go in?'

She nodded and he helped her up. The street was full of people, both neighbours and strangers, and she wanted to get away from their prying eyes.

'Do you have any idea how the fire started?'

She had sat down in the kitchen, and he wouldn't leave her alone.

'I'm pretty sure it was the wood burner,' she said. 'That he lit a fire and then went to bed.'

Everything she had said was true, yet it felt like a lie. There was more she could add, about everything that had been on the floor, fuelling the flames. The chair that wasn't usually on its side by the stove, the magazine rack that should have been in the hallway.

'So you think it was an accident? That he was careless somehow?'

'Could have been,' said Eira.

Once everything had calmed down and Eira had spent a few hours dozing on the sofa, too unsettled to go upstairs, she grabbed her computer.

She had opened all the windows in an attempt to get rid of the last of the smoke, but she knew the smell would linger for a long time. The voices from the street were like a rippling murmur, people walking past, pausing, adding details to the story they would tell future generations. About the day the Westin place went up in flames and the neighbour, the police girl, got him out.

He'd been lucky, poor Allan Westin.

Eira brought up the preliminary investigation that had just been opened. Until they could establish another cause, the case would be classified as arson, which meant that it fell under the jurisdiction of Violent Crimes. *Lead investigator: G Georgsson*.

She felt a twinge in her pelvis, the baby putting pressure on it again.

Why had they given it to the most experienced investigator on the team? Was it a sign that GG really was on his way out, that he'd given up the big cases? Or was it because he'd heard her name? There would be talk about what she had done, was that why?

The thought made her feel warm inside.

They hadn't been able to interview Allan yet; or hadn't

uploaded the report, at the very least. Maybe he was resting – there was no real urgency. Why bother a fragile old man with something that could wait? Until the technicians got a chance to go in and take a look around, there wasn't much to report at all. Just the facts: the call came in, and so on. A brief description of her own actions.

As yet, Eira was the only person who knew what Allan had said.

How could she have missed it? As though there was no way an eighty-two-year-old man – she had never really thought about his age until she saw his personal ID number – who took in a stray dog and practically loved it to death could have committed such a serious crime. It came down to the most basic of things: don't be fooled into believing that people are simple.

Had Allan been crafty, or had she been blind?

Should she have noticed the signs? Like the fact that he hadn't dug up his potatoes like normal, that he'd let the weeds take over? Or that he asked questions when he came round to see her? But all those things could simply be signs that he was shaken. Hauling a body out of the river was no small thing; it affected the entire community.

Eira logged out and started writing, jotting down everything he had said when he regained consciousness.

Allan Westin.

He'd been in the woods, seen the killing – *was it premeditated murder or manslaughter?*

Made a call to tell someone there was a CIA infiltrator in Lunde, one of the deserters working at the dock – *who had he called?*

Had worked at the dock himself, stole the anchor from the tug – *what did he think when they recovered it from the depths, from the fog of time?*

Eira didn't feel any of the usual satisfaction as the pieces fell into place and the picture of the crime began to emerge more clearly, though the other man remained nothing but a shadowy figure. She realised that she imagined Allan as old back then, despite the fact that more than fifty years had since passed. *Who was he then?*

And what the hell did her own father have to do with any of it?

Your old man would've been happy to get rid of the lot of us, let me tell you.

It must be something to do with the old antagonisms, she thought. Union man Veine Sjödin and Comrade Stalin next door. They may not have been the best of friends, but that sort of thing fell away, got swept under the carpet; neighbours were neighbours, they helped one another.

. . . if I'd known then . . . none of it would've happened.

The confusion when Allan came round and saw his house burning, the realisation that he could have died. Had he wanted to die? Hadn't he said that it would have been for the best?

Eira went through her notes, trying to bring some sense of order to them. Some parts were clearly linked to the old murder case, but others didn't seem to belong.

She called GG.

'I'm not interrupting anything, am I?'

'How are you feeling?' he asked, sounding anxious.

'I'm fine, don't worry.'

'Has no one ever told you it's a bad idea to run into a burning building?'

'I took the course,' said Eira. 'Over on Sandö. It wasn't my first time.'

'The doctors say Allan Westin's blood alcohol level was nearly 0.3%. He would almost certainly have died if you hadn't been there.'

'Do you know how he's doing?' Eira had never been able to take praise, wanted to stop him before he said any more, or before he gave her a telling-off. Yes, she knew they weren't supposed to run into a blaze, that that was the fire brigade's job.

'Broken arm and a possible concussion,' said GG. 'But considering he was thrown out of a first-floor window, they say that's a minor miracle.'

'Will you be interviewing him tomorrow?'

'I'm not sure it'll be me, I've got a few other things on . . .'

Eira had to take a deep breath as a wave of pain washed over her, and she stifled a groan.

'Allan Westin was involved in the death of John Aiello,' she said.

'What?'

'He confessed to me when he came round. I've written down everything he said. Allan could actually have been the instigator of the whole thing.' It sounded absurd to use such dry, legal terms, though it also made it more real somehow. 'I'll send you everything I have.'

She heard a ping as her email arrived. GG clearly spent his evenings at his computer, just like her.

'Let me know once you've had a look,' said Eira. She really did need to pee.

'OK.'

Bent double, she made her way through to the bathroom, breathing deeply. Was this what contractions felt like? How were you supposed to know? She had forgotten everything the midwife had told her, would have to google it. Either that or calm herself down.

She felt a little better once she had peed and had some water. It was probably nothing.

Eira kept thinking about the look Allan had given her when she asked . . . What exactly had she asked?

Her muscles tensed again, pressing downwards. Eira paused halfway up the stairs, hunched over and focused on her breathing for a moment before continuing. She still had three weeks left to go, it was too early; this was probably just the shock from the fire finally catching up with her.

Who, Allan? Who was it that told you?

Was it my mum?

His confusion had been genuine, as had his denial, but there was something he had kept back, something in that bottomless look in his eye. Her neighbour had just confessed his involvement in a murder, so what could be worse than that? Seconds had passed, possibly even a full minute, and then they were interrupted.

It wasn't resistance she had seen, nor his own guilt. It was something else.

Compassion?

She slumped down onto the child-sized bed, the one Kerstin herself had slept in as a girl, tucked away in the

317

space beneath the sloping roof. Kerstin had had visions of her grandkids sleeping there, Magnus's boys, possibly even Eira's one day, but for now it was little more than a storage space for everything that had been stashed away.

Eira had tried to put everything back in the right order last time she looked through it. Papers and schoolbooks and, at the very bottom, a few stacks of handwritten letters. She dropped some of it to the floor as the next contraction hit her, a black-and-white photograph of her mother holding a newborn, Magnus by the looks of it, late 1970s. It was striking just how young she looked.

Love letters, tied with string.

She recognised her father's handwriting right away. The letters were all dated. 1972, 1971 – he had spent a long time trying to win Kerstin. Eira had heard it all before, how her mother had eventually given in to his insistent wooing. Veine had even bought her roses – who did that in a place like Lunde? The year Kerstin took a break from high school and went to work in Stockholm, Veine had written intensively. No long letters, more short notes and postcards. Addressed to *Dearest Kerstin*, signed *forever yours*. Eira struggled to imagine her father being so grand and romantic, almost poetic in his language: *the evening we sat so close that not even the rain could come between us.*

The first of the letters was dated April 1968, the same month Kerstin met Steve Carrano in the square in Kramfors. Had her parents really had something going on as early as that?

I've been thinking about you so much since Saturday evening . . .

318

She screamed out in pain, something twisting inside her, turning her body inside out. This really wasn't good.

You were supposed to time the contractions, she knew that much – assuming these really were contractions – but her phone was downstairs. Eira heard it start ringing and then stop again.

She crawled out from the space beneath the eaves on all fours, stopping dead as the next pain seared through her.

L ina lugged an old wooden cable drum over to the window at the back of the house, blackflies biting her neck as she climbed up on top. The garden was much more overgrown than she remembered it, stinging nettles up to her thighs. The house really had been abandoned.

She had taken a detour through the woods in order to get here without being seen, not that there would be anyone out and about in Geresta in the middle of the night. The hamlet was like a barely beating heart, the same torpor she remembered from those nights when she had snuck out and clambered back in again. The farmsteads were scattered across the countryside, a lovely valley, people said. But Lina had always struggled to see it as anything but claustrophobic, the forest and the mountains like looming walls.

She tugged down her sleeve and broke the window pane, then reached inside and lifted the latch. Ducked as she yanked the window open, a glittering shower of glass. Sure enough, the white curtains were still hanging on the other side. Those damn net curtains. Lina threw her rucksack and the rifle inside and pulled herself up onto the ledge.

It was one of those things she had learnt as a child, like swimming and cycling. Things her body would never forget. But she was less flexible than she had been back then, her back stiff. She was only forty-two, but she got aches and pains in her hip sometimes, like some old woman. She needed to open the other half of the window to get a good grip, accidentally breaking another of the panes as she gave it a shove. It really was stuck – had no one opened these windows since the day she disappeared? Once she managed that, she had to twist around so she didn't land on her head, dropping down to the rug below. She bashed her knee in the process, but it didn't hurt too much.

The rug, she couldn't believe it was still here.

Lina took in the room around her. The corner sofa. An animal seemed to have gone to town on that. The table-cloth her grandmother had embroidered. The shelf of knick-knacks. One of the little glass birds had fallen to the floor. The air smelled stale, like soap and wood. No, she told herself, it was just the memory of those scents, something her mind had conjured up. It had to be at least twenty-five years since anyone had last scrubbed these floors. The big painting on the wall had always scared her as a girl, squares and lines and dark colours; she could never work out what it was supposed to be. But looking at it now, she saw three faces.

Something had torn up the floor in the kitchen; possibly a badger had been thinking about moving in, only to change its mind. She could understand that. The pantry was empty, but all the cutlery was still in the drawers. Her parents really did seem to have just upped and left. Maybe they had only ever planned to go away for a short while and then failed to come back?

Or perhaps they'd thrown themselves into the river, giving the place a quick once-over first?

The stairs creaked in new places as she made her way up. It was summer, but the attic was cold. They used to hang their washing here, and store their winter clothing during the warmer months. The cold was good for the clothes, apparently, it kept the moths away. As though they lived in the 1930s, as though there weren't sprays and other ways of dealing with that crap, as though there was no such thing as a tumble drier. *Why waste electricity when we've got a perfectly decent place to hang our things? Those machines are so rough on clothes.* Lina remembered the girl who had once hidden between the sheets hanging on the line, pretending they were ghosts that had been trapped up there, playing hide and seek though no one was looking for her.

The door at the far end of the attic was locked. Lina pulled on the handle, wondered whether the wood might just be swollen, but no. She headed back downstairs to look for a key, but all she could find was a hammer, a knife, the poker.

As she hit and prised at the door, she imagined her younger self locked inside. Her body might have escaped, but her soul was still beneath the covers, eating toothpaste so they wouldn't notice that her breath smelled like smoke.

The doorpost gave way relatively easily. Old wood, homemade. The room on the other side was empty. Of course it was. Black spots on the crocheted throw, dead flies. They'd made the damn bed before they had her declared dead.

All traces of sixteen-year-old Lina were gone. The posters they were always fighting over: *But are they really good role models, these people? With all the drinking and the drugs and goodness knows what else.* She could just imagine her parents and the police rummaging through her things once she was gone. Collecting stray hairs and fingerprints, reading whatever they could get their hands on. She had never kept a diary, thank God, hadn't cared about any of the meaningless days that passed. The drawers had been emptied, nothing but the mirror left on her dressing table. She trailed a finger through the dust and tried to catch a glimpse of her own face, but the only image she could conjure up was the lame school photo they had used after she went missing. Lina had refused to let her parents buy those pictures, but her mother had done it anyway. Framed one of them and hung it downstairs while their real daughter slammed the door in the attic. Locked it behind her and then climbed out of the window; the ladder up to the roof was right outside. It was all so easy. Easy to lie, easy to run. Lina pictured her last moments here as though she had stepped out of herself, like watching a film. She had gone out the usual way that evening, wearing a summer dress and a cardigan, no more than her little rucksack on her back. *I'm staying at Elvira's tonight.*

She couldn't remember what her plan had been, probably hadn't had one other than seeing Kenny, pretending they were going to run away together. Whatever it had been, the whole thing had gone to shit and now she was tired. She tore back the bedspread. Her pillow was still there, an old blanket too.

A place where no one would ever look for her.

There was a thudding sound in the distance, too far away to be any help.

Something seemed to have happened to Eira's leg, and she couldn't get to her feet. She'd curled up on the floor instead, possibly in an attempt to delay the inevitable.

She counted the seconds, little more than two minutes between contractions now. They were getting longer, too, some lasting almost a full minute, and she remembered that this was when she was supposed to go in, or maybe she should have done that a long time ago. The closest maternity ward was fifty miles away. Did the people who wrote the information brochures know that?

I don't want to give birth in an ambulance, she thought, but a moment later that had become: I just hope an ambulance shows up at all.

It wasn't until she heard someone shout 'Hello?' that she realised she wasn't alone in the house.

'I'm here,' she whimpered, yelling as loud as she could when the next contraction hit her. 'Upstairs!'

Footsteps, hands, a scent she would recognise among thousands of others.

'Where did you come from? What are you doing here?'

'You weren't answering the phone.'

GG got her up onto her feet and guided her down the stairs, Eira clinging to his arm.

'There's something wrong with my leg.'

'Trapped nerve, I should think.'

'What, are you a doctor now?' His arrival seemed to have opened the floodgates, and she broke down in tears. What the hell was he doing there? Thank God he had come.

'Don't forget I've done all this before,' he said, helping her onto a seat in the hallway. 'Have you packed a bag?'

'No,' Eira screamed as the next wave surged through her. 'I haven't. It wasn't meant to happen yet.'

'Of all the ways to go into labour . . .' He smiled and got through to someone on his phone, she wasn't sure if it was the emergency services or the healthcare helpline; whoever it was he was arguing with them, about the ambulance that was supposed to be stationed in Kramfors, ten minutes away. Someone had crashed their car on the way to Nyland, it seemed and GG swore and hung up.

'I'll drive you. You're going to Örnsköldsvik, apparently.'

Eira didn't have time to pack a bag – what was she even supposed to put in it? A toothbrush, baby clothes? Did it matter? She sprawled on the back seat as GG broke the speed limit, telling her it was all going to be OK, such a blatant lie. Her waters broke as he slowed down for the roadworks in Herrskog, damn it, all over the seat of his new Audi.

He could hear that something wasn't right during their call earlier, but he had hesitated to call her back so late in the evening. When he eventually did – because he'd had a bad feeling and, like he said, he'd done all this before – and she didn't pick up after five attempts, he had jumped straight into the car and driven the fifty or so miles to Sundsvall. Eira had run into a burning building, after all, and he had seen enough over the years to know what shock could do to people. He had knocked on the door, pounded, eventually trying the handle; the door wasn't locked.

She wasn't going to give birth on the side of the road. GG was on the phone to the maternity ward during the last few miles, asking her whether she was OK every thirty seconds.

'Yes,' Eira snapped. 'Stop nagging!'

The midwives were waiting with a trolley when he pulled up outside the hospital. Warm voices surrounding her, experience and competence. GG gave way to the crowd of medics running tests and examining her, sticking their fingers into her to check the dilation and attaching electrodes to the baby's head. And then he was back, stroking her hair, telling her that everything was going to be OK, and then it was time. She only just made it into the delivery suite when she felt a sudden urge to push, and everything that had come before was like child's play in comparison. 'Don't scream,' said the midwife beside her, 'put that strength to use instead.' Eira yelled for water, swatting away the hand that gave it to her. 'Don't push, just go with the contractions when they come,' the voices told her, but it was all bullshit and agony, a few blissful seconds of rest before the next pneumatic drill got to work on her.

'I can see the head, you're almost there now,' someone shouted from between her legs. Someone else gripped her hand, and then it was as though a hurricane tore through her, breaking every tree in its path.

The calm once it was over. Whimpering, a pitiful cry, a tiny body on her chest, pale and blue.

'It's a boy.'

So small, Eira thought as she sobbed with exhaustion, the midwives mopping her blood from the floor and pulling a clean sheet over her. He'll break if I do anything wrong.

'Can you take him, please? I think I need to use the toilet.'

The little one had been given some clothes and was fast asleep in a plastic trolley when August arrived. He unpacked more clothes from a bag. Tiny sleepsuits with teddy bears on them, soft fabrics.

Were those tears she could see in his eyes?

'I don't know how I could have left you on your own, I was there just a few hours earlier.'

'I didn't feel anything then,' said Eira. 'And you were working.'

'Still.'

'It all worked out fine in the end.'

Was she really supposed to carry his guilty conscience, on top of everything else? Yes, he had left, but wasn't she the one who had told him to leave, that she was fine? Why did she say these things when nothing was fine? Why wasn't she capable of accepting help from a single person?

GG had come over and given her a hug once it was all over, and Eira had thanked him in a way that felt much too small and awkward. They had laughed at the slightly embarrassing fact that some of the staff had assumed he was her father. Theoretically, of course, that was perfectly possible. She had never considered that before. Eira had told him to check in to a hotel to get some sleep, but she wasn't sure whether he had done that or driven back to Sundsvall.

Don't think about the fire or the murder now, he had told her, *I'll take care of it.* And with that, there had been nothing she could say to keep him there.

'Still, the fact it started while you were on your own,' August continued. He was upset she hadn't called him, bringing a hint of tension to a room that should be calm and peaceful. 'So far from the hospital, too. It's kind of worrying.'

Eira thought she could detect an undertone in everything he said. *You should live your life the way I live mine. Wouldn't everything be so much easier then?*

Or was she just imagining it?

August leaned over the little trolley again.

'When do you think we'll find out?'

He had already been to give a DNA sample. It would be sent off to the same lab that dealt with police DNA tests, and they both knew it would take however long it took. Until then, the baby would be left in limbo in his see-through trolley. A sense of panic gripped Eira again: that he was too delicate for this world, that she wasn't the right person to protect him. She still couldn't quite access all the incredible feelings everyone had said she would feel. What kind of mother ran into a burning building and put her baby's life at risk before he was even born, had to turn to the National Forensic Centre to find out who his father was . . .

August stroked his downy head, delicate as glass.

'Don't wake him,' said Eira.

'Don't you think he looks like me?'

She laughed. 'I need a favour.'

'Anything, whatever you need. I've already told them I

might be taking some time off at work. I wonder if you're allowed to take paternity leave if you only *might* be a father. What do you reckon?'

August was so worked up, wanting to laugh and hold her hand. The way he kept looking at her felt different, too. Admiring, because she had managed it, but also the opposite, as though this was his moment to step in and take charge. The baby whimpered, stirred. August held out his arms.

'Is it OK if I . . .?'

'Sure. You know to support his head, right?'

'Of course I do.'

It was touching to see how careful he was as he picked up the boy, tender yet confident.

He sat down on the edge of the bed, cooing and stroking his cheek, trying to catch the little one's eye.

'I need you to stop off at Ricken's place on the way back,' said Eira.

'You're kidding?' She got the sense that August was clinging to the child, backing away from her though he was sitting perfectly still. 'Why would I do that?'

'He doesn't know,' she said. 'I need to let him know that he might be a dad.'

'Why don't you just call him?'

'This is Ricken we're talking about. He doesn't have a mobile phone – he's convinced they're surveillance tools, that everything we do on them is stored somewhere.'

'Sounds like a responsible father . . .'

'He does have a landline,' Eira continued, 'I'm just not sure he actually uses it. He never picks up, anyway.'

'So you want *me* to tell him?' August laughed, and in that moment Eira realised she didn't like him all that much.

'Can't you just stop off there?' She could always ask someone else, but she wanted August to do this, to give him a chance to prove it wasn't all just talk. That he could handle things, even when they were uncomfortable.

'OK. Yeah, I guess so.' He passed the boy over to her, smiling when he saw his mouth searching for her nipple, his tiny fingers stretching. 'Maybe I should get us both a cigar?'

Eira woke to the sound of her phone ringing and realised that she had dozed off with the child on her breast. If she had turned over in her sleep, rolled on top of him, let go of him . . . She gently lowered him into his little trolley.

Less than two hours had passed since August had left.

'Seriously,' he said, a little too loudly. 'Do you really think it's a good idea to let your kid grow up there? How does he even make a living, this Ricken guy? I ran a search—'

'What did he say?' Eira felt a little dizzy when she got up, had lost quite a bit of blood, but she walked over to the window all the same. The world was still out there. 'About the baby, I mean. Did he seem happy?'

She knew what was in Ricken's record. Theft, assault, a few charges for growing cannabis a long time ago. She didn't need August to tell her any of that.

'Yeah, he was totally beside himself, started doing some weird war dance in the garden. Shouting "Fuck, I'm a dad" for everyone to hear, as though he already knew the kid was his.'

Eira couldn't help but laugh. She was pleased that Ricken was excited, a man who had never wanted to bring a child into the world. She wasn't sure she had ever seen him dance. Maybe once, as they ran singing around the old oil tanks over on Svanö? Had they danced then, before she lost her virginity to him?

'He said he'd swing by,' said August.

'Thank you for going to see him,' said Eira.

'But he refuses to give a DNA sample.'

'What?'

'Not a chance in hell, that's what he said.' August tried to imitate Ricken's soft, melodic accent. 'Then he started asking if I knew what they do with all the DNA they collect, how much information they have on all of us. "Sure, you're a cop, no harm in that, there's a cop I love too, but you're part of this bigger structure and so is she . . ."'

'Did he really say that?'

'I mean, if he can't even step up and take responsibility for fathering a child how do you expect him to actually look after a baby? My son won't be growing up among any wrecked cars, I'll tell you that.'

That wasn't what Eira had meant, but she couldn't exactly ask whether Ricken had really said that he loved her. She didn't bother pointing out the illogical aspect of his words, either. That the boy obviously wouldn't be growing up in Strinne if August was his father. Nor if Ricken was, for that matter.

'I guess it doesn't really matter,' she said. 'The test will show whether it's you, and if it's not you then it's him.'

'Still, it's the principle,' said August.

'I've got to go,' said Eira, gripping the window frame. The city seemed to be swaying, multiplying in the shiny new facades and expanses of glass looking out to sea. 'I think I need to lie down again.'

A fter three days she could no longer remember the pain; all memory of it was gone.

'We're supposed to forget,' said Stina, who had come to the hospital to give them a ride home. 'Otherwise no one would ever do it. Did yours go away the minute you managed to shit again? That's always how it's been for me. Pretty weird, but I guess it makes sense.'

Her deft hands got the little one into a tiny jacket and leggings, pulled a hat onto his head. Lifted him into a lined carry bag.

'You can't call him "the boy" forever, you know.'

'It's not forever,' said Eira.

She had phoned her childhood friend to ensure that the drive would be a quiet one, without having to discuss anything with August, for example. She also thought she owed it to Stina after everything she had done for Eira – including lending her the car seat that was ready and waiting for them.

'You can keep it until I become a granny,' said Stina.

Eira got into the back seat, letting the boy grip her fingers. He was calm, possibly pacified by the fact that something new was happening.

'Have you always felt like a mother?' she asked. 'After giving birth, I mean.'

Stina glanced up at Eira in the rear-view mirror. She had just joined the line of traffic through Docksta, tourists heading up to Skuleberget, lorries pulling in and out of the roadside café. 'It can be that way first time round,' she said. 'They don't cause much fuss when they're this age, you know. They don't sit there in their prams, thinking "Who's this useless woman I've been lumped with? Can't I swap her for a better model?"'

Eira laughed, which was a bad idea considering the stitches she had needed, still not quite in control of her bladder.

'So, come on then, can you see any similarities? Which of them are you hoping it is?' Stina knew all about her dilemma and had previously laughed and teased Eira. She seemed to be holding back slightly now, as though the boy could understand.

'I guess it doesn't matter.' There had been moments when Eira thought she could see a hint of blue in his eyes, like August's. Or was it a flash of green, of Ricken? What about the dimple in his chin, where had that come from? 'He'll get the dad he gets. They'll love him either way, right?'

Stina turned off after Ullånger, escaping the traffic on the E4 for the tranquil valleys and fields. As they passed the little swimming beach in Butjärn, Eira saw that the kiosk was still open, kids eating ice creams and racing down the slide into the water.

'So are you planning to stay up here now?'

She caught a hint of something searching in the eyes in the mirror. Of uncertainty. But there also seemed to have been a shift in the power balance.

When Eira left Ådalen to continue her studies, her friend had also transformed. She had become the One Who Stayed Behind. Stina had become a mother while she was still in high school, doing precisely what the older generation of women warned their daughters about. *Use protection, live your lives, get an education and be careful not to get stuck with a bloke too early.*

Four babies later, she had a level of knowledge that Eira would never come close to.

'Is it OK if we take a detour through Kramfors?' Eira asked.

The staff met her in the doorway, Eira with the baby in her arms. She had been given a sling, but it was too early for that yet, too many straps and clips to wrap her head around; the whole contraption seemed lethal.

'Ohh, what a lovely little lad.'

'You had a boy!'

'All ten fingers and toes – and he certainly knows how to grip! What a strong little thing.'

'How wonderful for your mum, that she gets to meet him.'

Eira had called ahead to let them know she was coming, and they had helped Kerstin into one of her pretty blouses. Her reading glasses had disappeared a while back, and the book in her lap was unopened.

'Hi, Mum.'

'Oh! Who's this, then?'

Eira pulled out a chair so that she could sit right by her side with the boy in between them. A brand-new sensation rose up inside her, one she struggled to put into words. A feeling of belonging. A focal point outside of themselves.

'There she is,' said Kerstin.

'He,' Eira corrected her with a laugh. 'He's a boy, Mum. You've got a new grandson.'

It wasn't so surprising that Kerstin had made that mistake; August had consciously bought gender-neutral clothing, no pinks or blues. He wanted people to address the baby as an individual, first and foremost, rather than simply a boy or a girl.

She held out her arms, wanted to hold him.

'Gosh, she's so lovely, come here, my dear . . .'

Eira hesitated to hand over her son. If Kerstin couldn't even understand that he was a boy, was she really in a fit state to properly support his head? What if she dropped him? Eira felt a pang of guilt when she saw her mother's outstretched arms, the look of expectation on her face. She knew how wrong it would be to deny her this, the woman who had birthed two children of her own. Didn't that knowledge run deep, becoming part of the muscle memory? Eira lowered him into Kerstin's arms, hovering close by so that she could react if necessary.

She watched as her mother immediately tucked a hand beneath his neck. The instinct was still there after all, she needn't have worried. They could enjoy this moment together, Kerstin humming and stroking his cheek.

'Oh, sweet girl. Nora, my love, my little love.'

'No, Mum. This is my baby, your grandson. I've just come from the maternity ward in Örnsköldsvik. I came here as soon as I could, so you could meet him.' Eira could hear the disappointment in her voice, and she fought back the grief that threatened to overwhelm her. At the fact that Kerstin was unable to be lucid in this moment, that Eira was never quite enough, not even when she turned up with her newborn son. At the fact that she had actually mixed him up with another child, as though he was any old baby. Or maybe she had misheard her, maybe her mother had said Eira. Was Kerstin really so muddled that she thought she had just given birth?

A realisation: holding him seemed to have made her happy, in any case. At one point in time, she had wanted to hold the baby she named Eira.

'He was seven pounds five ounces,' she said, matter-of-factly, trying to bring Kerstin back to the present. 'Which is great considering he arrived a few weeks early. I haven't decided what to call him yet, he's only three days old. I've been thinking about Albin or Jonathan, maybe Tore, but it's not just up to me.'

Kerstin rocked the little one, captivated by his gaze. He was calm and quiet, at the very least. With Stina's help, Eira had given him a quick feed in the car outside, so she was lying when she told her mother.

'I should probably take him now, we need to get home.'

'No, no, I don't think so.' Kerstin gripped the baby tight, clutching him to her chest.

'Come on, Mum, I'll bring him back tomorrow or the day after, I promise. We only just left hospital, so we're both tired.'

Eira lifted the boy from her arms, and Kerstin no longer put up any resistance. Her hands hung briefly in

338

the air, nothing left to hold, then slumped down into her lap.

'I'm sure you must know some nice boys' names from the family?' said Eira. 'We can talk about that next time we're here.'

She felt a real sense of victory once she finally managed to feed him at home. It took a lot of desperate searching for her nipple, prodding and squeezing, but she got him there in the end, damp patches on her top from where her other breast was leaking, small pads tucked into her bra to soak up the milk.

Eira pushed the pram through to the kitchen, rocking it back and forth to get him to sleep. Babies found that motion reassuring, she had read. And music! She switched on the record player, that felt much more soothing than voices wittering away on the radio, and grabbed a few records from the collection.

They were Kerstin's, music from her childhood. Bob Dylan and Joni Mitchell, perfect for someone trying to sleep. She skipped over a Hep Stars LP. Of course, the Kramfors band that had played the shake evenings at the old temperance house.

Eira continued to rock the pram with one hand, opening the investigation into John Aiello's murder with the other.

GG had taken care of it, just like he had said he would, and she brought up the transcript from his interview with Allan Westin.

AW: I couldn't find work. That's how the whole thing started, I suppose.

GG: How what started?

AW: That damn summer. Yup, Maarit . . . I wasn't one to say no to a drink either, if you catch my drift.

GG: And what does that have to do with John Aiello?

AW: Someone had been sharing the names of communists, that's why I couldn't get work. They were scared of people like us.

GG: And you thought it was John Aiello who was sharing that information?

AW: Yeah, I s'pose I did. Or something along those lines. And if it wasn't him, then at least we wouldn't have someone like that here. Not in Lunde.

GG: Who did you call after you heard that John might be working for the CIA?

AW: A number.

GG: The Communist Party?

AW: No, like hell. Hermansson and that lot had taken over by then.

GG: Hermansson?

AW: C.-H. Hermansson, he was the chairman of the party, but he betrayed the revolution. Started collaborating with the Social Democrats, protested when the USSR entered Czechoslovakia. Well, that told us all we needed to know.

GG: So who did you call?

AW: The revolution won't be won by kissing the Social Democrats' arses, that's what I thought.

GG: And now?

AW: What?

GG: Do you still believe in the revolution?

(Silence)

AW: The workers didn't get enlightenment, did they? They went home and watched TV instead. That's what happened.

GG: Who did you call?

(AW clears throat)

AW: I can't give you a name. It was a group. The revolutionary Welfare Committee. Our brothers in the east would support us if we took back power in the party. But in the end there was nothing but division, all to silence us.

GG: The Welfare Committee?

AW: Yup, not even the Security Service could guess what they stood for.

(Laughter)

It went on and on in much the same vein, with GG going back and forth in an attempt to get the details out of Allan, confusing digressions about a political landscape that felt incredibly distant. Several of the questions were Eira's, ones she had written down and sent to GG along with Allan's statements after the fire.

He hadn't uploaded a summary yet, but an outline was starting to emerge, bitty and recalcitrant.

Allan had been denied work because he was a communist, a true believer who wanted to see Sweden forge closer links with the Soviet Union and was convinced that armed revolution was the only way.

Someone had seemingly been keeping track of people

like him, compiling lists and sharing them far and wide, meaning that prospective employers hundreds of miles away had known exactly who he was when he tried to find work with them.

This new information set a bell ringing somewhere at the back of Eira's mind, something she had read or heard. The name Jan Guillou appeared out of nowhere. He was a famous author now, but as a journalist in the 1970s he had served time in prison for revealing something along those exact lines.

Hold on, could it have been Ricken who told her? One of his many rants about the surveillance society, how little privacy anyone really had. Eira had rarely paid much attention to all that stuff, even in the past, when she was blinded by infatuation for him.

She put the interview to one side and opened Google. The IB Affair, that was it. 1973. Two journalists had revealed that prominent members of the ruling Social Democratic party had been working alongside the unions to conduct an illegal surveillance operation against communists, using workplace representatives as informants. Eira's jaw dropped when she clicked on another article and saw that the situation had been particularly acute in Norrbotten, where the communists had gained a foothold. If they had taken over, that would have represented the first step towards revolution.

Prior to the revelations of 1973, all of this had taken place in secret. There could be some truth to what Allan had said, in other words; someone really had been keeping an eye on him. Eira found herself thinking about Steve

Larsson, who had been convinced he could see the CIA everywhere. It had clearly been a time of real paranoia, but that didn't mean it couldn't also be true.

She opened the interview again.

GG: If we could circle back to when you first heard the rumour that John Aiello was working for the CIA ...
AW: OK.
GG: Who told you?
(Silence)
AW: It was all so long ago.
GG: You seem to have a pretty good memory, Allan.
AW: Yup.
GG: I have information suggesting that one of the few people who knew was someone you now know well – Kerstin Sjödin. Is she the one who told you?
AW: No, bloody hell. Kerstin? I didn't even know her then, she was just a young lass. I can't believe that.
GG: She was involved in the anti-war movement, in a relationship with one of the deserters.
AW: I had no idea. Was she?
GG: So you're sure it wasn't Kerstin Sjödin who told you?
AW: No, I'm telling you.
GG: Logically, then, you must remember who it was. Who was it, Allan?
(Silence)
AW: There were probably a few of them there.
GG: Where?
AW: Over by the People's House, at the end of the day. Booze, plenty of that too. A man gets angry.

GG: Who was there?

AW: Social Democrats, union men. I gave them a piece of my mind, said it was probably one of them who'd been spreading muck around the country.

GG: You suspected that one of these people was keeping a secret list of communists?

AW: I was just so angry. I'd been drinking too, like I said. Ran my mouth off a bit, you know how it goes. They needed to be told a thing or two. And then one of them said I should be focusing on the docks instead, on those Yanks who'd run away from the war.

GG: That one of the deserters was working for the CIA?

AW: Yeah. Never would've thought that. The Americans and their world domination, sure, but on your own doorstep?

GG: Who told you?

(Silence)

GG: As I mentioned earlier, Allan, the statute of limitations has passed. You won't be charged with anything. No one is going to go to prison for any of this. But for the sake of the dead man's family, we need to know what happened. You understand that, don't you, Allan?

(Silence)

AW: Can I use the loo yet?

Eira kept reading, but she couldn't see any names.

No names.

Rabble leapt up as she got to her feet, seemed happy to have her home. A neighbour had been looking after him while she was in hospital. Eira had called Mette at the old toll house and told her that the key was under a rock by the right foot of the hammock stand.

The boy had woken up, and Eira fed him as she ate a sandwich, which worked just fine. She remembered what GG had said about what mattered right now: making sure he was fed and cared for. Rabble could go out and relieve himself; he'd be back soon enough. Gulls screeched and soared above the river.

She changed his nappy, wiped his bottom. Pictured – once she had finally crawled into bed and dared close her eyes after checking repeatedly that the boy was still breathing – the men sitting on the steps outside the People's House.

As they sometimes had when she was a child, too. She had often been sent over there to tell her father that dinner was ready.

The boy had made it through the night. He woke every other hour or so, and Eira had picked him up, nursed him, even fallen asleep with him in the bed beside her at one point. She had shut Rabble out of the room, had to draw the line somewhere.

The dog had whined pitifully at first, but then he had settled down.

It took forever to shower, with the little one on a blanket on the floor, and then to get breakfast into two people. Fortunately there was bread in the freezer, and Mette had left some toppings, juice and milk in the fridge, fresh tomatoes. 'I remember what it was like,' she had said.

Once their bellies were full and they were both dressed, Eira went out with the pram. She heard delighted shouts from the gardens she passed, people stopping to peer down at him as he slept.

Kalle Molin lived behind the old Näslunds' place, the one that had once been a shop. She found him in the garden, eyes closed as he enjoyed the sun, listening to the radio.

Good Morning, World!, about the storming of the Capitol and the investigation that was now under way.

'Hi, Kalle.'

He raised a hand to block out the sun, almost as though he was saluting her.

'Sjödin? I'll be damned, have you got a little one now?'

'Is it OK if I sit down?'

'I don't have a quarrel with the police, do I?' He laughed and attempted to get up, which wasn't especially successful. His chair was a low recliner, and he had to be almost eighty. Tall and strong, but still. Eira remembered him as one of the louder ones, the men who made their presence felt and raised their voice over everyone else. Telling jokes she hadn't understood as a girl and likely wouldn't find funny now.

Kalle Molin gave up trying to get to his feet. Probably didn't want to show his frailness.

'Help yourself from the kitchen, if you want anything to drink.'

'Thanks, but I brought my own.' She gestured down to the pram. 'I have a few questions about my dad, if that's OK. The two of you were pretty good friends, weren't you?'

'I suppose you could say that.'

'Through the union?' Eira saw that the boy had opened his eyes, and she rocked the pram to keep him calm.

'Yeah, that and the Social Democrat association.'

'I know I've asked you about this before, but did you have much to do with the deserters who were here in 1968?'

'Is this about the murder of that American?' Kalle Molin forced himself up so that he was sitting instead of reclining, squinting up at her to where she was blocking out the sun. 'Can't a cop take maternity leave these days? Have they cut that back too?'

'I'm just trying to tie up a few loose ends,' said Eira, turning the pram so that he could see the baby. 'They mostly just sleep at this age anyway.'

'Boy or girl?'

'Boy.'

'His dad must be proud.'

Kalle's words hung in the air, waiting to see how she would reply. All this fishing for information, the gossip that was a part of living here, it could be hard to separate from genuine concern. Maybe they ultimately boiled down to the same thing.

People cared, for better or worse.

'Yeah, really proud.'

'Veine was so damn proud of you, too. You should know that.'

'There's so much I don't know about him.' Eira sat down, sparing him from looking up into the sun and enabling him to see her face. 'You know how it is, you don't ask enough questions when you're younger and then suddenly it's too late.'

'Bloody cancer,' Kalle Molin nodded, reaching for a bottle of water. 'It's a damn shame he never got to meet his grandson.'

'I'd like to talk to you about something that happened in the summer of 1968.'

'Is it the cop talking now, or is it Veine Sjödin's daughter?' There was clearly nothing wrong with his mind, even if his body was struggling to keep up.

'Both,' Eira replied with a smile.

'Shoot.' The old union man gestured for her to start talking, his curiosity now piqued by something other than the identity of her baby's father. 'Did you know that Veine asked me to be your brother's godfather? I said no. Didn't want to be a hypocrite by going to church and promising to give him spiritual guidance. What the hell did I know about any of that?'

They both laughed.

'To think that he got her in the end, your mum. Veine fought hard for Kerstin, let me tell you. I remember when she went to Stockholm. He still didn't give up. Doubt he ever even looked at anyone else, not until their divorce.'

Kalle Molin stroked his chin, pulling on a stray hair he had missed while shaving. On the whole, he was well groomed, handsome in an ageing way.

'I wonder if you remember a specific occasion,' said Eira, 'when you were sitting outside the People's House. It could've been just you and Dad, or there might have been some others there. I'm guessing there might have been a meeting, maybe a party?'

'Well, there were a lot of parties. Dances every other weekend back then.'

'Allan Westin walked past. He was probably pretty drunk, and he started shouting at you. I'm sure you know he was an enthusiastic communist?'

'Ah, Allan, he was part of the old guard. We had our fair share of clashes over the years. How's he doing, by the way?'

'He'll be OK.'

'Glad to hear it.'

Eira told Kalle what Allan Westin had said about Luleå, that someone had spread word that he was a communist and that, on an evening like she had just described, outside the People's House, he had heard that there was a CIA infiltrator among the deserters in Lunde.

That he had drunkenly, angrily, drawn a link between that and his own situation.

She studied the old man's face as she talked, saw it grow serious and introspective. His mind was whirring, she was sure of that. Debating with himself, which caused him to sit quietly for a moment once she had finished.

He cleared his throat, reached for his water again.

'It was a different time back then,' he eventually spoke up.

'So you do remember?'

'Maybe,' he said. 'But are you sure you want to know?'

The baby had started fussing, and Eira had no choice but to pick him up and try to give him a dummy. She didn't want to start breastfeeding during an interview, even if it was taking place in a lush garden, partly masquerading as an innocent chat about her late father.

'I would have asked him myself, if I could,' she said.

Kalle Molin studied her for a moment.

'And Veine would've told you, I'm sure of that. We had nothing to be ashamed of. Didn't need no damn CIA to deal with the commies in this country.' He sat tall, his crooked back now poker-straight. 'No, we handled them all on our own.'

He then added that it was understandable, really, that the Americans would want to keep an eye on those long-haired types who'd run away from the army. It was the middle of the Cold War, in so-called Red Ådalen, but his jaw had still dropped when Veine Sjödin brought up that business about the CIA.

And then he had thought: well, it was actually pretty logical, in a way.

'Not that we supported the bombing of Vietnam, of course. Even Palme protested against that, fell out with the Americans over it. But a country needs order.'

'You said you dealt with it yourselves,' said Eira, rocking the boy against her shoulder, keeping her voice low. 'What did you mean?'

'You're too young to remember,' said Kalle Molin, 'but it's not a secret any more, even if it was back then. We knew there was a risk they would take over the unions, that was how they did it. And you have to remember that the Iron Curtain was just over there.' He pointed eastwards, towards the sea, Russia.

'Was my dad working for the IB?' She already knew the answer, but she still had to ask.

'We both were.'

'So you reported on communists, stopped them from getting jobs? Allan Westin, for example?'

'You should be happy about what your old man did, if you ask me.' Kalle Molin swatted an insect away from his face, tried to catch it in his hand. 'Or would you rather have grown up in that kind of society?'

S he had gone straight home after leaving Kalle Molin's place. Fed the boy, who seemed so content, who didn't yet know a thing about life.

That it could turn against you in the blink of an eye.

Eira had worshipped her father, always thought of him as the one who had comforted her with open arms. By her teens, she had decided he was a loser – especially when he told the same stories over and over again, about all the people who came before her, all the hard work that had enabled her to grow up in comfort.

But he had never mentioned a word about the secret intelligence agency known as IB. Of course he hadn't.

She dropped a slice of bread into the toaster and reminded herself that she really would have to go over to Kramfors to buy some proper food soon.

So what did this mean?

If her own father was one of those who had prevented Allan Westin from finding a job up north?

If he and Kerstin had been close then, and she had, for some reason, told him what she'd heard?

But why would he repeat it to a drunk, argumentative Allan? To deflect the blame? Or was it jealousy, to discredit the deserters, one of whom was getting too close to Kerstin?

Eira realised she would have to go up to the attic again,

to all of the papers and letters, the only things she had left. She rifled through the love letters from her father: *Do you remember the rain that couldn't come between us, that first evening? My love is greater than the mountains and the sky and the river, my longing cries for your warm skin and your glances . . .*

He was no poet, that was for sure.

Their wedding photograph had come down from the wall after the divorce, but she found that too. Yes, Kerstin was beautiful, and there was no doubt he was proud – Veine standing just behind her, his hands protectively gripping her shoulders – but was she happy?

Eira searched for memories of how they had been together, other than the silence of their last few years. There were a few political arguments in there. 'You don't know what you're talking about,' Veine might snap, the sort of thing she remembered so clearly because it soured the atmosphere so badly. 'If you'd got your way, we'd all be on the other side of the Iron Curtain.'

As a child, Eira had thought the iron curtain was a real thing, and she'd had terrifying visions of herself trapped alone on one side of it.

But what about before that, when Veine was in love and Kerstin had chosen someone else, back when the political situation was more heated than ever?

Had he been jealous? Did he badmouth the NLF and the deserters, warn her about the American? And what about Kerstin? Perhaps she had been tougher back then, stood up to Veine, told him he didn't know a thing. What could she have said? That Steve wasn't the threat, that

Veine's beloved Social Democrats were two-faced liars, criticising the war while collaborating with the USA, doing deals with NATO behind the scenes? That she had heard that the CIA's tentacles stretched all the way to Lunde?

It wasn't entirely implausible.

And yet she had married him in the end.

In their wedding photo, Kerstin's hair was short and wavy, her dress tight yet sober somehow. It was 1974, six years after her love affair with Steve. She was only twenty-three, but she looked much older than she had in the pictures from the late sixties that Eira had been preoccupied with lately.

Five years later, Magnus was born. Eira remembered the picture she had seen of Kerstin holding him in her arms, remembered that she had been struck by just how young her mother looked when she became a mother, a black-and-white image.

It was at the bottom of the pile, beneath all the letters. Kerstin with long hair. She looked like a girl, with some of her youthful wildness still intact, a lock of hair hanging loose over the infant in her arms. The baby was wearing a white dress. Had Eira reacted to that, to the fact that it looked a little strange? The lacy white hat. Was that really how people dressed a boy in the late 1970s?

She turned the image over. There were no names on it, just a date.

3 June 1969.

It wasn't Magnus Kerstin was holding. No wonder she looked so young; she was only eighteen. The year she should have graduated from high school but took a sabbatical in Stockholm instead.

June 1969.

The next thought was dizzying. That was nine months after Steve vanished from Lunde, after her mother had paced back and forth along the river in despair, eventually giving up and dropping out of school, leaving for Stockholm.

Was it possible to keep something like that a secret? It would definitely make her silence over Steve more understandable.

Eira heard the boy crying downstairs, and she was in such a rush to get to him that she almost slipped on the stairs. She picked him up and uncovered her breast, and as she slumped down into a chair, she remembered her mother, the confusion when Eira turned up to introduce her son.

Nora?

Kerstin had called the baby Nora.

It was tricky to log in to the police database as she coaxed her nipple into his mouth, milk running down her stomach.

She had never had reason to look up her mother in the databases only the police had access to, in which all personal details were stored.

Kerstin Sjödin, née Backlund. Married 1974, divorced 1990. There were her grandparents' names, there were the kids. Magnus, born 1979; Eira, born 1987.

So many years between them, yet Eira had never really wondered why. Perhaps Kerstin hadn't wanted another child, or perhaps they just never had sex? Had she been looking for a way out of an unhappy marriage even then?

And then she saw it, right there in black and white. Four digits that seemed to scream out at her. 1969.

A girl.

Born 3 June at Sabbatsberg Hospital in Stockholm. Father unknown.

Born, but not dead. Eira had started to wonder whether Kerstin might have lost the baby not long after birth. That would have explained a lot, but apparently not.

Adopted the very next day.

The girl's name hadn't been registered. Perhaps she was never officially called Nora.

Eira closed her eyes, felt the boy's stubborn sucking.

A sister.

She had a big sister out there somewhere. Wasn't this what she had always dreamed of when she was younger? Someone who could be there for her, who understood.

A sister Kerstin had managed to keep secret until dementia tore down her defences and brought the girl back. Lost in memory, where time flowed freely.

Nora.

The name that never was.

Eira moved the boy over to the other side, remembered the midwives' clear instructions: use both breasts, otherwise you might suffer blocked ducts and other issues.

Kerstin hadn't taken a sabbatical because she needed a break from school. No, it was so that she would be out of sight, 300 miles away. So that she could hide her pregnancy and give birth in secret. Did Veine know? Her grandparents? Or had she snuck off to Stockholm before she was showing, without telling a soul?

Then returned to Ådalen and married someone else.

Loved her son unconditionally when he was born a few

years later, but struggled to take to the girl she gave such a similar-sounding name.

Nora.

Eira.

The boy had fallen asleep on her breast, and Eira carefully lowered him into his pram. He needed to be burped, but she didn't want to wake him. She could feel a headache building as she scrolled down her contacts list and hit dial. It was all just too much to process; she was exhausted from lack of sleep.

The silence on the other end of the line spoke volumes.

Unni knew. She was Kerstin's closest friend; she had always known.

The seconds passed. Half a minute. An eternity.

'How did you find out?' she eventually asked.

'Mum gave herself away,' said Eira. 'She got my baby mixed up with hers, thought he was called Nora. Was that what she called her?'

'Have you had a boy?! Did everything go OK?'

Eira gave a brief recap and then interrupted Unni's congratulations.

'I asked you about that time,' she said. 'And you told me about Steve. He was the father, right? Why didn't you say anything?'

'You have to understand, I made a promise to Kerstin. My head was spinning when you came over with that old picture, but what was I supposed to do? She'd hate me if I blabbed. Friendship, you know.'

'It was over fifty years ago,' said Eira. 'You're both old

women now. Kerstin doesn't even know what year it is. Should it really take a police investigation to find out you have a sister?'

'We're not *that* old.'

Eira could hear Unni pacing around her apartment as she spoke, probably pouring herself a glass of wine. And as ever, she had to pay close attention to her tone of voice to work out whether or not she was telling the truth.

Unni explained that October had come around, but Kerstin's period never arrived. 'And it wasn't like you could just go to the pharmacy and buy a quick test back then, you know.' Kerstin's parents had been furious when she announced that she wanted to drop out of school and move to Stockholm, lecturing her on how they'd slaved away to give her this opportunity, but Kerstin just shouted back at them. They didn't understand the way the world worked now, didn't understand a thing. She left before she started to show. Found herself a job at a hospital with staff accommodation, worked until the very last minute.

'Why didn't she want to keep the baby?'

'I suppose she had different ideas about what she wanted from life.'

'Such as?'

'Oh, you know Kerstin. She wanted to study and see the world, to write, to become an author; she dreamed of sitting in Parisian cafés.'

'And yet she went home and married my dad, which makes no sense.'

'Like I said, I never understood that. But what do we really know about other people? Veine kept writing his letters, telling her he loved her, and there she was in Stockholm, with leaky breasts and an ex who had got her pregnant and then dumped her. She probably wasn't as strong as she wished she was. Needed a bit of love after everything she'd been through. It's not easy to resist when someone has their heart set on you.'

Eira studied the boy as he slept, felt a rush of reverence.

'But it's always been there in your mother, don't you believe anything else,' Unni continued. 'That drive. You know what I'm talking about. The dream of getting away – even if she only did it through books. Ever since you were born, she's always said, "This girl is going to get out into the world, no one's going to hold her down." She wanted to make sure you were tough, she said, not some little wimp.'

'Was that why?'

'Why what?'

Eira couldn't explain what she meant; they weren't even fully formed thoughts, just a muddle of emotions and fragments of a mother who had pushed her away. *Become someone, get out of here, don't cry, get up.*

'Once, when I asked her how she felt about everything,' Unni went on, 'whether she ever wondered what happened to the girl, Kerstin said no. Waved my question away. It wasn't something she was interested in, something she ever thought about. She'd put it out of her mind.'

'Did she call her Nora?' asked Eira.

'Yes.'

'Then I guess she hadn't forgotten after all.'

'No, I suppose you're right.'

Eira had just let Rabble out into the garden and lowered the sleeping, sated baby into his pram when she noticed the car by the burnt-out house. It looked like a rental car, a red Toyota with stickers on it, and her first thought was that it must be someone from the insurance company. She watched as an older woman got out of the driver's seat, a bluish tint to her hair, a slick suit with flared trousers.

'Maarit?'

The woman didn't hear her. She was too busy taking in the remains of what had once been her home. Eira pushed the pram into the shade beneath the overhanging roof and made her way across the grass.

'Hi, Maarit.' She could feel the powerful emotions, everything that coming home to such destruction stirred up in a person, and Eira put a hand on her shoulder.

Maarit Westin sniffed, turned ninety degrees and studied Eira for a few seconds, then wrapped her arms around her.

'I don't want to think what might have happened if . . . that you . . . Oh, little girl. If you hadn't dared go in.'

'I'm not so little any more,' said Eira.

Maarit's tears were infectious, and the older woman dug out a tissue and passed it to Eira.

'I should never have left him. When men are left alone like that, it's as though they get lost.'

'You did what you had to do,' said Eira. Her mother had told her about Maarit's anguish before she finally made up her mind to go, that she couldn't bear to be so far from her grandchildren, growing old without ever really getting to know them.

'He said he would come, but time just kept marching on. It's as though he was stuck here. I think it could have something to do with . . . all this business.'

'The murder?'

Maarit didn't reply, just walked slowly around the corner and looked up at her former home. Eira followed her in silence. Broken windows, sections of facade charred by flames.

'Allan must have told you?' she said hesitantly.

Maarit had paused by the garden furniture to the rear of the house, all remarkably intact.

'That man!' she said. 'Lying there in a hospital bed, hooked up to drips and goodness knows what else, trying to act like everything is normal. Honestly. How can someone keep quiet about something like this for so long? How?'

'So have you spoken to the police? You know what happened in the sixties?'

A grunt, or possibly a murmur, a noise that told Eira that whatever might have happened back then, Maarit was done talking about it now.

'Either way, he's coming back to Stockholm with me once they discharge him. He can't stay here. All this brooding on his own. No, nothing good will come of that.'

Maarit's gruffness, the thing Eira had always been slightly frightened of as a child, was back. She wanted to ask how anyone could live with that knowledge, a murder that had been hushed up, a man who wasn't who he seemed, but there was no need. Strictly speaking, she wasn't currently a police officer; she was on maternity leave.

'It would be good,' said Maarit, 'if you could keep an eye on the house. Just until we hear from the insurance company. We don't want anyone else to move in while it's empty.'

It was a warm evening, an August dusk full of soft darkness and bright moonlight. The boy could stay outside, Eira thought as she headed back. Not all night, of course, but for a while. Sleeping in the fresh air was the best, according to Stina. It would also be a good chance for her to get a bit of work done in the garden. She wasn't going to start mowing the lawn or anything like that – she didn't want to wake him – but maybe she could tackle the edges around the house with a pair of secateurs? Pull up the dandelions that had been left to their own devices for too long, start getting rid of the lupins everyone was always moaning about.

She couldn't hear a peep from the pram, so Eira went over to make sure he was still sleeping soundly. She had turned it towards the house, which meant she couldn't see the boy at first glance, and a wave of fear washed over her. Had he slipped under the blanket somehow? Could he have suffocated under there?

She tore back the cover.

The baby wasn't there. The scream that rose up inside her got caught in her throat, and Eira wheeled around, but there was no sign of anyone. She ran over to the road. No one there either.

She had to think logically now, not panic. The other side of the house, of course. Someone she knew must have stopped by. Maybe the boy had been fussing, and they saw her chatting to poor Maarit. The other house was no more than twenty metres from hers, but how could she have left her baby all alone, so far away?

She ran around the house, but no.

They must have gone inside, she decided. Magnus, he must have been let out on day release again, he said he was going to put in a request so he could meet his nephew, he'd sounded so excited on the phone, the proudest uncle on earth, he said.

As she flung the door open, she immediately knew something was wrong. The dog. He didn't come to greet her.

'Hello? Rabble? Is there someone here?'

A low growl, a bark, but he didn't come.

Eira paused to listen. Moving slowly, she walked through her own house as a police officer, taking in every detail, being as quiet as she could.

She spotted the dog before anything else. Standing in the opening between the kitchen and the living room, his hackles up.

The woman was next. A woman she didn't know, blonde and vaguely familiar, sitting in the armchair. The baby was by her feet, on the bare parquet floor.

'Who are you? What are you doing here?'

'Don't you recognise me?'

Eira took a few steps towards her. Bent down without taking her eyes off the woman, stroked Rabble's back, telling him that it was all OK, that she was here now. He

364

was still growling non-stop, ready to attack. Protecting the baby, that was what he was doing. He had transformed since she brought the little one home, pacing around the place, keeping watch, his senses primed. Eira's past investigations raced through her head. It wasn't uncommon for a police officer to be threatened – a probation worker she knew had recently been attacked by one of her clients in her own home.

'I'm just going to pick up the baby,' Eira said calmly. She could do this, she had been in high-pressure situations before, she just needed to think like a police officer to stop herself from screaming.

The woman was still smiling.

Eira took another step forward.

'Stay right where you are.'

That smile. Eira felt like she had seen it before, but where? A long time ago?

'I want to talk to you about a few things,' said the woman.

'Absolutely,' said Eira. 'We can talk. I just need to see if he's hungry, if that's OK with you. He's only four days old, we don't want him to start crying.'

Was it the sound she heard first, or did she catch a glimpse of the weapon by the woman's leg, partly hidden behind the armrest? A hunting rifle. She was gripping it in both hands now, but she wasn't pointing it at Eira. The barrel was trained on the floor, on the boy, lying defenceless on his back.

'Don't do anything stupid,' said Eira. 'Put that down and we can talk. You can ask me whatever you want and I promise I'll answer, you just need to put that down first.'

Always assume that a gun is loaded. During training, she

had heard plenty of stories about officers who had made that mistake.

'I can't believe you still live here,' said the woman, looking around the room. She seemed perfectly calm, like an old friend paying a visit. 'Have you never thought about getting out of this dump?'

Someone who had been here before, a long time ago.

That smile, as bright and fake as it had been back then.

'Lina? Is that you? Lina Stavred?'

The woman laughed.

'Yeah, I thought you might remember me.'

Her features were sharper now, her teeth no longer quite so white. Eira couldn't make out the colour of her eyes in the gloom. Three years ago, when she found Lina Stavred in a Stockholm café, she had been much plumper.

The tattoo. Teenage Lina had had a heart and some birds on one arm, but the pattern she could see beneath the rolled-up shirt sleeve in front of her now was completely different. Over-the-top, violent.

She must have noticed Eira's gaze, because she scratched the skin there. Tattoos could be removed, covered up. The fact that it was different didn't mean a thing.

No, what it meant was that she was keen to conceal her identity, to avoid being recognised. That she was planning to get away once again.

Or maybe she just didn't like it any more.

'Sorry, I should ask how you are,' said Eira, trying to gauge the distance to the armchair. Six metres, the boy slightly closer than that, by the woman's feet. 'It's been a while since I last saw you.'

She kept her voice calm, as though there was no danger whatsoever, refusing to let her emotions take over, however much they were building up inside her. Don't think about the fact that this woman has killed twice before, she told herself – or was the number higher?

'Not so long,' said Lina. 'You came to the café where I worked. I know you're Magnus's sister, I know you're a cop. I read about you in the paper, after you fished the dead guy out of the river. Pretty funny that they thought it was me, no?'

'Why are you here?' asked Eira. 'Do you need help with something?'

Don't provoke, instil a sense of calm.

'I want to know what you've got on me. I want to know what the police know.'

Eira tried desperately to find her way back to her usual professionalism, to dull her fears. Weighing up her options, thinking strategically. You don't know what she knows, she reminded herself, so don't lie. Stick close to the truth.

'They found fingerprints at the crime scene in Täby,' she said. 'And they matched them to yours, so the police there know that Lina Stavred is alive.'

'Am I a suspect?'

'Not technically, no. They don't know what happened in the house, just that you were there. He had a history of drinking and abuse, so if you came forward you could probably get away with voluntary manslaughter, maybe even involuntary.'

'He was such a fucking loser.'

Eira found the courage to glance down at the baby. He

367

made a noise that sounded like language, as though he wanted to be a part of whatever was going on, snapping up how the world worked.

All that mattered now was protecting him.

'It must have been awful living with someone like that,' said Eira. 'I can understand. I don't wish you any harm. You can take my car, get away. I won't report you.'

Lina's laugh was worse than her coldness. So heartfelt, despite everything. As though she found this funny.

'I remember you,' she said. 'You were such a little brat. Spying on me and Magnus, constantly hanging around him. I'm sorry, Eira Sjödin, but I don't think you're capable of keeping a secret.'

'Magnus told me what really happened that night,' said Eira. 'Over in Lockne, the night Kenneth Isaksson died. He said it was you, but he still took the blame. He's doing time for that, but I haven't said anything.'

'Yeah, my God,' said Lina, slapping a hand to her forehead. Eira realised she hadn't closed the door, and the blackflies had followed her in, nothing now stopping them from feasting on the boy. Was that what was happening, why he had started whining?

Hush, my love. Please just be quiet.

'What a sanctimonious little pig you are. Do you seriously believe him? You think there's no way he'd lie to you, just because you're his sister? Didn't Magnus tell you that he hit my new boyfriend over the head with a metal pipe? That I had to help bury him so we didn't both get sent down. No?'

For a brief moment, everything seemed to sway.

'You can stop whatever you're doing with that fucking

phone, too,' said Lina. She had noticed that Eira's hand had crept down to her pocket, maybe she had heard it vibrating. Damn it. 'Give it here.'

'Sure, here you go,' said Eira, throwing it to her. Lina's reaction was lightning fast, reflexive, her hand shooting up; it was the reaction of one of Kramfors School's star volleyball players.

Eira seized her chance and hurled herself forward the minute Lina's attention was elsewhere, snatching up the boy. She didn't manage to support his head, but that would have to not matter now, she just needed him close. If one of them was going to die tonight then she had to be holding him when it happened.

It wasn't until she was sitting with him in her arms that she realised she should have gone for the gun instead. It was pointing straight at both of them now, Lina on her feet.

Eira heard a bark, saw a quick shadow; Rabble barking furiously, a chaos of snapping and tugging around Lina's kicking legs. And then the shot rang out. Always assume that a gun is loaded. Eira hunched down over the baby, her mind blank. She couldn't hear anything, couldn't see anything, but the baby was warm in her arms. I'll never let you go, she thought, never, ever again.

'Get up,' said Lina, jabbing her in the back. With the gun? Her foot?

Eira felt something sticky as she lowered her hand to push herself up, and she opened her eyes at last. Blood. The boy was still warm, still breathing, and she couldn't feel any pain.

That was when she saw the black fur, his tongue lolling out, his eye meeting hers. Rabble wasn't dead yet, but there was so much blood.

'What the hell have you done?'

She heard Lina load the weapon again, somewhere above her head. Turned around and looked straight down the barrel.

'The fucking dog went for me, what did you expect me to do? It's savage. Someone should've put it down ages ago.'

'Is it OK if I stroke him?' asked Eira, reaching out to touch his trembling neck as his panting grew weaker and weaker beside her.

'Just don't try anything else.'

'I didn't, I just wanted to give you my phone.'

'I need money,' said Lina.

'I don't have any in the house. You can take the jewellery, though. My mum's. It's all here, up in her old room.'

'She's still alive, then?'

'She has dementia, she's in a care home in Kramfors.'

'Sounds fucking great,' said Lina. 'Forgetting all the bullshit. I really wish I could've forgotten this place, that goddamn house, my parents, all the lame boys who thought I needed protecting. Like your brother, he was the worst of all. Followed me out there, to the fucking forge, thought I needed someone like him. It should've been him who died, not Kenny. Everything would've been different then.'

'How?' asked Eira, still stroking Rabble's soft fur. 'What did you want to happen?'

'Christ, I don't know. Isn't that the point? Not having to know what's going to happen, what life's going to be like?

Studying and planning, all that shit, when you know you're ultimately just going to die.'

She had to keep talking, thought Eira, to stop Lina from realising that there was someone else here. The sound of a car pulling up, right outside. At least Rabble wasn't alone when his breathing stopped and he slipped away, the light in his eyes fading.

'I know what you mean,' said Eira, immediately realising that had been the wrong thing to say. Lina Stavred didn't want her understanding. 'Or, I mean . . . I'm impressed. That you managed to disappear, to do whatever you wanted to do, that you don't care about anyone else. I wish I was a bit more like you.'

Footsteps on the gravel. Come in, she thought. Please let it be someone who sees the open door and walks straight in, wondering what could be wrong or wanting to see the baby, anything at all so long as it's someone who knows how to handle a weapon.

'You can take the car keys,' said Eira. 'They're in the basket in the hall.'

'And the money?'

'Mum's jewellery is upstairs.'

'What the hell am I meant to do with jewellery? I need cash.'

'I told you, I haven't got any. But my cards are in my bag outside. I'll give you the codes.'

'Thanks,' said Lina. 'That's nice of you. I also need you to log in to the police database and delete my records.'

'I can't do that,' said Eira. 'But I could add something to say that Lina Stavred's body has been found, that we think it's you. That would buy you some time. It takes forever to identify a body if it's found in water, for example. Or I could make up a witness. Someone who saw you in Finland or wherever the hell you want. You can take my passport, too. Dye your hair.'

Eira ducked as something flew through the air. What was it? A pan? A cycle helmet?

It was followed by something else, something that hit Lina's arm and made her drop the gun. She didn't have time to react before he was on top of her, roaring at the top of his lungs.

Eira backed into a corner with the boy. He was crying now, or was he?

She saw their bodies in the dim light, wrestling on the floor, and she reached up and flicked the light switch, filling the room with brightness.

Ricken.

He had the upper hand. Lina was biting and hissing and lashing out, but he was sitting on top of her, his knees on her arms. Wonderful, wonderful Ricken. He'd done this sort of thing before.

Eira scanned the room for her phone. Where had it landed? She needed to call the police, now.

Protect the child.

Run?

Eira saw Ricken lunge to the right and grab the gun without letting Lina break free. He then got up and pointed it at her, and now she was the one lying defenceless on the wooden floor.

Shoot her, Eira wanted to say. *She's already dead. That's what everyone thinks. We could get rid of the body and no one would even miss her.*

'Don't shoot,' she said.

Ricken gripped the rifle. Eira knew he wasn't much of a hunter, that he liked animals too much. His dad had done what fathers do: taken him out into the woods, let his son carry the dead hares home.

'It's not worth it,' said Eira. She had found the courage to move now, but she was still clutching the little one, ducking down to check beneath the sofa for her phone.

'Come on, it's me,' said Lina. 'Rickard Strindlund. Hey, look at me. You know me. It's been a while, huh? But you still look the same as ever. Hang on, just let me sit up. I don't want to hurt anyone, OK?'

'What the hell?' he asked, turning briefly to Eira before focusing on the woman again. 'Who is she?'

'Lina Stavred,' she said. 'I know, it's been a long time.'

'But . . . ?'

'Yeah, she's alive,' said Eira. 'Be careful. She's the one who killed the guy over in Lockne. Magnus just helped her to run.'

'I saved Magnus's life,' Lina snapped. 'Don't forget that. I had no idea he'd been locked up for it. I only just found out. I'm sorry.'

'Is that true?' Ricken whispered. He took a step back and Lina shuffled up against the bookcase, her eyes fixed on him, smoothing her hair.

'She's wanted,' said Eira. 'Involved in the murder or manslaughter of the man she was living with in Täby. God knows how many different names she's had over the years.'

He looked worryingly uncomfortable with the gun – had he ever fired one before? The assault charge on his record was from a fist fight, and the other man had attacked first. She could feel his hesitancy; it was all too familiar, the way he kept shifting from one foot to the other, never making a firm decision either way.

'I need my phone,' said Eira. 'So I can call this in. I threw it to her, but I can't see it anywhere. She must have it.'

'I'll confess to everything,' said Lina. 'But you need to let me go. I can't be locked up. You get that, don't you?'

She fixed her big, blue eyes on Ricken, fluttering her lashes. Eira saw it happen, the way she seemed to transform now that there was a man in the room.

'Hang on, look, I'll record this.' Sure enough, Lina had Eira's phone, had been sitting on it. 'Just give me the code. I'll say that I killed Kenny Isaksson, that it was an accident, and then I'll go. I'll leave the phone somewhere you can find it, we can agree on a place. Magnus will get out, and you can go on with your sweet little lives.'

'Don't listen to her,' said Eira.

'Seriously, what the fuck . . .'

'Or call the police,' Lina continued, playing with the phone in her hands. 'Do it. I'll confirm Magnus's version of events. I read about it in the paper, so I know exactly what he said. He was jealous and got into a fight with Kenny, I wasn't even there. I ran off because I was scared of him. I remember you, Ricken. The two of you were such great friends, always together. And you, Eira. I know you don't trust me, but I think you want your brother to be free.'

374

Eira shushed her, needed to calm the boy, couldn't think clearly with him screaming in her ear.

She watched what happened next as though it was a film.

Lina Stavred got up from the floor, and Ricken backed away. He followed her with the barrel of the gun as she walked towards the door.

Did she take the car keys from the basket?

The front door slammed.

'No!' Eira blurted out as she came back to her senses. 'We can't let her go!'

Ricken's arms were around her, the smell of oil and sweat.

'Easy, Eira, easy. It's all OK now, it's over.'

'Don't you get it? She's a killer, she'll do it again.'

'But Magnus . . .'

'You're such a fucking idiot.' She pulled free and pushed Ricken away from her. 'Don't you realise she'll get away with it? We need to stop her.'

Eira was on her way to the door when she remembered the child in her arms. She heard an engine start outside, realised the little one was howling, and she slumped onto one of the chairs in the kitchen.

She managed to tug up her top and her nursing bra as she grabbed the computer to call the emergency services. Someone picked up in Umeå, and Eira told them her name and address, her breasts aching and full to bursting, his little mouth unable to latch on. She had to squeeze her breast, squirting milk onto his face and the screen, but he managed it in the end, sucking rhythmically, a sting of pain from her cracked nipple. Life. Eira described her car, a black

2019 Volkswagen Passat, an estate, reeling off the registration number and everything Lina Stavred was suspected of doing, adding unlawful detention and making threats at gunpoint, plus the murder of a dog. 'She shot him.'

'Who did she shoot? Is this person dead?'

'No, Rabble, the dog. He's not technically mine, I've just been looking after him while . . .' She began to sob as the shock finally hit her, or perhaps it had been unleashed as her milk flowed into the boy's little body. He was alive, *he was alive*, and that realisation was so powerful that she started to shake, out of gratitude and relief and something bigger than both. And then she noticed the email that had just arrived.

From the National Board of Forensic Medicine in Linköping, the geneticist she knew there. Eira had asked whether they might be able to do her a favour and speed up the DNA analysis. Breaking the rules like that wasn't OK, of course, exploiting her professional contacts for personal gain, but she just couldn't bear to wait weeks for an answer.

Once she had hung up and the call handler had dispatched a unit, Eira went back through to the living room where Ricken had spread a blanket over the dog and slumped back on the sofa.

'I'm sorry I didn't come to the hospital,' he said. 'I was going to, but then I got all nervy.' He kept blabbering away, as though they hadn't just been through a traumatic event. Threats, a dead dog on the floor in front of them. He was in shock, of course. The boy had fallen asleep in Eira's arms, so rosy-cheeked and calm, but she couldn't bring herself to put him down amid the chaos. The chair that had been knocked over, the blood. She would have to clean that up, she thought, bury poor Rabble as soon as the technicians had been; she couldn't touch anything until then.

'I don't know whether I can handle being a dad,' Ricken continued, 'but I decided I had to come over this evening, so you wouldn't think I was completely fucking useless. I wanted to see him too, this little guy. He's beautiful, just like you. I wanted to say that I hope he's the other bloke's. August would make a far better dad than me. He's a real man. Pretty snobby, but what the hell. I've got nothing against him, even if he is a cop. That's what I wanted to say, that it's all OK.'

Eira was still clutching her computer.

'It's negative,' she said.

'OK, but don't say that, Eira. You know me. I want to say one thing and something else comes out. Christ, maybe you're right. I shouldn't have let her go.'

Eira angled the screen so that he could see it.

'The paternity test,' she said. 'August isn't the dad.'

With that, she saw his face change. Confusion, joy and fear, one shock followed by another.

'It's me? Are you serious?'

'It's you,' said Eira.

E ira spotted him in the distance. It was dusk, almost
dark, but the passing headlights illuminated his frame
as she walked towards the crown of the bridge.

'Thank you for coming,' said Frank Aiello.

'Of course,' Eira replied, applying the brake to the pram
and keeping a firm grip on the handle. He had told her that
she didn't have to come, that he could do it alone. He didn't
want to bother her with something that wasn't *entirely*
legal. Strictly speaking he was supposed to apply for permission, but he couldn't stay long enough to wait.

He had a life in America, a job to get back to.

'I just don't have the energy to fight with my siblings over
the family grave,' he said. 'I thought about burying him in
El Segundo, where I live, but John had no ties to the area,
and I'm not a member of a church there, could never bring
myself to join one. Besides, would he have wanted to go
back? I don't know. Coming here was his choice.'

The American lowered his shoulder bag to the pavement,
right by the railing, and carefully took out a plastic bag.
The urn was inside. Eira had never seen one like it before,
bright white and made from something resembling paper. It
looked more like a wrapped gift than anything.

'Biodegradable,' Frank explained. 'It'll start to dissolve
after just a few minutes in the water.'

'That's good,' said Eira. She had been imagining something far worse, the dead man's ashes swirling in the wind, blowing back in their faces, drifting across the road and hitting windscreens and people cycling by.

Frank Aiello wrapped his arms around the little container.

'In some sense it feels like I've got my brother back,' he said. 'However strange that might sound. It's like I can feel his presence, a glimpse of the person he was.'

'I understand.'

He mumbled something Eira didn't catch, possibly a prayer, waited until a timber lorry had thundered by and then held the urn out over the railing. After a moment, he let go. Eira leaned forward and saw it sail down towards the water fifty metres below. It hit the surface without a sound, bobbed briefly and disappeared. Perhaps it had sunk, or maybe it had disintegrated, meaning John Aiello's body was already flowing out to sea.

She stood quietly, leaving Frank to his thoughts.

'I've been thinking about what John said, about freedom.' He turned to Eira once the moment had passed. 'That he's free now. No longer shackled down there, in any case.'

'I've got a brother who talks about freedom too,' said Eira. 'But he's locked up. In Umeå, where you went to collect John's remains.'

'What is he in prison for?'

'Stupidity. Loyalty. He says he's filed a petition for a new trial, that he wants to be an uncle to my son, but I don't know. He talks a lot.'

Legally, it wouldn't be easy. Magnus was prepared to

take back his confession, had called to say he wanted to do the right thing for once. Ricken had also put his convictions to one side, dropping his refusal to have anything to do with the authorities and submitting a statement about everything Lina had said and done. Maybe it would all work out.

'He's hopeless,' said Eira, 'but he's also my brother.'

As they walked back together, she thought she could feel the black dog trotting alongside her, though he was buried by the roses in the garden.

Frank pushed the pram the rest of the way after the boy woke up and Eira lifted him out to carry him. She had no idea where his fluffy sleepsuit had come from, whose child it had previously belonged to. Eira walked in the middle of the pavement, at a safe distance from both the cars and the railing, the dizzying depths always so near, an irrational fear of falling. She clutched him firmly but gently to her chest, felt his soft breath on her throat.

Don't worry, Tore, I'm here.

Don't worry, Hugo, Edvin, Joel, so many possible names.

With a bit of luck she would get a sense of who he was before long.

He wasn't a Bernhard, in any case, like his paternal grandfather. Nor a Dylan, like the great Bob. Ricken called with new suggestions from time to time, had plugged his phone into the landline after all.

You'll like this one day, she had thought when she took the boy over to Strinne for the first time. You'll love exploring these cars, learning all about them, and no matter who your dad is you'll love him above all else.

Tore wasn't actually a bad option. Tore Sjödin. A little like Nora. Maybe that way it wouldn't matter if his granny got it wrong every once in a while.

Adoption records, she had recently learnt, were sealed for seventy years. In just thirteen years' time, she would be able to turn to the authorities to ask about a baby girl who was put up for adoption in June 1969.

Or maybe she could delve deeper into the police databases, looking up everyone born that day. Checking and ruling out, eventually finding someone who might not even realise she had been adopted. Tearing open wounds and turning a woman's life upside down. Did she have any right to do that?

Did she even want to?

Frank Aiello hugged her and said thank you before he headed off to the bus stop, gazing out into the calmness that came with the dusk.

'This feels like a good place for a child to grow up,' he said.

'I hope so,' said Eira.

From *The Ångermanland News*

A car was discovered on the bottom of the Ångerman River yesterday, close to the old deep-water dock in Marieberg. Police divers made the discovery following a tip-off from a member of the public who had seen a car driving out along the wharf at high speed. The driver has not yet been found, but private images from the recovery show that the driver's side window was open.

The car is a black 2019 Volkswagen Passat, and the police have confirmed that it had recently been reported missing.

The search continues for a body.

Afterword

This novel is a work of fiction, but as ever I have leaned heavily on reality. The seed of an idea was first planted when I read that two marine archaeologists had discovered 300 wrecks and taken pictures of the collapsed Sandö Bridge on the bottom of the Ångerman River. I enrolled on a diving course in the hope of maybe, just maybe, being able to go down there to see 'The Church' with my own eyes, but I never quite made it that far.

So thank you, Lennarth Högberg and Jens Lindström, for so generously sharing your knowledge of diving, marine archaeology and everything lurking in the deep.

A Russian ship dating back to the Tsarist era really has been found on the bottom of the Ångerman River, and while some are convinced it is the *Berkut*, others believe it is her sister ship, the *Kondor*. Either way, I've taken the liberty of moving her around nine miles, so it's probably best not to use this book as a diving map.

The deserters John Aiello, Steve Carrano and Terry Anderson are all fictitious characters, but I built them using a whole host of different people and stories taken from real life. I'd like to extend my warmest thanks to Vincent Strollo, Gerrie Warner, Norman Burns and Herb Rains for sharing your memories with me. Of all the reading I did while researching this novel, I would like to mention a few titles in particular. *Operation Chaos*, in which the British journalist Matthew Sweet attempts to get to the bottom of the CIA's infiltration of deserters; *Waiting Out a War* by Lucinda Franks, *Vietnam's Prodigal Heroes* by Paul Benedikt Glatz, *Desertörerna* by Johan Erlandsson and *Desertören och Vietnamkriget* by Johan Romin. The real-life Swedish collective where a number of deserters settled was in Torsåker, Gästrikland, but I took the liberty of moving it a couple of hundred miles north, to a community of the same name in Ångermanland.

As always, I'd like to say a huge thanks to everyone in Ådalen for answering my strange questions, for giving me a ride whenever I don't have the energy to cycle, for sharing stories and checking details; there are so many of you now that I hope I haven't forgotten anyone. Thank you to Göran Andersson, Kerstin Nylander and Mette Bäverbäck for sharing memories from Lunde; to Bengt-Olof Näslund, Bengt Westin and everyone else involved in documenting the history of traffic on the Ångerman River.

Thank you to Ragnar Forsberg from Chepp Steppers and Tom Sahlén of the NLF in Kramfors, to Raimo Laukka and Ingvar Ohlsson for their memories from the filming of *Ådalen 31*. Thank you to Fredrik Högberg, Mats de Vahl, Tony Naima and Nina Andersson, Ylva Aller, Lena

Persson and, last but not least, Ulla-Karin Hällström-Sahlén and Jan Sahlén for their eagle eyes on all things Ångermanland.

Eira would be a terrible police officer if it weren't for the vast knowledge and expertise of Veronica Andersson at the Violent Crimes unit in Sundsvall, crime scene investigator Zorah Linder Ben-Salah, Johanna Loisel at the National Forensic Centre in Umeå and Cajsa Älgenäs at the Department of Forensic Genetics and Forensic Toxicology in Linköping, prison officer Eva Linder and former officers Rune Lindström and Per Bucht. Thanks also go out to Källa Bie and Åsa Rylander for reminding me of everything I'd forgotten since I myself was pregnant and gave birth.

Any mistakes or flights of fancy are, of course, entirely my own.

Heartfelt thanks also go out to those of you who were there during the writing process, and who make it all so much less lonely. Göran Parkrud, for the difficult questions and the long chats; Liza Marklund, Gith Haring, Anna Zettersten, Malin Crépin, Kicki Linna and Claes Josefsson for reading and providing feedback on my characters and texts. Without you, I'd never manage it.

To Kristoffer Lind, Kajsa Willén, Anders Gustafson and everyone at my publisher, Lind & Co: it's such a joy to get to work with you. To Astri von Arbin Ahlander, Kaisa Palo and the rest of the gang at Ahlander Agency: I'm so glad that you took on my books.

Last but not least, and most important of all, to Astrid,

Amelie and Matilde. Thank you for every minute I get to spend with you; for caring and being there for me; for being the wonderful people you are.

Tove Alsterdal